The Darkest Summer

Ella Drummond lives in Jersey with her husband and three rescue dogs. She was described as *One to Watch* by Good Housekeeping magazine, and also received a *Special Commendation* in the Harry Bowling Prize. Ella has written two novels for Hera, *My Last Lie* and *The Darkest Summer*.

the
DARKEST
summer

ELLA DRUMMOND

hera

First published in the United Kingdom in 2019 by Hera Books

This edition published in the United Kingdom in 2022 by

Hera Books
Unit 9 (Canelo), 5th Floor
Cargo Works, 1-2 Hatfields
London, SE1 9PG
United Kingdom

A CIP catalogue record for this book is available from the British Library.

Print ISBN 978 1 80032 996 6
Ebook ISBN 978 1 912973 14 9

Look for more great books at www.herabooks.com

Printed and bound in Great Britain by Clays Ltd, Elcograf S.p.A.

1

To my mum, with love.

Chapter One

Sera

'Sera,' Mum shouted, through my half-awake state. 'Hazel's old farm is on fire.'

I threw back my duvet. Mum was an actress and had a tendency toward the dramatic.

'Are you sure?' I whispered, straining to hear if her theatrics had woken my four-year-old daughter, Katie.

'Of course I am,' she snapped, waving me towards her bedroom. I followed her to the large window overlooking the back of the house. 'Look.'

We peered at the orangey glow. Until tonight, there had been little excitement in our lives since I'd returned to live back at Mum's with Katie after my husband Marcus' unexpected death three years previously.

'It is a fire, isn't it?' Mum asked, a tremor in her voice.

'I'm going to see if there's anything I can do to help.'

'It could be dangerous. Anyway, I've already called the fire brigade. They shouldn't be long.'

Not wishing to argue, but unable to simply watch and do nothing, I said, 'I have to go and see if there's anything I can do. The new farmer lives there alone.'

1

'Do you even know the man?' A fearful glint appeared in her eyes.

'Mum, I'm twenty-seven.' She opened her mouth to argue, but I added, 'And I'm going to the farm. Now.'

'Fine, but you're not going alone. Paul can come with you.'

As Mum's boyfriend and I drove closer to the farm the smell of smoke increased until I could taste it. My heart pounded. I wasn't feeling nearly as brave as I had done watching from the safety of my mother's bathroom. Paul and I stared open-mouthed. I had never been this close to a fire this size before. I squinted as the flames lit up the area like a massive orange spotlight. I wasn't sure how much help we would be, but some help was better than none.

I raced through the high stone pillars either side of the farm entrance. From what I could tell, the ancient barn was on fire. It was devastating seeing a beloved place from my childhood going up in flames. I parked on a grassy area and we got out of the car. The intensity of the heat slammed into us as we ran into the yard.

'Bloody hell,' Paul shouted, his eyes wide with shock at the reality of the scene close-up.

'Hello.' I battled to make myself heard over the sound of screaming timbers as the flames consumed them. 'Hello?'

'Over there.' Paul pointed at the farmer. I could see the man was limping badly as he stepped forwards, his attention focused on spraying water from an almost useless hose.

'Any animals?' I asked, running up to him.

Startled, his head turned sharply to stare at Paul and me. I had to force myself not to react to the damage to one side of his tanned face. It was old scarring from a previous injury. I suspected he was in his late thirties.

'No,' he replied, wiping his forehead with the back of one hand, brushing sweat across his soot-smeared face. The tension in his expression relaxed a little and I knew we'd done the right thing coming here. He nodded his head in the direction of the field to the side of the house. 'I take the animals out,' he said with an obvious French accent. 'My dog, Patti, she is up there also.'

I stared up at the inferno. 'What can we do to help?'

'I have one more hose at the back of the house, you can attach it there.' He indicated a standpipe. 'I must control the fire.'

Paul hurried to do as he'd been asked. Doing my best to avoid the farmer's devastated expression, I took the hose from him and pointed it at the flame-engulfed timbers.

'My mother phoned the fire brigade,' I said, hoping this information would comfort him. 'They should be here soon.'

He limped to the side of the barn.

Aware I was doing very little to help, I carried on pointing the hose at the flames. Paul joined me, dragging the second hose around the side of the farmhouse and spraying water against the barn walls.

The farmer returned. He gazed across the yard, confusion and misery etched on his distorted face. I couldn't help wondering what had happened to him to damage him so cruelly. I presumed it must have been an incident when he was in the army, if the village gossip about him was true.

I pushed the thought away and concentrated on what I was doing. He grabbed a metal bucket and filled it from the standpipe in the yard. Running as close to the barn as he could, he threw the water onto the fire. Our pathetic efforts to quell the flames were pointless, but I supposed it made him feel as if he was doing something.

The flames were darting up into the night sky and I spotted the paint on the shutters of his farmhouse bubbling in places. Desperate, I turned my hose to the side of the house nearest the barn and sprayed it with water, hoping to cool it before that too began burning. He didn't need to lose his home as well as his livelihood.

'Oh, hell,' I groaned, spotting that the window I was aiming near was open. 'I'll go and close those windows,' I shouted, coughing when the wind changed direction and I breathed in too much woody smoke.

He looked horrified at my request. 'No, it is much too dangerous. I will go.'

He dropped his bucket and hurried as quickly as he could into the house. It would have been far quicker to let me run inside and do it, but I sensed he was more concerned about what I might see inside his house rather than my safety. I kept my suspicions to myself. It was his house, after all, and he could play this whichever way he chose. Within a short time, the windows were slammed shut and he came back out to join me.

'They're coming,' Paul bellowed, pointing out towards the main road. He looked as relieved as I felt to hear the clanging bells from the fire engine.

Thankfully, it hadn't taken them long to get here. 'Thank you for coming tonight, and to your mother for her help,' he said, hurrying to greet the firemen.

Paul and I stepped back to let them do their job. We stood silently by the gnarled lilac and apple trees that had grown so entwined that it was almost impossible to imagine them as individual trees.

The large fire engine emerged carefully between the stone pillars into the middle of the yard. The firemen leapt out and immediately began unrolling hoses. Seconds later gallons of water coursed down onto the flames slowly bringing them under control.

I yawned, exhausted from the shock of what we had witnessed. The farmer grabbed hold of me, jerking me backwards. I shrieked in surprise, just as ancient timbers screeched and crashed to the ground nearby. Stunned, I watched as first one and then all the barn walls followed suit. It was obvious that there wasn't much left to save of this once beautiful building. The thought saddened me.

He let go of me and went to join the firemen. I watched him limp painfully away, sad that he should be going through such a dreadful experience. He was slightly stooped on one side, but still about six feet in height. I realised that this wasn't the first terrible thing to have happened to him.

Chapter Two

2018 – Oakwold, New Forest

Sera

The following morning, the farmer appeared at my front door with a bag of potatoes and a plait of garlic.

'It is only a token, but I want to thank you for helping with the fire,' he said. 'It took courage to come to my aid with everything they say about me.' I must have looked surprised, because he added, 'I've heard the stories.' He gave me a half smile. 'Some of them, although maybe not all. There are villagers who wish me to know how unwelcome I am.'

'You think someone did this deliberately to force you to move out?'

'I think it's possible.'

One of the neighbours walked past the house and peered at us, not bothering to hide his interest. I stepped back and waved the man inside. 'Please, come through.'

He looked a little unsure then followed me along the tiled corridor. His limp seemed worse than the night before as he navigated the three steps into the pale blue farmhouse kitchen. He stood awkwardly inside the doorway. I motioned for him to take a seat at the bleached pine table that ran most of the length of the room.

'Coffee?' I asked lifting the garlic and hanging it temporarily on the handle of the small window above the bread bin.

He nodded. 'Please.'

'I'm sorry, I don't know your name,' I said over my shoulder.

'It's Henri.'

I poured us both a mug and sat down opposite him. 'So, apart from what happened last night, how are you finding living in the New Forest?'

He gave a slow shrug with his right shoulder. 'It's a beautiful area, much better than some places I've lived. I am not certain how long I will remain here.'

I could understand his not wishing to stay. What had he ever done to anyone here to deserve their distrust? 'Where did you live before coming here?'

'Many places. I grew up in Paris.' He hesitated frowning thoughtfully, then added, 'I moved many times, but lived mainly in Marseille.'

I sensed that he didn't often share information about himself and was only doing so to be polite. There was something slightly mysterious about him. However, I still didn't think that excused people's suspicions about him. It infuriated me to think of customers in the supermarket whispering behind their hands as he shopped for basics.

At that moment, Katie ran into the room. 'Nana Mimi said she wants to speak to you in the garden.'

Sensing someone else was in the room with us, Katie turned and shrunk against my legs, one arm wrapped around the back of my thighs, the other tugging my skirt.

'This is my daughter, Katie,' I said, ruffling her bed hair.

'I'm Henri.' He looked at Katie. 'I live on the farm near the woods.' Katie murmured a barely coherent greeting and Henri's face softened. It was the first time I'd seen him smile. 'How old are you, Katie?'

'I'm nearly five,' she said letting go of my skirt and edging closer to him. I willed her not to say anything she shouldn't. 'Why have you got a hurt on your face?'

I winced.

Henri raised his hand to touch the scarred cheek. 'I was bitten by a dragon,' he said quietly, bending slightly towards her.

Katie's eyes widened. She glanced at me to gauge if he was telling the truth. 'Is it sore?' she asked.

He seemed younger than I'd assumed him to be initially, maybe in his mid thirties. It was hard to tell. 'Not now. It was for a while though.'

'Do you have animals at your farm?' she asked, leaning against the long bench, bored with his scars.

He nodded. 'I 'ave the horses, sheep, hens… and a dog, Patti. Patti is 'aving puppies soon.'

Katie jumped up and down gleefully. 'Can Mummy and I come and see them, please?'

I hated that she'd put him in such an awkward position; how could anyone say no to an innocent request from a four-year-old?

'But, of course.'

'Mummy?' She came to me and placed her hands on my skirt, a pleading expression on her face, willing me to agree. It seemed I had another actress in the making living with me.

I nodded, liking the idea of seeing them myself. 'Yes, when the puppies have been born,' I said, not wishing her to visit when the ruins of the fire were so fresh and probably still smouldering. 'Now, run along and tell Nana Mimi I'll come outside to see her soon.'

We watched Katie leave the room. 'Thank you for bringing these,' I said, pointing at the garlic. 'Did you grow them?'

He nodded. 'On my previous farm.'

'How lovely, thank you.' I held the string of garlic up to my nose and sniffed. Heavenly, I couldn't wait to use them in my cooking.

'Do they know yet if the fire was started deliberately?'

He looked at me. 'It seems an accelerant was discovered at the side of the barn. I didn't put it there.'

Fury coursed through me on his behalf. 'How could people be so vindictive?'

'There are a lot of evil people in this world, er—' he struggled to think of my name.

'Sera. Short for Seraphina,' I explained.

'It's an unusual name,' he added after a slight pause.

Used to this sort of comment, I said, 'My mother wanted a glamorous name for me and that's what she came up with.'

'It suits you.' He cleared his throat and glanced at the kitchen wall clock. 'I must go. The animals are restless. I don't want to leave them for long.' He positioned the palms of his hands against the table and pushed himself up to stand, wincing in pain. I resisted taking his elbow to help him, not imagining he would take kindly to my assistance. 'I worry that if I am away from the farm they might come back.'

Disturbed by this thought, I stood up to show him out. 'Call to see us again if you're in the village. I've only been back here a couple of years myself, so I know what it's like to have few friends.'

'That is kind of you,' he said.

I watched as he walked down the front steps and closed the front door quietly. I turned to go and join Mum in the garden, but was surprised to see her walking in the back door.

'Has he gone?' my mother asked a second later, as Katie ran past her up the stairs.

'Mum, don't be mean.' Her attitude really annoyed me sometimes.

'He's not the sort of man you should get involved with, Sera.' There was no mistaking the distaste in her tone.

I laughed, shocked by her histrionics. 'Really, Mum. He brought a thank-you gift, that's all.'

Sometimes I wondered if returning to live in Oakwold with my mother after Marcus' death had been the right move for me. It might be a pretty village, but it could be a little suffocating at times, especially when she treated me like I was still a teenager.

'I don't know how you think you can tell what sort of man someone is by having a sneaky look at him from a distance,' I added, walking upstairs to find Katie, my heart pounding with irritation.

'I know I'm right about this one,' she said following me into Katie's room. 'But you never did listen to my advice.'

Probably because I never thought she knew any better than me, I mused. I reflected on my childhood filled with her rules and regulations.

'Nana Mimi, can we go to the sweet shop today?' Katie whispered.

'We'll go tomorrow when Mummy is at work,' Mum said, grabbing Katie and tickling her.

Katie's giggles made me smile. Their closeness never ceased to amaze me. For some reason, she was able to show her love to Katie in ways that were still surprising to me. I watched them for a moment. At Katie's age I'd craved attention from Mum. I now realised that as a single mother she had needed to accept any acting jobs she was offered to make enough money to keep us giving her little time to focus on me.

'How would you like to come to the shop with me, Katie?' I said, yearning for ten minutes in an air-conditioned store.

'Nana Mimi, you coming?'

She shook her head. 'No, darling,' Mum said, smiling at me over Katie's head. 'Nana has to learn her lines.'

'Boring lines.' Katie pouted, then remembering my offer, gave me a beaming smile and grabbed hold of my hand. 'Sweets?'

'Yes.'

'That little one will go far,' Mum said as we all walked back downstairs and into the kitchen where I'd left my short shopping list. 'You two go and enjoy yourselves and leave me in peace with this.' She pulled a creased script towards her and waved us away.

–

Ignoring my mother's prophecies of doom and determined to help Henri feel more included in the community, I drove up to the farm moments later. Maybe he needed me to fetch him something from the shop.

The heat gave the roads a watery sheen. I lowered the sun visor to shield my eyes and turned off the main road onto the dusty dirt track leading to his home. Even the birds seemed quieter in the intense heat. A light breeze did nothing to ease the temperature, but swept across the heads of corn in a nearby field giving the impression of gently rolling golden waves.

'Henri,' I called from my battered Golf. It was thirty-five degrees inside but still cooler than standing in the direct sunshine. 'I'm going into town; do you want me to pick anything up for you?'

I waited outside the run-down farmhouse, its stone walls almost completely covered with rampant ivy. The front door didn't open. I wasn't sure if I'd done the right thing coming here. As I was tempted to go and knock, the weathered oak door was pulled back and Henri, scowling, looked across his dusty yard at me.

'No, thank you' he said, before going back inside, his shoulders stooped.

Not wishing to overstep the boundaries of our fragile acquaintance, I didn't say anything further, but couldn't help wondering if his limp was always this bad, or if he'd been hurt trying to put out the fire.

I started the ignition. I wasn't certain, but thought I felt him watching me from one of the windows. I wished he would let me in, just a little, but maybe me coming here so soon after the visit to Mum's house had unsettled him. We all needed friends and I suspected he needed them more than he let on.

'Mummy, do you think Mr Henri is sad?' Katie asked from the back seat. 'Nana Mimi said he isn't nice.'

My grip on the steering wheel tightened. I wished my mother would keep her opinions about Henri to herself. I didn't want her worrying Katie about someone who hadn't done anything wrong.

'Nana Mimi doesn't know Mr Henri. He is nice, but sometimes when people like to be left alone it makes them seem sad.'

There was a moment's silence as the car drew out of the farmyard, while she contemplated this notion. 'Like you, when you're working?'

'Yes, just like that.'

As much as I loved living back in Oakwold, I also enjoyed leaving the peace of our village with its quiet, tree-lined lanes, red-brick cottages and pretty colour-filled gardens, and the wild ponies coming looking for food if you didn't keep your gate shut. It was picturesque, like the perfect backdrop on a social media post. And just like so many filtered posts, looks could be very deceiving.

Chapter Three

2018 – Oakwold, New Forest

Sera

The following morning I washed and dressed Katie, leaving early to take her to pre-school. I was relieved that it was one of the three days each week that I drove into Southampton to my workshop where I renovated old enamelled signs. It was good to get away from the house and Mum repeating her lines. I needed the peace of my studio after the shocking fire two nights before. Living at Mum's house meant that I didn't have to pay rent, just contribute to the upkeep of the place and our food, so Katie and I were able to survive on the small policy we received that Marcus had thankfully set up for us about a year before he died.

Sourcing and renovating the signs gave me an interest and added income. It also gave me a reason to drive to different markets looking for stock as well as keeping me from spending too much time at home dwelling on Marcus' death. After a shaky start when my shyness threatened to hold me back, I now enjoyed selling the signs weekly from my market stall in Southampton.

Today, though, I was looking forward to spending a solitary day in the studio. The day was still and the heat heavy. I loved summery days, but this year the consistently high temperatures and feeling like I was trapped inside a thick blanket was exhausting. Determined to lift my mood, I pressed on the car radio. As I turned into to a road passing nineteenth-century town houses and hinting at the past wealth the region had enjoyed, I sang along to 'If Tomorrow Never Comes' by Ronan Keating. My best friend Dee and I had sung it and I'd played it endlessly after she and her family had disappeared on the hottest night of a heatwave in 2003.

The song's title gained a new significance when I rounded a corner and thought I'd spotted someone I hadn't seen for fifteen years.

'Leo?' I shrieked as the car in front stopped at the last minute, when the traffic lights changed to red. It was pure luck I didn't cause a smash. My heart pounded, although whether it was from the shock of the near miss, or thinking I'd seen Dee's younger brother, I wasn't sure.

I could still recall the months I'd waited for a letter from her. I'd wasted hours trying to trace them online and via electoral rolls, even contacting the Salvation Army, desperate to ascertain if they were still alive, or what might have happened to them. All to no avail.

I was about to drive on, but what if it was Leo? I couldn't miss a chance to speak to him. Excitement bubbling inside me, I looked for a parking space, checking back in his direction, but unable to see him. My stomach churned at the lost opportunity, but then I saw him walking towards an office along the street.

A car pulled out of a space in front of me. Parking my Golf badly, I got out, almost forgetting to lock it, before running towards the imposing stone building that housed the branch of the town's main bank. I took a deep breath and pushed the heavy oak doors open.

Running up to him wasn't the way to reintroduce myself, if indeed it was Leo. I watched the broad-shouldered man speaking to the receptionist, willing him to turn his face slightly towards me so that I could get a better look. Why was he here? This wasn't a financial district and this man looked the epitome of a financier, if the cut of his suit was anything to go by.

Then the potential humiliation of what I was about to do dawned on me. What was I thinking? Surely, if either Leo or Dee had wanted to get in touch with me, they could have contacted Mum. Losing my nerve, I turned away. Walking out of the building, the heat of the day hit me. Maybe listening to that song had conjured up one of the people I'd longed to find.

My tired mind must be playing tricks on me. Embarrassed at getting carried away, I hurried to my car. I dropped my keys when a hand landed heavily on my shoulder.

'Sera, is that you?' the man asked, bending down to retrieve my keys from the gutter.

The voice was much deeper, but the inflection belonged to Leo. A thrill of excitement shot through me.

'Leo,' I whispered spinning round to face him. 'I thought I was going mad.'

He held out my keys and shrugged. 'Yes, it's me.'

I took the keys with a shaky hand and couldn't help staring at him as he took a deep breath and smiled. 'Where the hell have you been for the past fifteen years?'

'Let's not worry about that now, shall we?'

'But…' Why couldn't he tell me? He must know how lost I'd been when his family vanished?

Taking my shoulders, Leo held me at arm's length and studied my face. 'I always knew you'd grow up to be a beautiful woman,' he said, his cornflower blue eyes twinkling with more confidence than I could ever have imagined him possessing. My stomach contracted as I looked up at him. He was even taller than Marcus' had been.

Leo frowned, then pulled me into a bear hug. I stiffened for an instant, unused to being held by a man since Marcus died. Despite my best efforts my face reddened. How could this handsome man be the same scruffy boy his sister and I had teased as teenagers?

'I just can't believe it,' I said, my mind whirling and trying to come to terms with what was happening.

He held me away from him again and gave me another wide smile displaying perfect white teeth. He looked wealthy, as if he'd done well for himself.

Desperate to find out more about his family, but not wishing to give him an excuse to leave, I asked, 'Dee? Is she well? She's not here with you, is she?'

His smile slipped. 'No. Dee's not here.'

I waited for him to continue, but he glanced at his watch. 'I have to go. I'm already late for a meeting.'

I followed his gaze to the large building. 'Will I see you again?'

'That would be great.' He thought for a moment. 'Where should we meet?'

'I've moved back to Mum's place. How about coming to the house this afternoon, if you're free?'

'I should be able to get there for around two-thirty. Would that suit you?'

I nodded. 'That's perfect,' I said. 'I'll see you then.'

The mystery of their disappearance had plagued me since my teens. I had almost given up hope of ever finding out what had happened to Dee and her family, but it looked as if my wait wasn't quite over. I smiled as I unlocked my car. At least I knew they were alive. Glancing back to the majestic bank, it dawned on me that Leo hadn't actually answered any of my questions. What *was* he doing back here?

Chapter Four

Young Sera

I almost lost my footing on the gnarled branch of the apple tree as I raised one plimsoll-shod foot and reached out to Dee's windowsill, missing by inches. I held my breath for a second. I'd never known Dee's mum to ground her before. I couldn't imagine what she must have done to upset Hazel this badly.

'Shit.' I grimaced, silently praying that I could hold on long enough for her to realise I was there. I could hear her mum's raucous laughter as she partied with her friends on the other side of the barn where it opened out onto the meadow.

Having no siblings of my own and a mum who had long since disconnected with her relatives, the people at the farm were like my family. I could confide in Dee about anything and she understood how it felt not to know the identity of your father. No one, not even Hazel, was going to stop me seeing her.

I didn't want to insult Mum by letting her know how much I wanted to be a part of Dee's home where everyone chatted openly about their thoughts and dreams. At home the only dream that mattered was the size of the next part

Mum might get. I understood that she needed to earn enough money to pay for everything in our lives, but did she have to be so controlling? Hazel wasn't married either. She needed to find ways to pay for her farm and kids, but unlike Mum she was carefree and fun to be with.

Someone put on another record and Hazel began singing. It was safe to carry on. I braced myself ready to propel forward once again. Grabbing hold of the sill with one hand, my nails grazed one of the wooden shutters. I groaned as two nails broke near the quick, tearing the skin.

'Dee,' I almost hissed, trying not to be overheard by her mum.

Something clattered onto her wooden floor and Dee's face appeared at her half open window. 'What the hell are you doing up here?' she asked, barely able to stop from giggling. I noticed her headphones dangling from around her neck – no wonder she hadn't heard me.

'Bloody help me,' I said through gritted teeth. 'I'm stuck.'

She pushed the other window wide open and leant out. She pulled me to her by the elbows. 'Shit, you're heavier than you look.'

I didn't have the strength to argue, but pushed my feet hard against the branch, launching myself towards her, and together we fell back heavily onto her floor.

'Oof. Get off me.' She tugged at the wires now wrapped tightly around her throat.

Relieved to be safe, I pushed myself off and lay next to her, willing my heart to slow. 'I thought I was a goner then.'

We stared at each other in silence for a couple of seconds, before amusement washed over her face again.

'You looked so funny hanging on for dear life,' she giggled. 'I never knew your eyes could go that wide.'

I punched her playfully on the shoulder, wincing as the broken skin under my nails tore further. 'Ouch.'

'You hit me after nearly strangling me?' she teased, tears of laughter running down her face.

'It was your headphone wire that nearly strangled you, not me,' I argued. 'Anyway, I was terrified,' I said in between hysterical bouts of laughter. 'You know I'm scared of heights.'

Dee wiped her eyes with the bottom of her T-shirt. 'Why did you climb the tree then, moron?'

'To see you.'

'You can't use the front door, like everyone else?' She threw her iPod Classic onto the bed.

'When I saw your mum earlier at the greengrocer's, she told me I wasn't to come here. She said you were in serious trouble.' I sat up and crossed my legs. 'What did you do to piss her off?'

She sat up opposite me, frowning and stared at the floor in contemplation. 'It's that idiot boyfriend of hers, Jack.'

I didn't like him much either. There was something odd about him, though I had no idea what. We'd discussed our thoughts on Hazel's relationship many times, while stuffing our faces with popcorn and watching *10 Things I Hate About You* on DVD, desperately trying to work out ways that we could meet Heath Ledger. I suspected that our nastiness towards Jack had mainly been due to boredom.

'What did he do?'

'He shouted at my brother.'

Anger coursed through me. 'Why?' Leo was a quiet kid. He never really got into trouble and I couldn't imagine him having the courage to give Jack any lip.

'Leo said he saw Jack push Mum, but she denied it.'

I thought about how I'd feel if I saw someone being rough with my mum. 'Why are you grounded if Jack was the one in the wrong?'

'That's precisely what I said when I walked in on her shouting at Leo.' She traced a series of circles in the light dust on her bedroom floor with one finger. 'She's been acting a little odd lately.' She hesitated. 'I think she's doing more than smoking the odd spliff, Sera.'

I wasn't sure what to say next.

Dee shrugged. 'Never mind that, you know how I never stand up for Leo, so that must tell you how nasty things got earlier.'

She was right, she didn't. It must have been a bad row for her to defend her brother. 'True.'

Dee hadn't finished. 'I couldn't believe it when she turned on the pair of us and sent us to our rooms, so she could be alone with him.'

Despite Dee's comments about her mum and what she was getting up to, it still didn't make much sense to me why Hazel had been quite so angry with her. I voiced my concerns.

She sighed. 'Well, she also caught me cutting up one of her dresses.'

'What?' I shrieked. 'Why would you do that?' But Dee was always braver than me so I could picture her doing such a thing.

'She slapped me.' Dee put her palm up against her left cheek and I saw it still had a pink tone to it under her tan.

'Won't do that again then, will you?' I asked, stunned to think of Hazel raising a hand to either of her kids.

She shook her head. 'No. I don't know what all the fuss was about; she hadn't worn it for years.'

'Can I see your creation?' I asked, but had no idea where Dee thought she'd wear a new dress, if she had managed to make one. There was little to do in our village. There certainly wasn't anywhere you'd bother dressing up for.

'I can't,' she pouted. 'She threw it away.'

I hated seeing her cross, she was usually so cheerful. 'At least you have a mum whose clothes you can make into something you'd choose to wear. Imagine me trying to do that with my mum's stuff?' We sat contemplating this amusing notion for a bit. 'So,' I said, standing up. 'Are we going to sit here all night, or are you coming down to the woods for a swim? It's stifling in here.'

I was worried I'd get caught by Hazel: while she could be odd at times, I loved her and didn't want to get into her bad books. Coming to this farm in my free time was what I enjoyed doing most. I wished my mum and Hazel were friends and she could see how lovely and open this family were, but Mum would have none of it. She didn't really like me spending time here with them.

Mum wouldn't even take me to visit her mother and sister and it didn't matter how many times I tried, she never answered any questions about my dad. Giving me a name would have been a start. I couldn't understand why she wouldn't give me that, at least.

'Stifling?' she said, mimicking my voice.

'What?' I said, realising I hadn't been listening to her.

'You been listening to your mum talking posh again?'

'Shut up,' I pushed her, unable to stop smiling.

She got up and pulled open the middle drawer of the wide chest next to the window and lifted out her pink bikini. 'I think I could do with cooling down a bit,' she said stripping off and changing, and I knew she wasn't just referring to the heat in the stuffy bedroom. She was angrier about what had happened between her and her mum than I'd realised.

We stepped out onto the landing, stopping to listen for Hazel's voice, or any one of her cronies who might have come into the house for drinks. Then we tiptoed down the stairs, covering our mouths with our hands to stifle our giggling. As soon as we were outside, we glanced at one another, and without speaking, tore off, running as fast as we could towards the wood. Dee shrieked as we neared the coolness of the dense trees circled around the natural pool.

When we were younger and first discovered this place, Dee had insisted it was a fairy glade. I didn't believe her, but now I was sure that the pool had magical properties.

'Remember when we thought time stood still for everyone else when we were in here?' Dee asked. Without waiting for a reply, she dropped her towel, and ran into the water. She didn't stop until she was in the deepest part of the pool, instantly lowering her head.

I imagined it must be spooky here at night-time, but right now it was an oasis cooling our hot skin. I followed her, my breath catching as the cold water reached my ribcage.

'This is brill,' she shouted, splashing me and cheering as if she hadn't been out here only the day before. 'I love this place. One day I'm going to buy this wood. I'll make sure I never leave it.'

'You have to leave it sometime, you can't stay here forever.' Dee gave me a sad look and I wondered if maybe the situation between her mum and Jack was worrying her more than she was letting on.

'How come you're here tonight?' she interrupted my thoughts. 'Your mum doesn't usually let you out this late.'

'She's away filming, again.'

Dee's mouth fell open. 'She never leaves you by yourself in the house.'

'I know.' I just couldn't imagine my controlling mother leaving me alone in the house for several days. 'She's got another babysitter from that agency to stay with me.'

'That doesn't explain why you're allowed out,' Dee said, lying on her back floating, her arms and legs outstretched. 'Where is this babysitter?' she asked, emphasising the word 'baby'. 'How did you escape from her?'

I hated my mum treating me this way. I was twelve, not six. I sulked as I stared up at the dusky sky through the trees, copying what Dee was doing.

'Her boyfriend snuck around to the house about half an hour after Mum left. I told her I had loads of homework to be getting on with and needed to be left in peace in my bedroom to do it. I said I'd see her tomorrow morning at breakfast. I think she was relieved to be left alone with him.'

Dee turned to look at me, a look of admiration on her tanned face. 'And she believed you?'

'Yup.'

'Fab.'

We floated silently in the cool water after our tedious day spent in a humid classroom. I was almost dozing off when she splashed me. The shock made me sink slightly, so that I swallowed a mouthful of water. I frantically attempted to clear my airways.

'What did you do that for?' I eventually managed to splutter.

'Sorry.' She grabbed hold of me and helped me swim to the side of the pool. 'I had a thought.'

We both giggled, amused that her thought had caused me to almost drown. I grabbed my towel and sat on it, patting the space next to me for her to join me. 'Go on then, spill.'

She raised her shoulders and gave a little squeal. 'Why don't we ask your mum if you can come and stay with us every time she goes on location?' She gave a satisfied grin. 'Brilliant idea, don't you think?'

I shook my head. 'She'll never go for it. You know odd she is about Hazel.'

'I suppose my mum is very different to yours, but it doesn't mean that you won't be looked after. We'll just have to work on her and persuade her it's the best option.' She thought for a moment. 'We could tell her how much money she'd save by not hiring nannies for you so often.'

I grimaced. 'Nah, she'd hate anyone to think she didn't have money. No, it'll have to be something else. But what?'

Dee hugged me. 'We'll think of something. Imagine you being able to stay at my house night after night, it would be fun. We could have midnight feasts at midnight.'

I laughed. 'Not at seven-thirty in the evening, you mean?'

'Yes. And we could sneak out and meet boys.'

I pushed her so hard she fell backwards, leaves from the ground getting caught in her damp hair. 'We don't know any boys, silly,' I said, wishing we had the nerve to do as she suggested. 'Only the stupid ones from school.'

'True, but we could meet some if we sneaked into the village at night.' She lowered her voice despite us being alone. 'I heard that Frankie was caught snogging Steve by the bins near the chippie the other night.'

'No, really?' I didn't like Frankie very much, she was often spiteful and teased me about not having a dad, but I couldn't help being impressed by this news.

'It would be fun. We just have to think of a way to get your mum to agree.'

I had to admit I liked this plan of hers. Staying at the farm and sharing Dee's bright bedroom would be much more fun than having to make small talk to an endless round of babysitters. 'What about Hazel? We'd need to ask her permission first.'

She shrugged. 'You know my mum would love you to stay with us. Especially if it kept me quiet and out of her way.'

This was true. 'Fine then, we'll make a plan. I'll hint to my mum when she gets back.'

Just as I'd expected, my mother's initial reaction had been one of horror. She looked over her shoulder as if expecting to find someone lurking there. I was used to this odd behaviour. She'd always worried about strangers and checking doors were locked even when it was the middle of the day and the house was busy with people. In fact, I was sure that her slightly neurotic manner was the reason I pushed myself to be more open and trusting of others.

'Leave you in the care of that mad woman and her wild family? I don't think so, Sera.'

'Why not?' I said. 'At least there's someone to have fun with there. You're always learning lines. Why don't you talk to me? We could spend more time together and you could tell me something about your family, or—' I braced myself for her tone to change '—you could tell me a bit about my father.'

'No.'

'But…'

Mum's expression changed to one of irritation. 'But, nothing.'

For once I didn't care about her issues. It irritated me that she had this unspoken rule never to talk about her life before Oakwold, and never to mention Hazel's name. It was ridiculous and I'd had enough.

'If you met her and tried to get to know her you'd probably get on well,' I argued. 'She's kind and funny.' I laughed, picturing Hazel's silly antics. 'And she's an incredible singer…'

'Shut up,' Mum bellowed. 'You don't know her.'

'I do,' I shouted, confused. I bent towards her, hating her at that moment. 'Hazel's much nicer than you.'

Grabbing me by the shoulders, she shook me so hard my neck hurt.

I cried out, shocked by the uncharacteristic violence of her reaction. The loathing in her face scared me. I writhed away from her, frightened.

'I hate you,' I shrieked, running away from her to the safety of my bedroom.

'Hazel isn't the perfect person you think, Sera,' she screamed, as I slammed the door.

Chapter Five

1990 – London

Mimi

The pretty girl with the wild strawberry blonde hair dropped her faded denim jacket onto the chair and held out her hand. 'Hi, I'm Hazel.'

I couldn't understand why she looked so pleased with herself. This crummy guesthouse I'd found through a newspaper ad was even worse than I'd imagined. I was relieved my mum and sister couldn't see where I was intending to live.

'I only got here a month ago,' Hazel added, snapping my thoughts back to the present. 'I don't know many people yet.'

'I'm Mimi,' I said trying to look friendlier than I felt. 'I'm an actress. I'm eighteen.'

'Me, too,' she giggled. 'Eighteen, that is, not an actress,' Hazel giggled again. She reminded me of an over-excited puppy. 'Where've you come from?'

'Dalingbrook, it's a small village near Northampton.' That would be the last time I'd mention where I grew up, I decided, wishing I hadn't told her. 'You?'

'York,' she said beaming at me. She whooped in delight, her hair bouncing around her cherubic face.

I stifled a groan. I'd hoped to escape childish friends, but it looked as if I was going to end up having to spend my nights sharing a room with one.

'I'm a singer,' she said. 'Have you acted in anything I might have seen?'

'Nothing much. Not yet anyway. That's why I've come to London. I want to make a name for myself.'

Hazel clapped her small hands in delight. 'Me too. Oh, I knew we'd be great friends.'

I wished I shared her enthusiasm. 'Is that my bed?' I asked, looking at the one covered with an array of discarded clothing.

Hazel nodded, her face reddening. 'Sorry, I've always been a messy bugger. Let me move them.' She scraped the clothes together and dumped them onto her creased sheets.

Hazel beamed at me. 'We're going to get along well, I can tell.'

Could she? I wasn't so sure.

'Do you have any contacts here yet?' I asked, thinking that I may as well make the most of having to put up with this messy girl.

She pursed her lips together. 'There's a party tonight at a club in Soho. I've been invited by this really cool guy who runs it. Vince. He owns a few bars and nightclubs. It's where all his theatre-type friends hang out.'

My mood lifted immediately. This was more like it. I might finally meet some famous people. I sat heavily on my newly cleared bed. 'Really?'

She nodded enthusiastically. 'Yeah, there are actors and singers and their agents go there, too.'

'Theatrical agents?'

'Yes.' She lowered her voice to a whisper. 'I heard that Vince grew up in the East End and until a couple of years ago ran things for this older guy.'

'What happened to him?'

'He died,' Hazel said staring out of the window briefly.

'How?'

'Look, I don't know all right? No one talks about it.'

My stomach fluttered nervously. 'He sounds a bit dodgy, if you ask me.'

Hazel pushed my shoulder playfully. 'He's great,' she laughed, but it seemed forced. I wondered if maybe she was panicking that I might repeat what she had told me. 'He's always immaculately dressed,' she added, if that made up for any shortcomings in his character. 'If someone upsets him, though, he fires them and sees to it that none of the other clubs will employ them.'

I wasn't sure he sounded like the sort of person I wanted to get to know, but it wasn't as if I knew of anyone better.

Hazel pulled a face. 'I think that if they're stupid enough to cross him then it serves them right.'

I decided that if Hazel had the connections to help my future I wasn't going to annoy her by arguing.

'Do you think he'd mind if I came to the party?'

'Yeah, course you can. He said to bring a friend.' She sighed dreamily. 'He's a real hunk, you'll love him; everyone does.' Her pale cheeks reddened.

'I'll let you know what I think when I meet him.'

'Have you got a boyfriend back home?' Hazel asked.

I shook my head. I wasn't going to admit that I'd never had a boyfriend. One quick snog after a local church dance was all I'd experienced up until now. And that had been short-lived when my mother appeared from the shadows to shout at him.

'What time do we have to be at the party?' I said, changing the subject.

Hazel smiled. 'Any time after nine, so we've got hours yet. Time for you to unpack.'

'Time for me to try and find a job,' I said.

She thought for a moment. 'We can ask around. I'm working as a waitress in Dave's Diner,' she laughed. 'It's a greasy café down the road and they pay a pittance, but it's a job. I'm hoping to make a contact at this party and then I can give in my notice. Maybe Vince can get me a singing job at one of the clubs.'

Vince was sounding better and better. 'Maybe he might know someone who could help me?' I suggested hopefully.

Later that evening, we entered the club, the dark red walls giving a feeling of depth that was impossible to decipher. The flashing lights from the stage drew my eyes to the glamorous woman singing with the band. There was so much to gaze at that I almost forgot how my feet ached from traipsing around London looking for work.

I sucked in my non-existent stomach, trying my best to exude confidence. I didn't know if it was excitement or nerves, but my legs felt like they were made of cotton wool. I followed Hazel, noting that every woman we passed, beautiful or not, was immaculately made-up. This was a totally different world to the one we'd just left outside. The smartly dressed men lurking in the shadows appeared smooth and a little intense. They seemed to sense our naivety, as if they could smell it. None of them bothered to conceal their approval of Hazel and me as they exhaled smoke from their cigarettes and drank champagne. It was as if they were evaluating our worth in some way.

Hazel stopped in front of a small group, waiting for them to notice her. One of the women, a tall blonde, threw her head back in laughter. She almost spilled the pink cocktail she was holding in one manicured hand down a man's suit. He flinched, pushing her other arm from his broad shoulders. Then, glaring at her, he bent his head next to hers and whispered something I couldn't make out. She lowered her head briefly, and then raised it, a fixed smile on her face. I couldn't miss how her large eyes glistened suspiciously.

As if he sensed me staring at him, he turned to face us. The others in his group stepped back to clear his line of vision.

Hazel nudged me so I assumed this tall man, wearing a tailored, steel-grey suit, must be Vince. He had a self-assured air about him that I had never witnessed before.

Suddenly breathless, I cleared my throat as his deep blue eyes connected with mine. He was mesmerising. His dark, almost black, hair was shorter than the other men's in the club; his tanned face set his perfect white teeth off to perfection. It was easy to understand why she liked him. He watched me silently. I blushed under his intense scrutiny.

'Mimi,' Hazel snapped, glaring at me.

He motioned for us to step forward.

Hazel took me by the arm and pulled me over to stand in front of him. I jerked my arm from her grasp, and smiled.

'Vince,' Hazel said, her smile not reaching her eyes. 'This is Mimi, she's my flatmate.'

Flatmate? We shared a box room, but, hey, if she wanted to give them a more upmarket impression of us then who was I to argue.

Vince held out his hand without taking his eyes off me. I shook it, still holding his gaze and did my best not to feel intimidated by the blonde he had pushed away seconds before who now glared at me. She raised her arm, resting it on his shoulder. He stepped closer to me and her arm dropped.

'Mimi,' he said, saying my name slowly in a rich, deep voice. 'It's good to meet you.' His grasp tightened on my hand and pulled me gently into his group. Then, putting one arm around my waist and the other around Hazel's, he led us towards the bar. 'You, gorgeous ladies, are coming with me. We could do with some fresh faces around.'

I heard laughter behind me and thought someone said, 'Fresh meat,' but ignored them and exchanged delighted glances with Hazel. We had arrived.

'I think you both need a drink and proper introduction to this place.'

Hazel giggled.

'Is this your first time in London?'

'Yes,' I said, desperate to appear sophisticated like the blonde woman. He seemed too worldly to be fooled by any façade, however.

Vincee caught the attention of the barman. 'A bottle of champagne and four glasses, Joe.' Then he turned back to me. 'So, what have you come to this vibrant capital for, Mimi?'

'She's an actress,' Hazel chirped before I had time to reply. 'She's looking for work and we thought maybe you could help her find something?'

I glared at her. I didn't want Vince to think I was too shy to speak for myself.

'Hey, it's okay,' he said spotting my reaction. 'She's right to tell me. I always do my best to help friends.'

'Friends?' I asked, laughing a little too loudly. It was partly out of relief that he liked me, but also because I had never received such rapt attention from any man before, let alone one as charismatic as Vince. 'But we only met five minutes ago.'

The tanned skin around his dark blue eyes crinkled in amusement. 'Maybe, but we'll soon get to know each other, and I'm sure we'll become firm friends.'

'Okay,' I said, sounding ridiculously grateful.

He winked at me. Picking up the bottle of champagne, Vince pushed at the cork with his thumb until it flew out. He poured the bubbly, golden liquid into the four glasses and passed one each to me and Hazel. He then passed one to the blonde woman, holding the glass in mid-air for a few seconds when he spotted her scowling at me. 'This is Alice,' he said, finally passing over the drink.

I assumed she must be his girlfriend and my mood plummeted. If she wasn't a model, she certainly could pass for one. How could I ever compete with someone so glamorous? There was something about her that I ached to duplicate. I resented her immediately.

'So, you're an actress,' Vince said, ignoring her and focusing on me.

'Yes.'

'Have you done much acting work?' I shook my head. 'Never mind. If you're determined and have any talent then you might stand a chance.' He narrowed his eyes and drank some of his champagne. 'I might be able to help you, at least with an introduction or two, but you're going to have to work for it.'

I didn't care what I had to do. 'That would be perfect,' I said, taking a sip but the champagne went down my throat the wrong way. I began coughing, mortified to have made such a fool of myself. Unable to catch my breath I held out my glass, trying to place it on the bar. My eyes streamed. It was all I could do not to cry. My first impression and it had been a bad one.

'Here,' Vince said quietly, taking my glass with one hand and patting my back with the other. 'Joe, get the kid a glass of water. Now!'

I fought to draw breath and Vince's hard pats on my back helped a bit.

'Here,' he said, his voice gentle. 'Take a few sips of this water, it should help.'

I did as he said, taking first one sip and then another few. Gradually the coughing ceased, and my breathing began to return to normal.

He handed me back my glass. 'Come with me,' he said as if we were the only ones there. 'There's someone I'd like you to meet.'

I did as he asked, nervously hoping that this would be my life-changing moment. Vince put an arm around my waist again and lowered his head slightly towards me. 'The guy I'm taking you to meet is a business contact of mine.'

My mouth dried up instantly. I could barely contain my nerves. 'Really?'

He gave me a little squeeze. 'Yes, really.'

Hazel had been right; Vince was lovely. We drew up next to a short, skinny man with thick glasses.

'Vinnie,' he shouted, raising his arms in the air. 'Where've you been hiding all night?' The men standing with him moved away. I noticed one nudge the other and grin in my direction. I shivered for some reason I didn't understand.

Vince placed his palm against the small of my back and propelled me forward. 'Gerald, this is Mimi.'

I almost lost my footing. When I regained my composure, I came face to face with the second person that evening who took more time to study me than I was used to. His tongue moistened his fat lower lip thoughtfully. 'Mimi,' he said in a high-pitched nasal voice. 'You are a cute one.'

His attention unnerved me. He had the smallest eyes I'd ever seen on a grown person, but they seemed to bore right through me. I was a little unsure how I should react. 'Thank you.'

'You're an actress?' He puffed on a short, fat cigar, removing it to reveal how wet it was at one end and waved it in the air.

I was flattered that he could tell just by looking at me.

'You're pretty. And tall. But can you act?'

I nodded, my previous confidence vanishing.

'And you want me to find you work?'

'Yes, please,' I said, a little less sure about how much I actually wanted his help. I spotted Hazel and Alice watching my conversation with great interest. Maybe Gerald wasn't such a bad person to be introduced to, after all. I forced a smile, wishing to appear a little friendlier, and less afraid.

'I think I might be able to do that.' He took out his wallet and withdrew a business card. Handing it to me, he said, 'Here's the address for my office, be there at ten

37

o'clock sharp on Monday. We'll have a chat. See what I can do for you.'

'Thank you,' I said breathlessly.

Delighted, I couldn't help standing a little taller, confident that I'd just experienced the moment I'd been hoping for all my life. It was. Meeting Vince did change my life, just not in the way I'd expected.

Chapter Six

Sera

After a few unproductive hours in my studio in Southampton, I arrived back at the house. It was another sweltering day and I had stopped off at my favourite bakery to buy a box of fresh cakes. The heat was so intense that everyone felt drained and lacking in energy, so a sugary treat would help all of us.

I had spent the morning struggling after yet another exhausted, fretful sleep wondering what had happened to Dee and her family to make them disappear. The last time I saw them it had been to deliver a letter from my mother. Had she said something to make them leave? Today, I hoped to finally discover what really happened to them.

Checking the kitchen wall clock yet again, I ground fresh coffee beans and set them to percolate on the range. I tried not to get too excited and pottered about the house, finally giving up and sitting to wait for Leo's arrival.

I glanced at the clock. What if he changed his mind and wasn't ready to speak to someone from his past? I stood up and wiped down the worktops; then, when he hadn't arrived by two-thirty, I washed the kitchen floor to keep busy, wondering if he was coming.

The doorbell rang just before three; my heart pounded as I hurried to answer it. Could he really be on the other side of that door? Was I about to discover what had happened to my best friend and her family all those years before? I'd imagined this moment many times since their disappearance that hot summer night when Dee and I were barely twelve. Although I wasn't going to see her today, at least I might learn where she was now and how I could contact her.

I turned the brass handle and pulled back the front door. There he was, smiling back at me. I wasn't sure who was more delighted to see the other.

'Come on in,' I said, my voice wavering. I waited for him to enter the bright hallway.

He walked in, stopping at the base of the staircase and gazed around the room and up towards the landing.

'I remember coming here with Dee a few times and you two would always make me go and play in the back garden. You never let me join in with whatever you were doing.'

I walked past him towards the kitchen, laughing at the memory. 'That was because we were practically teenagers and always talking about boys. You were what, nine?' He nodded. 'We didn't want you spying on us and reporting back to your mum.'

'Hah, you think she would have noticed?'

I pictured Hazel, her mind elsewhere whenever she was harvesting her crop of lavender. She seemed perpetually happy as she picked the scented purple flowers, the hem of her colourful flowing skirt tucked into the elastic waistband and a wicker basket by her feet slowly filling up, singing as she worked. Later, she placed the stems into oil-filled bottles, or plaited hearts with the longer stems to sell on her occasional market stall in the village.

'True, we could pretty much do whatever we liked at her farm,' I said, happy to be able to reminisce about those blissful days. In my mind it was always a hot summer's day. 'As long as we didn't overstep the mark when it came to pinching the odd tot of whatever cocktail someone had made, or sneaking off with a suspicious-looking cigarette.' I hesitated. 'She was besotted with Jack, wasn't she? Always trying to please him. I suppose they eventually married?'

I thought I noticed his smile slip slightly.

'They never did,' Leo considered. 'Jack was okay, but I think he got tired of the constant stream of people visiting the farm.'

'It was a bit full-on, sometimes, wasn't it?' If she wasn't trying out a new idea to make money, Hazel was entertaining her eccentric friends.

'It was.' He hesitated. 'Have you been there at all?' He glanced out of the window. 'To the farm?'

I picked up the coffee percolator and pointed at it. Leo nodded.

'As it happens, yes,' I said, pouring us both a mug.

He seemed surprised by this, though I wasn't sure why. I had lived here most of my life and the farm was only down the road. I indicated the plates and napkins and told him all about Henri and the fire burning down the barn.

He groaned. 'Hell, that must have been frightening.'

'It was, but I mostly felt very sorry for Henri. He's new to the town and a little, um, reserved. The people around here haven't really taken to him.'

'Because he's interesting, you mean?'

I laughed, choking on the mouthful of coffee I'd half swallowed. 'Stop it. There's nothing wrong with the people around here. Anyway, neither of our mums are from here and they didn't find it hard to settle in.'

He pondered my comment for a moment. 'We don't really know that, though, do we?'

'No, we don't.' I hadn't considered how little I knew about Mum's early years here when I was tiny.

'They had kids,' Leo continued, breaking my reverie. 'Us being born and brought up here and attending the local schools would have helped them fit in. He's a stranger with no connections, I guess.'

That was true. 'I'm not sure why they have such an issue with him.'

Leo stared at me for a moment. 'We were always slight outsiders, probably because our mothers were quite different in their own ways to the other local mums.'

My mum was always flitting here and there, either going to auditions in London or filming her latest bit parts somewhere. I think the people around here were slightly in awe of her lifestyle. At least Hazel, despite her barely concealed ambitions to be a professional singer, had fewer airs about her and tended to make friends a little more easily.

'Our mums had their own odd ways,' I reflected. 'No matter how much they tried not to stick out from the other locals, they never quite fitted in properly, which is probably why people thought we were different.' And, I mused, probably also why the three of us gravitated towards each other.

'Our mums were entertainment for the locals, I always thought.'

I smiled, recalling Hazel's battered Land Rover with coloured beads strung along the inside of the back windows. 'They were probably too stunned by your mother's antics to find the right words to criticise any of us.'

Leo laughed. 'You're probably right. And as for your friend, Henri, is it?' I nodded. 'You say he's quite reserved, maybe they take that as being secretive and untrustworthy.'

I could see his point. I hadn't picked up any bad vibes from Henri, but Mum certainly had. Unwilling to dwell on any negativity about the farmer, I pushed the plate of cakes towards him. 'Please take one.'

'They look delicious. I've missed eating these. Are they from that local bakery we always used to go to?'

'They are,' I said, watching him choose a chocolate-covered choux bun and eat half of it before asking the one question I'd been dying to put to him. 'So, Dee, is she well?'

He looked up at me, wiping the sides of his mouth with the napkin before lowering his gaze and staring silently at the table.

'She's okay,' he added eventually.

He didn't sound that convincing. 'Has something happened to her?'

He seemed to be gathering his thoughts and then looked me in the eye. 'To be honest, she's had a rough time of it.' I waited for him to continue, not daring to put him off elaborating further. 'In fact, I'm rather concerned about her, Sera.'

'Why?' I asked, trying not panic. 'Is there anything I can do to help?'

He shook his head. 'No,' he hesitated. 'I couldn't ask you. I've only just met up with you again, and you haven't seen Dee for years.'

'If there's something I can do for her, please promise me you'll let me know.'

He looked so sad. Once again, he seemed like a small boy with a mountain of trouble weighing him down. He'd always been a worrier, but then it had been about his mother's latest boyfriend, lack of money, or an unwanted guest who was refusing to leave their farm.

'I'd want to, Leo. Promise me.'

He sighed. 'Thanks. I'll bear that in mind. Now,' he said, pointing at the cakes, 'all right if I take a second one of these?'

'Of course,' I said, irritated that he was changing the subject so soon. 'Help yourself.'

I could see my questioning was making him uncomfortable. 'Be careful, though, you don't want to make yourself sick,' I teased, trying to raise the sudden dip in the atmosphere.

He pulled a face at me. 'I was what, seven, when I ate all my mother's Black Forest gateau?'

I laughed at the memory of how furious Hazel had been to discover that not only had Leo eaten most of her boyfriend Jack's birthday cake, but that he'd then gone upstairs and thrown up all over his freshly made bed. 'I didn't think she'd ever forgive you for that incident.'

He shook his head and grimaced. 'Nor me.'

'I was always envious of you and Dee growing up at the farm with your colourful mum and her floaty friends,' I said.

'Floaty?' he asked, confused. 'That's a good way to describe them. Most of them were off their faces on something they'd smoked.'

It had all seemed so lyrical to me, as if their farm was in an invisible bubble. 'It was their long flowing skirts and scarves I adored. My mum always wanted me to dress conservatively. She was all sleek hair, tailored clothes and primary colours, but I craved Dee's wardrobe.' I smiled, warmed at the memory. 'Hazel was always reinventing herself,' I said, thinking back to the vivacious woman I'd hoped to emulate when I grew up. One day she was a bleached blonde glamorous singer, the next rushing off to an ashram somewhere deep in the French countryside leaving Dee and Leo with whichever boyfriend was living at the farm at that time. 'Jack calmed her down a bit, don't you think?'

Leo drank some of his coffee while he contemplated my comment. 'I suppose he did. He certainly lasted longer than most of her boyfriends.'

I took a sip of my coffee, relishing the hot, rich liquid. 'You can't say we had dull childhoods, though, can you?'

'A little normality would have been a treat sometimes.'

I agreed. Sitting here with Leo and reminiscing made me aware how different my childhood seemed from an adult's point of view. My past had always been a bit of a mystery to me. Mum would never discuss where she grew up, despite my pleading. All she'd once said was that she'd spent her childhood planning her escape from her home town. I learnt not to press her from an early age. I began to think her airs were probably put on a bit as I got older and mixed with different kinds of people.

'I wish our mothers had been better friends.' It had been a relief that she hadn't minded Dee and Leo, but despite her being a pretty good actress she could never fail to show her loathing of Hazel whenever I mistakenly mentioned her name. 'Do you think she was jealous of Hazel's carefree ways?' I asked.

'Maybe.' A key rattled in the front door and Leo turned instantly to face the hallway. 'Could that be your mum?'

'Probably. She'll be amazed to see you here.'

The rapid tapping of her heels click-clacked on the tiled flooring as she neared. I waited, anticipating her look of astonishment when she spotted who was with me. I wasn't disappointed. Her initial expression was one of delight to find me talking to a man at the table; she was always nagging me to start dating again, irritated when I tried to insist that I was perfectly happy by myself. Then my mother stepped further into the kitchen. She squinted, realisation slowly dawning as Leo turned around to her, a smile on his tanned face.

'Leo, is that you?' she asked, raising a perfectly threaded eyebrow.

He stood up and gave her a brief hug. 'Hello, Maureen. You still look the same.'

'I don't, but it's very kind of you to fib,' she said, smoothing down her immaculate hair. 'I think I need a cup of tea, Sera,' she said, sitting down at the end of the table, all the time staring in disbelief at him. 'You look so different.'

'Mum, we'd find it odd if he hadn't grown up at all.' I poured hot water into the teapot and added a few spoons of tea leaves, before placing the pot in front of her on the table. It was only when I turned back from taking a cup and saucer from the dresser that I realised she looked troubled. I decided to ask her why later, after he'd left.

After an awkward silence, she asked, 'How are Hazel and Dee? Are they well?'

'Mum's living in a village in a remote part of Wales. She helps run a donkey sanctuary with her boyfriend.'

'That doesn't surprise me for some reason.' Taking the silver strainer from the table and placing it on the rim of her cup, she concentrated on pouring her tea, forgetting to leave the teapot to stand for her usual requisite two minutes. 'There was so much gossip when you disappeared all those years ago, no one knew what had happened to any of you. There was even talk of dredging the pool in the woods at the back of your old farm.'

He shuddered slightly. 'I always assumed us leaving like that must have been the most exciting event to happen here for years.' He didn't smile at his own attempt at humour. 'It was a strange time for us, too,' he added quietly.

I took a breath, eager to discover more. 'Can you let me have a phone number for Hazel? I'd love to call her for a chat.'

'She uses the sanctuary office phone in an emergency, but I don't think I have the number with me,' he said, shaking his head.

He glanced down at his watch. 'Hell, is that the time? I should go; I was supposed to meet someone ten minutes ago.' He got to his feet. 'It was good to see you, Mimi.'

She nodded and gave him a sad smile. 'Will you come and see us again, or will you be disappearing for another fifteen years?'

I still hadn't found out what had happened to Dee and wanted to be sure I'd see him at least once more. 'I'll see you out,' I said, giving Mum a pointed glare as I passed her. She didn't seem at all bothered that she'd been rude.

47

It was very unlike her and I couldn't help wondering if seeing him here brought back her concern for me and the devastation I'd felt after his family had disappeared.

I accompanied him along the hallway, both of us walking to the door in silence. He opened it, stopping and turning once outside.

'It really was wonderful seeing you again, Sera.'

'But you haven't told me where you're living, or why you're here.'

He gave me a kiss on the cheek and smiled. 'I live in London, but I've been staying with Dee in France. She lives near Dinard. I spent a few weeks helping her sort a few things with her cottage, but I had to come back to the UK for work,' he explained.

Unsatisfied with his answer and determined not to let him go without trying to find out more about Dee, I placed a hand on his right arm. 'Will you give me her contact details, so I can get in touch with her?'

He shook his head. 'She doesn't have a mobile and I'm not sure she'd want me to give out her landline right now.' He considered his next words. 'Tell you what, I'll speak to her. I can put her in touch with you, if you like?'

I hid my concern that she wouldn't call me. 'Okay.' I was aware that I didn't have any choice in the matter. 'Please tell her I can't wait to catch up with her.' I reached out and took one of my business cards from the hall table, handing it to him. 'Here are my numbers and an email address. I'll wait to hear from you, or Dee.'

He took the card and read it before lowering his head and kissing me on both cheeks. 'It really is very good to see you again. I promise I'll be in touch soon.'

I watched him walk down the steps to the pavement and out of my life, once again. Aware he hadn't offered to give me his contact details either, I hoped he was a man of his word. I sighed, closed the door, and returned to the kitchen.

'What was all that about?' I asked, unable to stop myself.

Mum looked up, her perfectly made-up face seeming older than it had this morning. 'I'm sorry, I didn't mean to be rude. It was a shock seeing him here after so long. I never thought we'd see them again.'

'Nor did I.'

Feeling mean for being harsh, I sat down and told her all about spotting Leo that morning on my way to the studio.

'It was the weirdest thing. He looks so different, but I still sensed it was him, for some reason. Don't you think that's strange, like it was meant to be?' She didn't reply. 'He told me this is the first time he's been back since they left in 2003.'

'Serendipity,' she murmured almost to herself. 'At least we know he's still alive.'

She stared at her cup thoughtfully for a while and I watched, noticing a softness in her demeanour for the first time. I wondered again why there had been such antagonism between her and Hazel. Mum didn't make friends easily, but she didn't fall out with people either.

She straightened her cup in its saucer. 'Whatever happened to the rest of the family?'

'Their lives have probably been pretty much like ours,' I said, trying to picture Dee as she was now.

'I doubt Dee's husband was killed in a plane crash like Marcus. I can't imagine she's had to cope with the things that have happened to you.'

The reference to Marcus stung, as it usually did when I wasn't expecting to hear his name. I'd struggled over the past three years since his plane had crashed into a hillside on the way to a meeting. 'Maybe not, but apart from that difficult time our lives have been ordinary, wouldn't you say?'

Mum sighed heavily. 'Not really, no.' It dawned on me that her boyfriend Paul wasn't with her. 'Where's Paul?'

She took a sip of her tea. 'I ended our relationship.' She stood up, collected the crockery and carried them over to the sink. Pulling on the rubber gloves she always wore to do any housework, she turned on the taps to fill the sink. 'We're not as well matched as I'd hoped.'

I had experienced this before and unlike the occasions when she met someone I thought did suit her, I wasn't sorry to hear Paul wouldn't be coming to stay a third time.

She glanced over her shoulder at me. 'It's getting late. Shouldn't you have left to collect Katie by now?'

I was still unsure why Leo had come to the house, when he seemed reluctant to say anything much about his family. Was what happened to them more sinister than I had imagined? I had no idea. I did know that people could be surprising – and a part of me couldn't help wondering what secrets Leo had that he wasn't willing to share?

Chapter Seven

2018 – Oakwold, New Forest

Sera

A few weeks passed by and I'd almost given up ever hearing from Leo again. I still found it strange to picture him as the broad-shouldered man he had become. He was such a timid little boy, so skinny and shy. I couldn't help wondering why he had returned after all this time. Why meet with someone at the main bank in Southampton? Unless he was planning on buying a home or setting up a business here?

Soothed by this thought, I decided it made perfect sense. Maybe enough time had passed for him and Dee to return to where they had grown up? Perhaps he didn't want to confide in me until they had set themselves up. I hoped so.

I left Katie with Mum while I popped out to the village shop for a few bits. I was studying the dates on packets of ham when I heard a couple of the locals chatting.

'I've never seen him in the village,' a woman said as she stood at the counter. 'Does he darken your doorstep, Val?'

I was aware of an uncomfortable silence, followed by whispers. I couldn't help but sense she was looking at me for some reason. I was tempted to turn and see what was so interesting, but never wishing to involve myself with local gossip, I placed a packet of ham in my shopping basket and focused on which cheese to choose for a salad.

'He comes in here once in a while,' Val said. 'They say he only ventures into the village when he needs something. It's not often, though, I'm told he's mostly self-sufficient.'

'I heard he killed a man,' the customer said. 'Or that he was in the Foreign Legion.'

'I heard it was a woman he'd murdered,' someone else said.

Wishing I had the nerve to leave my basket and go, I walked up to the counter, trying to act as if I hadn't heard their conversation.

'You know him, don't you, love?' Val asked, obviously having no intention of letting me go until she'd gleaned as much as she could about our mysterious neighbour.

'I'm sorry?' I placed my shopping onto the counter.

'You and that bloke your mum's been seeing, you helped that French bloke at the farm when he set fire to his barn.' She waited for an answer. 'What do you make of him?'

'He didn't set fire to his barn,' I corrected her, determined that they weren't going to get away with accusing him of arson, as well as everything else. 'He seems perfectly pleasant to me.'

'Yes, well, I'd expect you to say something like that.'

Unable to help myself, I retaliated. 'What's that supposed to mean?'

Another customer who was queuing to pay for the newspapers tucked under her arm, said, 'You can tell there's something sinister about him. And that farm of his, you know better than most, Sera, strange things have happened there.'

'Anyway,' the woman next to me said. 'He should try and get to know us, if he wants to fit in.'

'Really? Why bother when you've all obviously made your own minds up about him?'

Too furious to be able to stay in the shop a moment later, I turned on my heels and marched out. 'Keep the bloody food, I'll shop elsewhere from now on.'

She was right about strange things having happened at the farm, but they had happened fifteen years ago. Doubting any of them would have bothered checking on Henri after the fire, I drove over to his farm with Katie after collecting her from school. We turned the last bend of his dusty driveway and I spotted him leaning on a rake, one hand up to his eyes to shade them from the glare of the sun. He peered towards us trying to see who was coming, uninvited, to his home.

I pulled up by the lilac and apple trees and stepped out of the car. Opening the rear door, I unstrapped Katie's car seat and lifted her down. Then I let her run around in the yard. 'I hope you don't mind us coming to see you?' I said, sensing he did, very much.

He stared at Katie as she crouched down to study a couple of chickens and shook his head. Resting the rake against the house wall, he said, 'Not at all.'

Feeling a little awkward, I turned my attention to the charred remains of his barn. 'Any idea when you'll be allowed to clear this away and start rebuilding?'

'No.'

He must have been nervous living here alone if the culprits were still out there somewhere. 'I hope they catch whoever did this soon.'

He gave a slow shrug of his right shoulder. 'I can defend myself if I must.'

I believed him. Despite his limp and scarred face, he was muscular, and I didn't doubt that somewhere along the line he'd learnt to look out for himself. There was nothing delicate about Henri. 'Good, I'm glad.'

He looked confused by my visit. 'You want to see the damage to the barn?'

I studied the stakes of blackened wood standing like rotten teeth where the ancient, slightly warped walls had once been. I remembered the stores of apples collected in the autumn months, next to Hazel's willow boxes containing her lavender harvests, the brown bags filled with sunflower seeds from previous years and the more recent drying heads of flowers hung up along two of the walls.

This barn had been majestic and filled with laughter, especially when Dee and I had been sent by Hazel to hang fresh bunting for one of her evening parties. I recalled the calming scent and flickering glow of the lavender candles resting in the elaborate candleholders Hazel favoured. Seeing it crushed by the fire was devastating. It wasn't just a building, it was part of my past that I hadn't ever expected to vanish.

'Yes, okay.'

I followed him, trying to summon Hazel's lyrical voice singing those long-ago songs and wished I could travel back to that time, so reminiscent of the sixties and seventies, if only for a few hours. I longed to revisit those magical days with Hazel and her friends dancing around in their flowing, brightly coloured dresses, the flowers woven into their long tresses, the men with their faded jeans and unfashionably faded T-shirts. Now I could only smell charred wood, but back then the aromas of lavender, mixed with the heady scent of patchouli and sandalwood, filled this space.

I thought back to my younger self with Dee, liking the latest nineties fashions and teasing me that I should have been Hazel's daughter as I fitted in so much better with her carefree world. I imagined how heartbroken I'd be if Katie went through the same mysterious loss of her closest confidante like I had and hoped her teenage years would be more settled.

It hurt that Leo hadn't been in touch. I couldn't help thinking that maybe it would have been better not to have seen him again because doing so brought back too many memories I'd spent years learning to suppress. Had Dee missed me in the same way after they'd left? Had she managed to find a way to make sense of our odd lives?

I realised at that second why my mother had been so odd with Leo. She'd watched me grieve for the loss of my best friend and a family I wanted as my own. It couldn't have been easy coping with your only child withdrawing instead of turning to you for comfort. Poor Mum, I thought, guiltily. I'd put her through so much back then.

I glanced at Henri and realised he was speaking. 'Pardon?'

He smiled crookedly, one side of his face not working as well as the other. It gave him an air of danger somehow. 'I was asking how you are?' he said, kicking a charred piece of wood out of his way.

I told him about my childhood friend reappearing and then not hearing from him again for several weeks. 'I miss not having many friends,' I said, thinking of the life I'd left behind in North Yorkshire. I had joined the local book club soon after Marcus and I had moved there and enjoyed getting to know the women. I had considered them friends, but after Marcus' sudden death they kept away. Their withdrawal from my life was painful and Mum suggested it was because they were unsure what to say to me.

'Some of them will feel threatened that you're now a beautiful young widow,' she had added. 'They'll be concerned you'll look to one of their husbands for comfort.' I had been angered by her comment, but looking back it made sense of their abandonment.

'Friends, what are they really?' he said matter-of-factly. 'Only people who talk to you but usually want something you're not willing to give.'

I wasn't sure what he meant exactly and didn't ask, but his comment saddened me. 'You must have some people you consider friends?'

He looked up at me for the first time since we'd entered the barn. 'You are my only friend in England, Sera.'

'Really?' I couldn't miss the intensity of his gaze. We barely knew each other. It occurred to me that if anyone else had said that to me I probably would have felt a little claustrophobic. For some reason I didn't mind it from Henri. Maybe it was because I felt defensive of the way he'd been treated. Perhaps rather than not liking people, he simply didn't need the company of others to feel secure.

'You don't think me strange saying this to you?' he asked, narrowing his eyes.

'No,' I said honestly. 'It's a compliment.' Again, that intensity as he stared at me. Why didn't it make me uncomfortable?

'Good.' He walked over to the other side of the barn, careful where he placed each step.

I glanced over to the yard to check where Katie had got to and spotted her sitting on the ground playing with Henri's scruffy Collie. She was so sweet. My heart constricted to think that Marcus, so full of hope and ambition when he died, would never get to see her growing up. I reflected on the stories I had shared with him about my time here with Hazel and her family. Marcus had wanted to visit the farm the next time we travelled to Oakwold, but we never managed to before he died. I swallowed the lump in my throat. Now wasn't the time to immerse myself in self-pity.

'Sera?'

Henri's voice snapped me out of my reverie. I hurried to the other side of the damaged building wondering what could be so interesting about lumps of burnt wood and earth.

'Here,' he said pointing down at the floor. 'They think there is a cellar below.'

'Seriously?'

He nodded. 'You knew this place when you were a child? Do you remember anything being stored down there?'

I didn't recall ever seeing a cellar and told him. 'I'm not sure Leo and Dee's family ever knew a cellar existed, I certainly didn't.'

'The fire burnt away some of the wooden floor covering it. Maybe it had been covered over for many years.' He frowned and bent down to study the area further. 'It will be interesting to have a look, no?'

I agreed. 'You could find out how large the area is,' I suggested, intrigued that I thought I knew every inch of this place and here was somewhere I'd never come across before now.

'Storage is useful. A cellar keeps stock cold,' he said. 'When I rebuild the barn, I will make much use of it.'

'Especially in the summer time,' I suggested.

Just then, he walked off. I went to follow him, but my ankle gave way as I stepped over a piece of wood, causing me to slam my hip against part of a brick step.

'Shit.' I winced as I fell, trying not to let on how much it hurt.

'Sera.' Henri hurried back to me. I held my hand up to stop him, concerned that he'd end up tripping in his haste and damaging his bad leg further. 'You are hurt,' he said reaching me and bending down to place his hand on my thigh. 'You should check it,' he said, pointing to my skirt and turning his gaze away.

I gritted my teeth, nervous to discover how badly I'd hurt myself. Then, gently lifting the cotton material until it exposed my skin, I grimaced.

'The skin isn't broken.' I could see a dark bruise already becoming visible. 'But I'm going to be pretty sore for the next few days,' I said, embarrassed.

'Give me your hand, so you can stand.' He took my arm and draped it around his shoulders, slipping his hand around my waist to slowly lift me.

'Thank you,' I said wincing. 'How stupid of me.' I touched the painful area lightly with the palm of my hand and rubbed carefully. 'Damn, that's sore.' I could hear Katie giggling and singing to the dog, grateful she hadn't witnessed my antics.

He stepped carefully over the debris in our path and led me out of the barn area. 'I have arnica in my house; it will help where you have bruising.'

We slowly made our way to his front steps and both limped up to the front door. Not wishing to leave Katie outside alone, I called out for her to come with me.

'Mummy, are you hurt?' she asked, her little face crumbling with fear.

'No, I'm fine. I just twisted my ankle, it's nothing. Come inside with me and Henri.'

'You want some water to drink?' he asked, as she ran up to him. He looked a little more at ease with her and I couldn't help wondering if he'd had his own family at some point.

We reached his kitchen and he motioned for me to sit on an old fabric chair by the fireplace as he went to pull open drawers looking for the cream. Finding it, he handed the tube to me and then crossed the room to pour Katie a glass of water.

'I have old books in another room,' he said to her. 'Would you like me to find them for you?'

'I'll come with you,' she said in a loud whisper. 'I can take them to the porch to read them to your dog.'

He glanced at me and shook his head. 'You talk with Patti,' he said, as he left the room. I heard her chattering away to the Collie telling her how she couldn't read yet, but liked making up stories when she looked at the pictures in books. Henri soon returned laden with a pile of books which he placed just outside the open door. Katie beamed at him and sat down, immediately immersed in the pages of the first volume.

Henri returned to sit in the chair at the other side of the cold fireplace. I watched him for a while, not sure why his mood seemed to have changed. 'Henri, is there something troubling you?'

He rubbed the palm of his left hand with his right thumb absentmindedly. 'I do not wish to offend you.'

'You won't,' I assured him, nerves building in my stomach. 'What is it?'

I waited for him to gather his thoughts and squinted at the instructions on the metal tube in my hand to distract myself.

'You said you grew up here and returned three years ago. What made you come back?'

Deciding that if I was hoping for him to open up a little to me then I needed to do the same, I replied, 'My husband, Marcus and I were living in Hambleton, in North Yorkshire, when he died in a plane crash. Mum suggested I moved in with her and so I came back to the New Forest.' I could see the pity on his face. 'It meant that Katie and I could start rebuilding our lives somewhere familiar. I could also look after Mum's house whenever she was away working.'

'I should not have asked.' He shook his head and looked down at the grate.

I hadn't meant to shock him. 'It's fine, I'm almost used to not having him around now,' I said. It was a half-truth as sometimes the pain of Marcus' absence shot through me. 'I still miss him, of course. Marcus was a good husband and a wonderful father to Katie, for the short time he had that pleasure.'

'A plane crash?'

I nodded. 'He was flying. Marcus always wanted his own plane. He and his business partner shared it. They both died.'

'Do you mind me asking what was his business?'

It made a nice change to speak about my past with someone who didn't have any pre-conceived ideas about it. I thought back to the smart functions Marcus and I used to attend, the plans we'd made and our dreams of the perfect future for us and our beautiful daughter. It took me a moment to collect my emotions enough to be able to reply.

'Initially I hadn't realised Marcus and his partner had overreached themselves, financially,' I admitted. Why was I telling him this much detail? 'The meeting they were flying to was with prospective buyers for the firm. Naturally, the sale fell through after their deaths and almost everything went to creditors.'

'That is terrible.'

'It was devastating at the time. I was left with very little. I sold our home, paid off our mortgage, and came back to Oakwold.'

'You have a new life now. You are happy again?'

He looked so guilty asking me such a personal question that I smiled to put him at his ease. 'Yes, most of the time. Mum and I have our moments, but that's bound to happen, I suppose.'

My last comment made him frown. 'I think your husband would be happy that you've made these choices.'

My mother had said almost the same thing to me many times and a part of me believed it, too. 'I find it difficult sometimes not having him here.' A sob caught in my throat and I coughed to be able to continue speaking. 'Marcus was a darling man. He was funny and very kind. It almost doesn't seem right that I enjoy seeing our daughter growing up while he's missing out on everything.'

'Life is cruel.' He spoke as if the pain of his own past weighed heavily on his mind.

'Tell me about you, Henri,' I asked, seizing the moment. 'What happened to bring you here?'

Chapter Eight

2018 – Oakwold, New Forest

Sera

'Loss, like you.' He looked thoughtful. 'A different loss, but one I struggle to accept. In that we are the same, I think.'

Seeing his mood dipping and not wishing to be the reason his day was made more difficult, I leant forward in the chair and smiled at him. 'We're a couple of miseries; we need to do something to cheer ourselves up.'

He narrowed his eyes suspiciously, unsure whether to take me seriously. 'You wish to do something, together?'

I could tell that my suggestion had unnerved him. 'Yes, we could go somewhere with Katie. Fishing maybe, or swimming in the large pool in the woods at the back of your farm. Have you ever been there?'

He shook his head slowly. I could see my suggestion disconcerted him, but it was too late to take back the suggestion.

'No. This makes it a little painful to walk far.' He tapped his thigh and once again I was intrigued to know what had happened to him.

I recalled my mother's warning about him, but remembered how she also mistrusted Marcus when she had first met him. Turning my attention back to Henri and my plan to encourage him to confide in me at some point, I said, 'We can drive part of the way, if you like?'

He considered this suggestion. 'It is hot. I do like to swim.'

'Then it's decided,' I said, happy to have persuaded him.

I asked him to fetch a couple of towels for us and went to put away the books Katie was looking through. Entering the living room across the hallway, I glanced around for a bookcase and not seeing one, walked over to a small table in the corner that already had a pile of papers spread out on it. I straightened them slightly. Hearing footsteps coming down the hallway, I waited for Henri to join me.

'You have found something?' he asked, frowning, three rolled-up towels under one arm. I opened my mouth to say something, but he shook his head. 'We must swim.'

I was aware he'd changed the subject, which I found a little odd, but before I could prod him for further inform-ation Katie ran into the room. 'Why is Mr Henri holding towels?'

She was such a nosy little devil. I walked over to her and picking her up, winced when she landed against my bruised thigh. She spotted my reaction and looked upset, so I tickled her to distract her. She tried to wriggle out of my arms, until I told her of our plans to go to the pool for a dip.

We reached the car and I strapped Katie into her car seat and waited for Henri to come and join us. He looked unsure as he stood on the steps in front of the farmhouse. Refusing to allow him to stay behind, I turned on the ignition and motioned for him to come over. 'Get in,' I said, before he had a chance to change his mind.

—

'I'm sorry I haven't been to see you in a while,' I said, feeling guilty. 'I've been busy with work. I've had a few extra orders to take care of.'

'It is good to be busy. Please, do not worry.'

We drove to the wood and parked the car. I'd already worked out that my dark underwear could pass for a bikini, and Katie's pants and vest worked well as a make-shift costume. Henri stood by the car. I could see he was unsure of the situation as he silently watched me remove our outer clothes and step in to the water.

I held Katie in my arms and crouched down so that we were up to our underarms in the cold water. She gasped as it connected with our skin, a shock to our systems at first after the extreme heat of the day. I purposely didn't watch Henri take off his trousers. He was shy and I didn't want to give him reason to not enjoy a swim.

Katie splashed about. I held her under her tummy as she kicked and pretended to swim. It was the first time I'd come here since Dee's disappearance.

'That's it, Katie, keep kicking.'

I heard Henri's feet step into the water's edge and glanced up, trying to hide my shock at the sight of the deep, vivid scars across and down his right thigh. The angry gashes depicted the pain of what had happened to him. It was obvious that he'd been lucky to have kept his leg, although his shocking scars and limp made me wonder how close he'd come to losing his life.

He sensed me watching and let his T-shirt, raised midway, drop back down to his waist. 'Hideous, no?'

I shook my head. 'Your scars are on the outside, mine are inside, but no less terrible.' I pulled a stern face. 'Now get into the water, it's glorious.'

His expression softened, and he stared silently at me. For a moment, I wondered if it was a look like this that had disconcerted my mother but reasoned that his discomfort must come from allowing a relative stranger to come socially close, albeit only for a short swim. I had seen his damaged body and hadn't flinched. I had thought him shy, but now I could see he was ashamed of how he looked. He had no reason to be.

'Come on, what are you waiting for?' I teased.

'You are bossy,' he said, hurrying into the dark, cold water, his breath catching for a second as the cold hit him. 'Sheesh, it is too cold.'

'No, it isn't,' Katie giggled. 'Mr Henri is being a big baby, isn't he, Mummy?'

'He is, Katie,' I mocked, smiling at him over her mop of damp curls. 'You're far braver than him.'

'Swim,' she insisted, bored with our chatter. I held her under her tummy once again and laughed when she kicked and paddled with her hands. She would soon be swimming by herself. We played for a while longer and then she wanted me to help her swim again.

'She is good,' Henri said, before diving under and disappearing for longer than I thought possible. I scanned the water for him and was beginning to wonder if his legs had got tangled in reeds when his head popped up away from us.

'Don't do that,' I shouted. 'You frightened us.'

'He didn't scare me,' Katie said. 'Mr Henri is a fish. I want to swim like him when I'm big.'

'Then you'll have to practise, little one,' he said swimming slowly back towards us.

Katie shivered. 'Right, that's enough. You're getting cold,' I said, taking her over to the side of the pool.

'No,' she screamed indignantly kicking her legs in temper. 'Swim, now.'

'We can come back another day,' I assured her.

'I want to swim now.' Katie began to cry. I held her close to me and carried her over to the car to dry her. Thankfully, it was so hot out of the water she soon warmed up. Tired from the excitement of the afternoon and being at pre-school earlier, she became dozy, closing her eyes as soon as I placed her in her car seat. I quickly strapped her in.

I looked at Henri. 'Any news on how the fire was started yet?'

He shook his head. 'They have found nothing apart from the accelerant, but I am hoping there will be soon. I would like to start working on the barn.'

I turned to pick up my towel where I'd dropped it closer to the water, but Henri bent down to grab it first. He straightened up and opening the towel, draped it around my shoulders, the water from his hair dripping on to my arms. He stood still, so close we almost touched. I wasn't sure how to react.

'Sera,' he whispered in his lyrical accent, so different to Marcus' harsh Scottish one that I'd loved so much. 'I must tell you…'

He was about to say something else when I heard a deep voice calling my name. Henri and I stared wide-eyed

66

at each other. Who could know we were here? I peered past him through the trees to try and see who it might be.

Twigs cracked underfoot as the person intruding on our intimacy strode through the undergrowth. 'There you are,' he said, his smile faltering as he spotted Henri still holding the edges of my towel.

'Leo?' I shouted, stunned to see him so unexpectedly. I sensed Henri tense. He let go of the soft material. I daren't look at him again, in case my gaze inadvertently slipped back to his scars. Not wishing to appear rude to Leo, I walked a few steps to the pathway to greet him. 'What are you doing here?'

'Maureen told me I might find you,' he said awkwardly. 'I hope it's okay, me coming here, that is?'

I didn't look at the silent man standing by the water's edge. 'Yes, why wouldn't it be?'

I wondered momentarily what Henri had been trying to tell me, but Leo's voice dispersed my thoughts.

'Great. I would hate to interrupt your afternoon.' Leo gave me a bear hug. 'Phew, it's a relief to be in this shade. I don't think I've ever been so hot.' He walked over to the pool, bent down and scooped up some water in his hands, wiping it over his face and hair to cool down. 'I'm sorry I haven't been back to visit you before now, but there's been so much going on at work. Now I'm here, I didn't think I should waste a moment coming to find you and giving you the great news.'

My heart pounded with excitement. Henri walked up to stand slightly behind me as if he were guarding me in some way, which I found a little irritating.

'Tell me,' I said, forcing a smile and willing away the tension pervading the air around us.

Leo glanced unsmiling over my right shoulder at Henri, still a little unsure of the situation. He returned his gaze to me. 'Dee is with me. I told her about meeting up with you and she insisted on travelling here.'

I hardly dared believe what he was telling me. 'Here? But that's amazing.' Then remembering Henri, I turned to him. 'Henri, this is Leo. Dee is Leo's older sister,' I explained. 'We were best friends when we were teenagers. Did I tell you that? They lived on your farm.'

His expression darkened; he watched Leo silently. 'No,' he said eventually. 'You have much to talk about.' He backed away. 'I will leave you to welcome your friend.'

I couldn't understand why he was acting so strangely but supposed Leo had interrupted whatever it was he'd been about to tell me. I thought of his bad leg. 'I'll drop you off at the farm.'

'It is not necessary,' he said shaking his head, droplets of water splashing down on his tanned shoulders. 'I will walk.'

'No, please,' I insisted, touching his arm lightly. 'I'll take you home. It's on the way.' I turned to Leo. 'Your car must be here somewhere?'

'Yes, it's not far. I'll go, and meet you back at your house. Good to meet you, Henri,' he said proffering his right hand towards Henri, who, after a moment's hesitation, shook it.

Leo walked back the way he'd come.

'I suppose we'd better get going,' I murmured. I hated how the carefree atmosphere between me and Henri had vanished. I got into the car and turned the key in the ignition, setting off as soon as Henri was seated. He sat resting one arm on the open window as the car exited the wood.

The full force of the sun pierced through the wind-screen and I lowered the sun visor to shield the worst of the glare from my eyes. It had been good to spend a little time with him after the drama of the fire. I hoped that despite Leo's interruption his day had been made a little better by leaving the farm for a bit.

'Henri,' I said hoping to entice him to finish what he'd begun telling me by the pool. 'Was there something you wanted to discuss?'

He didn't reply immediately. 'It is nothing.'

By the tone of regret in his voice I suspected it must be fairly important. Maybe it was a confidence that needed to be shared when he was in the right frame of mind. I wondered if he would tell me soon; I hoped he would.

Chapter Nine

2018 – Oakwold, New Forest

Sera

'Mummy's friend has come to visit us,' I explained, wishing I'd managed to find a parking space closer to the house. My skin was so hot and the blissful coolness of our swim now only a memory, as I carried Katie into the house, trying to distract her from her grizzling.

'We're out in the garden,' Mum shouted, hearing me slam the front door closed with my heel. 'Hurry up; you'll never believe who's here.'

I supposed it was living here alone when I moved away with Marcus that made her be more open to inviting people around. My teenage self would have much preferred this softer, friendlier version of my mother.

I put Katie down to stand on the tiled hall floor, watching as she ran out to the garden, her bad mood forgotten in the thrill of having visitors. I hurried down the stone stairs to the oasis I'd established as a subdued teenager needing to escape my inner torment.

I couldn't see Dee anywhere, but a little girl a year or so older than Katie sat quietly opposite my mum.

'Dee?' I called, spotting movement behind the largest hydrangea. A slim figure with dark, bobbed hair stepped forward. She looked timid and nothing like the Dee I remembered. 'You're all grown up,' I laughed, desperate to hide my shock at her tense, sullen appearance. I hurried over to her.

She stood stiffly as I put my arms around her skinny body, but she barely touched my back in response. Not wishing to make her uncomfortable, I cut short my hug. I stepped back, unable to miss the expression set on her pinched face, once so pretty and cheeky, and now so, what? Sad? Haunted? I couldn't decide. She didn't speak.

'It's fantastic to see you again,' I said willing my enthusiasm to pass to her, desperate to fill the strained silence. 'I couldn't believe it when Leo told me you were here. And—' I motioned towards the fragile-looking little girl, '—who's this?'

'I asked her name, but I'm still waiting for her to answer me,' Mum teased.

'Her name is Ashley,' Dee said, her voice monotone. 'She's shy. She also doesn't speak much English.'

I tried hard to hide my shock. 'She doesn't?'

'She's always lived in France and we've always spoken in French at home, so I could practise. We didn't expect to ever leave.'

I asked, 'Would she like to something to eat, or drink?'

Dee shook her head. 'No, thanks, we ate before coming here. She'll be happy as long as she's with me.'

Katie, oblivious to any nuance of awkwardness, had gone inside to fetch a couple of her teddies. She handed one to Ashley, who stared at it. Then glancing over to Dee, she waited for her to nod an approval before snatching it from Katie and holding it tightly against her chest.

'She can have that one, Mummy,' Katie said, looking a little startled by the other child's reaction.

I ruffled her messy hair and bent down to her. 'Thank you, Katie, that was very considerate of you.'

'Can she come and play in my room?' Katie whispered.

'If she wants to, but I think she'll probably want to stay near her mummy for a bit until she gets used to us.'

She twisted her teddy's crumpled ear and thought about my comment. 'I'll ask her later.'

I nodded, and she went back inside the house.

I was dying to ask my once extrovert friend more about her life but by the look of her, Leo had underplayed the difficulties she'd experienced since we'd last seen each other. It was hard to imagine we could be the same age. Her skin was lined and her once full mouth now tight and sullen. What had happened to diminish her enthusiasm for life so completely?

Disappointment welled up inside me. If I didn't hurry up and distract myself, I wouldn't be able to hold back my tears. I went over to the peach tree and raised my arm gently, careful not to bruise the round juicy fruit as I cupped it in my hand. It came away effortlessly, and I held it out to Dee. She'd always loved this tree and could never get enough of the sweet peaches whenever she had come to see us.

She shook her head. 'No. Thank you.'

I covered my disappointment and walked with her moving silently next to me. Unsure what to say next, I smiled at her.

She stopped. 'You must think me very rude.'

'No. I do think something has happened to you and I'd wish you'd trust me to share it with me,' I couldn't help saying.

'Because I didn't say goodbye and never contacted you?'

Saddened by her defensiveness, I said, 'I'm sure you had your reasons. You're here now; that's all that matters.'

Neither of us spoke for a few seconds. 'Katie's gorgeous and so like you when you were small,' Dee said, finally. She glanced over to her silent little girl sitting, eyes closed, hugging the teddy to her as if her life depended on it.

'Ashley is very sweet,' I said. I tried to see some resemblance to her mother but assumed she must take after her father. 'Katie would love to show her all her toys when she's feeling a bit more at home.'

Dee frowned. 'She's very timid.' We walked on further. 'I was sorry to read about your husband's death. Marcus, wasn't it?'

I hadn't expected her to know about his plane crash, and hesitated. 'You knew?'

Dee frowned in confusion at my question. 'Of course, it was in all the papers.'

Why hadn't she bothered to contact me then? I wondered, upset at her lack of concern. Surely it wouldn't have been hard to send a note to Mum's house, or give her a call; Mum's number – though only given out to a few people – had never changed.

'It was devastating,' I said, my voice breaking at recalling that dark time twice in one day. 'We were very much in love, and Katie wasn't even three years old when he was killed. She doesn't remember anything about him, but she does miss him when it's her birthday. I think it's because other children at her nursery school have mummies and daddies and she just has me.'

'Shit.' She stared at me before looking down at the lawn.

'Definitely shit.'

Dee put her arm around me. 'I'm a lousy friend,' she whispered. 'I know I am, but I'm here now and I promise I'll make it up to you.'

My heart ached for her. What had happened? 'I'm just glad to have you here now. We've got so much to catch up on and I can't wait for us to spend time together. How long are you going to stay?'

'Well...' She looked over at Leo who was watching us, his arms folded. I suppose he hadn't known how we would react in each other's company, after all this time.

He came over to join us. 'What?' He stared at Dee.

'Sera was asking how long we were staying,' she said. It sounded like an apology, which seemed odd. 'I wasn't sure what to tell her.'

I watched them exchange glances and tried to figure out what I was missing. It dawned on me that I hadn't offered to put them up while they were in the area. 'You must stay here,' I said quickly. 'We have the room and it would be the perfect way for us all to catch up properly.' I looked over at Mum and before they had time to argue, added, 'Mum? Don't you agree? Leo, Dee and Ashley must stay here with us?'

She smiled, looking pleased at my suggestion. 'I'd be insulted if they stayed anywhere else.'

'That's settled then,' I said, taking hold of one each of their hands. 'You stay with us for a few weeks. It'll be like old times.'

Leo threw his head back and laughed. 'You two were horrible to me back then.'

'We weren't that bad, Leo,' Dee argued, a fragment of her old self escaping. Her mouth pulled back in a tense smile.

'We were pretty vile to him, Dee.' I winked at her. 'Poor Leo. I'm surprised we didn't put you off girls forever. You can relax, though; we've grown up now.'

'We have,' Dee agreed.

'Yes,' I said. 'And we're far nicer than we were.' But I didn't have a clue how Dee was now, which saddened me. It was impossible to dismiss that life had been hard for her, just in what way I didn't know.

We continued chatting and slowly Dee relaxed a little. I could hardly believe I was sitting in the garden with her and Leo after all these years. We'd both been through a lot since that last summer together, but nothing was going to come between us now, I was certain of it.

'How is Hazel, Dee?' Mum asked suddenly. 'Leo mentioned that she runs a donkey sanctuary in Wales.'

I recalled Hazel mentioning something about my mother's determination when they were both trying to make it in show business. I hadn't missed the sarcasm in Hazel's voice, probably because she was usually so friendly and never had a nasty word to say about anyone. I had gone straight home and asked my mother to tell me about her time in London, but she refused to discuss it. But she had let it slip once that she and Hazel had come across each other when they'd both been trying to make a name for themselves in the late eighties in London. Back then, Mum was desperate to be the next Joan Collins, and Hazel saw herself more as Cyndi Lauper, yearning for a number one single. Hazel mentioned living in a run-down flat somewhere in Soho. Also, there had been an innate understanding that something had transpired between Mum and Hazel that had shattered their bond forever.

Why then, I wondered, had they both decided to live so near to each other, in the same village, in the New Forest? It was a strange situation and one that I was going to have to find a way to uncover, somehow.

I watched Dee contemplating her answer and my mother's concentration while she waited to hear it. 'Mum?' Dee asked. 'She's happy enough.'

It made me smile to think of Hazel doing something she loved.

'I'm not surprised Hazel's fine,' my mother interrupted. 'She always is.'

I nudged Mum, willing her not to be mean about Hazel. She closed her eyes briefly, probably fighting a need to criticise. I changed the subject and suggested I make up a couple of the rooms. When I stood up to go in to the house, Leo came with me.

'Only if you're certain,' Leo said. 'I'd hate to put either of you to any trouble.'

Horrified at the prospect of them changing their minds because of some misinterpreted comment from Mum, I shook my head. 'Don't be silly. Mum said she was happy for you all to stay and she meant it. I want to make the most of you both being here.'

'Well, if you're sure,' he said, looking relieved.

'I am. Anyway, Katie would love to have a friend her own age to play with for a few days. Even if they speak a different language, children still find a way to have fun together. You go and check out of whatever hotel you're booked into and come back. We can have supper together. Let's enjoy a long evening getting to know each other again?'

'Great,' he said, waving Dee and Ashley over. 'We'll collect a takeaway on our way back here to save on the cooking. What's your preference with wine?'

'I love rosé,' I said. 'Any one, as long as it's cool.' I joked, delighted to have persuaded him to stay so easily.

I wasn't sure why they needed to all go to their hotel, but didn't want to force the issue about Dee and Ashley staying behind. Dee seemed very dependent on Leo and I didn't want to cause her to feel uncomfortable around me by making trouble between them.

They returned about an hour later with a takeaway from the local Thai restaurant.

'This is delicious, thank you,' I said, wiping my mouth with a paper napkin.

'My pleasure,' he said, tucking in to his meal.

Mum stared at Dee and then Leo. 'What's brought you back here after so long?' she asked, having taken only a few mouthfuls of her food.

They seemed shocked by her question. I wasn't sure why, it seemed like an obvious thing to ask after all these years. I'd been dying to know, too.

We waited in silence for them to answer. 'We're thrilled you're here,' I said as they struggled to reply.

Leo nodded. 'Of course, you want to know why. I would too, if it was the other way around.' Dee cleared her throat, her large eyes wider than usual. After giving her a quick glance Leo smiled, and explained, 'The thing is, it's business-related. I'm not allowed to share details with anyone just yet.'

'Until everything's finalised, you mean?' Disappointed, I had to accept what he was telling us. 'You did look very official when I met you that day in Southampton.'

He nodded and placed a hand on Dee's arm. 'Poor Dee, even she doesn't know yet. Do you?'

She shook her head. 'I keep asking, but he's been sworn to secrecy.'

'Contracts to sign before I can say anything further,' he explained, giving us a reassuring smile. 'I don't want to say something to put the entire business deal in jeopardy.'

'You'll be moving back here for good then?' Mum asked. 'We can help you find a home to rent if you need us to.'

Delighted at the prospect of having my old friends back here permanently, I smiled. 'Yes, you only have to ask.'

After dinner, he brought their cases in from the car. I was a little taken aback by the small cabin bag in which Dee and Ashley's clothes were packed. Leo's case wasn't much bigger. I wondered why Dee hadn't thought to let her daughter bring a few familiar bits with her on holiday. I doubted Katie would go away without her favourite toys packed safely. It was obvious the little girl needed the comfort of something to cuddle. Even Katie had been aware of that as soon as she'd given the teddy to Ashley.

I suggested Ashley share Katie's bedroom, but Dee wanted her daughter to sleep next to her, which was understandable, so they took the larger room in the attic and Leo was happy to have the box room next door to them. After supper, we put the little ones to bed.

Katie came down about an hour after she and Ashley had been put to bed to tell me that Ashley was crying.

'I didn't know what was wrong, Mummy,' she said, clinging to me. She looked shyly at Dee and then Leo. 'I think she's not feeling well.'

Dee went up to settle Ashley and I took Katie back to bed. I peered around Dee's bedroom door to check there wasn't anything wrong. Dee was leaning over Ashley and whispering in her ear. Ashley had her eyes closed and was cuddling the bear Katie had given her earlier. I could understand the little girl being unsettled by this big old house and went back downstairs.

The evening had grown a little cooler and we all moved into the living room to enjoy a couple of the bottles of the wine he'd bought earlier.

I was conscious not to mention Hazel again and despite my intense curiosity, decided also not to try and push them on the intervening years. But I couldn't help staring at them both, enjoying simply being with them again, talking mostly about Mum's work and our daughters' funny ways.

-

The following morning, I rose early, and, not sure when the rest of the household would want to bathe, showered and dressed before going downstairs to put on the coffee ready for when anyone else wanted breakfast.

'Morning,' Leo said, making me jump when he silently entered the kitchen, freshly showered and dressed, this time in chinos and a slightly creased shirt. 'That bed is so comfortable I almost didn't get up,' he said, raking his hands through his blond hair, pushing it back only for it to flop forward onto his forehead once again.

I laughed, relieved he'd had a good night's sleep, noticing he'd made coffee in the percolator. Pouring a mug of the hot dark liquid, I handed it to him and picked up my own, leading the way out to the garden. 'It's a little warm out here, but I love sitting outside enjoying my first coffee of the morning. It's very peaceful.'

We sat down opposite each other. He leant back, cupping his mug in both hands, closing his eyes and stretching his long legs out in front of him, crossing them casually at the ankles. He breathed in the fresh morning air, and sighed. 'This is very relaxing.'

'I love it here. Coming into the garden before Mum and Katie are awake really sets me up for the day.'

'It's a good way to work through your thoughts, too.'

It was. 'It was relishing moments like these that gave me back the strength to carry on after Marcus' death,' I admitted, wanting to open up to him and hoping he might feel inclined to do the same. 'I needed help to look ahead and found it hard to work out how to make a future for myself and Katie.'

He widened his eyes and the sadness in them bothered me. He leant forward and took one of my hands in his. 'I'm sorry we never contacted you when he had his accident, Sera.' He looked guilty and any resentment I'd harboured dissipated. 'Looking back now it seems unforgivable that we didn't at least write to you, or your mum. I think we were embarrassed about leaving without saying goodbye and after that neither of us knew quite how to approach you.'

I dwelt on how it must have been for them. 'I was too devastated to care about reproaching anyone then,' I admitted. 'It was all I could do to force myself to get out of bed to look after my little girl. If I hadn't had Katie to care for, I... well, I don't see how I could have kept going.'

He sighed. 'But you did, despite your world turning inside out.'

'It was only because she was Marcus' baby and he adored her that I forced myself to give her the life he would have wanted for her,' I said, not daring to dwell for too long on the past.

Leo let go of my hand and sat back in his chair, studying me silently.

Changing the subject before I got too maudlin, I added, 'I'm intrigued about where you and Dee have been. Something's obviously happened to her. I can't help noticing how troubled she is.' I shrugged. 'I just want to put everything behind us and be there for her.' I realised I'd have more chance of finding out about them without her being here, so added, 'I want to do anything I can to help to bring back that spark she used to have.'

'You're a good woman, Sera,' he said, his face expressionless. 'Beautiful on both the inside and outside.'

He seemed sad when he said those words and it dawned on me that maybe Dee wasn't the only one who'd suffered. 'We'll work something out,' I assured him. 'She'll be fine; I'll make sure she is. It's a shame you're here for such a short time.'

He dropped his head, his chin almost resting on his chest, his shoulders stooped. I wasn't sure what I'd said to change his mood and waited for him to speak, busying myself sipping at my hot coffee. He got up quickly, making me jump, and mumbling an apology, hurried over to the corner of the garden by an old apple tree. I wasn't sure what had just happened. Then I noticed his shoulders shuddering and with a rush of dread realised he was crying.

I'd never seen a grown man in tears before. He obviously didn't want me to witness him in this state. But I had to do *something*. Not wishing the children to come down and see him like this, I put down my coffee mug and went to join him. I touched his arm lightly.

'Leo? What's the matter?'

He turned away from me, covering his eyes with one hand and gripping my hand with the other. 'I'm sorry. Please, you go inside, I'll be fine in a bit.'

I put my free hand up to his damp cheek and gently brought his face towards me. 'Leo, look at me.'

He groaned, looking away from me. 'I'll be okay, really.'

I stroked his back. I didn't wish to add to his humiliation, but wanted to help him. 'You can tell me. What is it?'

He didn't reply for a while and I could sense he was struggling to get his emotions in check. I was about to retreat from him when he gave my hand a squeeze. 'It's Dee and Ashley.'

'Go on,' I said.

He sighed. 'It's not my story to tell.'

'I understand,' I said, wishing I did. 'If you tell me, maybe I'll be able to help them.' When he didn't say anything, I added, 'Has she just got out of an abusive relationship? Or something like that?'

'What?' He faced me, and I couldn't tell if he was shocked or angry by my suggestion.

'Sorry,' I said, wincing with embarrassment at my nosiness. 'I shouldn't assume. It's just that she's so withdrawn.'

'I'm sure she'll tell you if she can.'

I hid my disappointment. 'Of course.'

'I've got to go away on business,' he said. 'I need to know they're safe when I'm not with them.' He sighed. 'I know it's a terrible imposition, but would you mind if they stayed here for a few weeks, until I manage to sort somewhere for them to live?'

'Of course,' I said, although a small part of me was apprehensive at the thought of their stay being lengthened from a few weeks. Dee and I barely knew each other after fifteen years' silence. Apart from Katie, I had only ever lived with Mum or Marcus and wasn't sure how I was going to cope with Dee for an extended period of time. However, I was so relieved he wasn't cross with me for sticking my nose into their personal problems that I pushed away my doubts and instantly agreed. 'They can stay as long as they need to.'

His shoulders relaxed, and he smiled. 'Thank you, Sera.' He bent down to kiss me on the cheek. 'You've no idea how much I appreciate this.'

'Don't be silly.' I gave his hand a squeeze. 'What are friends for, if not to help each other in times of crisis?' He tensed, his smile slipping briefly. I didn't want him to think I was being sarcastic about their lack of contact over Marcus' death and nudged him playfully. 'You know what I mean.'

We stood in silence, the atmosphere heavy between us.

'What was it like, yesterday, when you came to the farm to find me?' I asked.

'Sorry?'

I took a sip of my coffee. 'Your old farm. Haven't you ever wanted to go back and pay it a visit before now?'

He shook his head. 'No.' He rubbed his unshaven chin with one hand. 'I don't think I could bear to be reminded of everything we left behind.'

'I always remember how pretty your mum made everything in your home.'

He smiled. 'I suppose you're right. She loved her lacy bits of material draped in strange places.' He laughed at the memory. 'Who else have you ever known to hang silk scarves from fence posts, or branches in trees?'

Warming to the change in tone of our conversation, I thought back to her love of flowers. 'Her pots of geraniums were everywhere. I always loved their bright colours.'

He grimaced. 'Seeing them always reminds me of trudging through farmers' markets and the endless garden centres she dragged us to on weekends when we were smaller.'

I pictured Dee and Leo's boredom at their mother's infatuation with plants. 'Remember the field she insisted we help plant up with lavender?'

Leo studied his hands, turning them over as if looking for something. 'I was off school for two days with horrendous blisters on my hands. God, that was an endless day, wasn't it?'

I giggled. 'My mum went mad when she saw how exhausted I was that night.' I bit my lower lip gently. 'I never dared admit to her what I'd really been doing. If she'd realised that I'd been planting a field for Hazel, she would have been furious.'

'Thank heavens it was only a small field.'

We laughed at the shared memory. I pictured that blissful June and July when the lavender bloomed, covering Hazel's small field in an aromatic, purple hue, like something out of the Monet painting I'd later learned to appreciate. I suspected her passion had instilled my love of gardening, something my own mother had always found to be a curious hobby for a teenage girl to enjoy.

'It was glorious to look at,' I said wistfully. 'Such a shame Hazel never got the chance to harvest the plants and produce the lavender oil she'd planned to sell in the markets that summer.'

Leo's face took on a closed-off expression again and I could have kicked myself for referring again to what must have been a traumatic time for them. 'Poor Mum, she loved that farm so much,' he reflected.

'Why did you all leave then?' I asked, keeping my tone as gentle as I could. I knew I was pushing my luck, but couldn't help myself.

Leo's mood changed instantly. He rose to leave. 'It's been amazing catching up with you, but I really should go and see how my sister and Ashley are settling in.'

Aware I'd ruined the moment, I watched him go. Would I ever discover what happened that night when the heat had been at its peak and the dryness in the air made everything, even breathing, much harder work than usual? I was beginning to doubt it.

Chapter Ten

2003 – Oakwold, New Forest

Young Sera

'Put this on,' Dee giggled, throwing a pink crop top in my face.

'I told you I'm not doing it,' I argued, throwing it back. 'If you want to sing for your mum's friends at her party tonight, go ahead. You can count me out, though.'

'Grow some balls, Sera,' she mocked. 'You know you'll have fun once you get going.'

I didn't know anything of the sort. Just because Dee had no fear and loved showing off in front of her mum's drunk friends, I didn't know why she was insisting I do it, too. 'Looks like you've grown a big enough pair for the both of us.'

Dee tied her hair up in a high ponytail and studied her reflection in her dressing table mirror. 'I don't look much like Christina Aguilera, do I?'

I let her get away with changing the subject. 'Is that who you're supposed to be?' I put a finger up to my mouth and pretended to think. 'Let me guess, are we supposed to be singing Beautiful" for your mum's guests?'

She jumped up and down gleefully, spinning round to face me. 'You said "we". Yes!' She punched the air in triumph.

I instantly realised my mistake and opened my mouth to argue.

'No,' she said, grabbing hold of me and placing her left hand over my mouth as we fell sideways onto her bed. 'No arguments. Your subconscious wants to sing tonight and that's why you just said what you did.'

'Hmm.' I shook my head but her hand remained firmly clamped in place.

'Don't waste your time,' she laughed. 'You know I'm right.'

I grabbed her wrist and pushed her away from me, aware when I'd lost a fight. Not that I ever really won them where Dee was concerned. She was the most determined person I knew. She was also always the life and soul of any party, even Hazel's. And, if I was honest, I envied her natural enthusiasm for life and the way she saw opportunity in ordinary daily events. She made life so much more fun when she was around.

'Fine,' I said, reluctantly giving in. 'I'll put on the bloody crop top, but it's too hot to wear jeans.' I hurriedly changed, as Dee sang the chorus to 'Beautiful' loudly into her hairbrush. I kept my denim shorts on and slipped my feet back into my flip-flops, already regretting having given in to her.

–

Several hours later, as the sun set and Hazel's friends became noisier, I began to fret about standing up on the makeshift stage Dee had persuaded Jack to assemble out of some pallet boards. I noticed Dee watching me. She waited for Hazel to go and chat to someone before pinching two bottles of lager and waving for me to follow her outside to the back of the barn.

'Here, drink this,' she said, handing me one of the bottles.

I grimaced. 'You know I hate that stuff. It's disgusting.'

Dee's arms dropped to her sides and she stared at me, head tilted to one side. 'You are such a wimp sometimes. What would Mimi say if she knew you didn't have the guts to perform? It's only a little song. Just one.'

The thought of my mother's horror at finding me drinking and singing in front of Hazel's friends made me grab the bottle right out of her hand. 'Fine. Give me that,' I said defiantly. I drank it as quickly as I could, wincing as the revolting taste hit the back of my throat.

Dee drank her lager quickly, belching between each mouthful and making me giggle. 'You see, I knew you could do it.'

'Come on then,' I said, inspired by her enthusiasm. 'Let's show them what we can do.'

Dee took the bottles and hid them behind a stool. I grabbed her left hand and we cheered as we ran past Hazel's guests to the pallet boards.

'Everybody,' she shouted, waving at them to pay attention to us. 'Hey. Quiet. Sera and I are going to perform for you.' She sang the first few words and I joined in.

She was right, I was loving every moment. Just like I always did when I was with Dee.

Chapter Eleven

2018 – Oakwold, New Forest

Sera

Leo had been gone a few days, back to his job in finance. I assumed the more time Dee and I spent together the closer we'd become. However, after that initial evening when she'd relaxed a little, she reverted to her quiet mouse-like ways and still hadn't opened up to me. After almost a week I began to give up trying. My initial delight at having her to stay was beginning to wane. I couldn't help wondering if maybe it would have been better to have been left with the memories I'd lived off for so long. She was a stranger, that much was obvious, more so now than ever.

Dee complained that the surrounding fields were causing her hay fever to flare up. Even the little girls didn't play together in the way I'd hoped. Like me, Katie gave up trying so hard to please Ashley. I'd never been around such a solemn child. I wondered if she was like this because of some sort of reaction to Dee's trauma, whatever it had been. I hated to think what this little girl might have witnessed at home.

The temperature was intensifying each day and the longed-for rain to water my garden and save my plants from drying out completely didn't come. Even the pavements felt hot beneath the soles of our shoes whenever we walked to the row of small shops at the end of our street. No one wanted to spend long outside, preferring to wait until after sunset. Even then it was almost too hot to stand. Mum insisted this heatwave was even more unbearable than the one she'd endured in 1990.

'Drama always happens to this family during intense heatwaves,' she predicted the previous night before going up to take a shower. 'You mark my words; it's going to happen again this year.'

I tried to brush off her ominous prediction, but it stuck in my head. That night I had nightmares that Dee and Leo were strangers masquerading as my friends.

—

Mum joined me in the kitchen later that day catching me mid-yawn. 'Sleepless night?'

'Nightmares,' I said.

'Me, too.' She picked up an old copy of the local paper and fanned herself. 'I think it's probably hotter than when Dee and her family disappeared.'

I thought back to those stifling days when the summers seemed to last for months and everything had been easy and enchanted.

'Coffee?' I held up the percolator.

She nodded. Her face crumpled up and she sniffed the air. 'What is that horrible smell?'

'What smell?'

'I'm not sure, but it's been driving me mad for days.' She took her cup of coffee from me and placed it on the table in front of her. 'It's getting worse, but I can't think what it must be.'

I sniffed a few times; there was a definite air of something. I looked around, unsure.

'Look up,' Mum said, hands on her slim hips when she figured out what was annoying her.

'What?'

'There.' She pointed over my head. I turned to see Henri's plait of garlic still hanging from the window.

'Bugger, I meant to take that down to the cellar to keep cool.' I lifted it from the window catch and as I held it closer to my face my eyes watered slightly. 'Blimey, it is strong.' I winced as I carried it out to the hallway to hang in the cellar.

'I think I'll take my bed down there later,' I joked to Mum when I returned to the kitchen. 'It's lovely and cool.'

Mum went out to meet some friends for lunch and I thought I should spend time with Dee after dropping Katie at pre-school. I went to join them, but she barely looked up from the book she was reading, sitting with one arm around Ashley's narrow shoulders as the child sat sucking her thumb.

'Hi there.' I sat down on the armchair opposite them. 'I was reminiscing about when we were younger and all the dreams we had. Do you remember?' I went to share some anecdotes with Ashley, but before I could, Dee shook her head.

'No, I don't.'

She couldn't have forgotten everything we'd shared, surely? 'Do you remember that day I climbed into your room from the apple tree?'

Dee's gaze slowly lifted from the book to me. 'Not really,' she said before looking down again.

Maybe it upset her to think about the past. So, trying a different tactic, I said, 'We should spend some time together today. Maybe the three of us could go for a walk in the New Forest? What do you think?'

'It's too hot,' Dee said, without looking up.

'We'll keep to the shady paths; it'll be cooler there.'

She gave a sullen sigh. 'We're reading.'

Finally getting the message, I left them to it. Irritated, I washed my hair and without bothering to dry it, grabbed my car keys and left for Henri's farm. If there was any breeze at all, the farm was the place to find it.

The three-minute drive couldn't pass quickly enough. I hadn't seen Henri since our swim in the woods and I couldn't help feeling a little guilty that I hadn't been in touch with him. It was a bit of a cheek, especially after inwardly criticising Leo for doing the same thing to me.

'Henri,' I called as I stepped out of my car, the punch of the heat hitting me.

There wasn't any sign of him outside, so I walked up to the front door and knocked. No reply. Determined to see him, I jogged around to the back of the house where I found Henri fast asleep. He was lying in the shade on an old wooden bench, earphones plugged in, his feet resting either side on the ground, one foot tapping along to the beat of the bass.

He was only wearing shorts. I watched his tanned chest moving up and down, his breathing calm as he enjoyed the music. I savoured being able to watch him uninhibited, believing he was alone. I was aware it couldn't last very long and wished he didn't feel so ashamed of his scars. I didn't want him to get a shock when he found me there, so slowly moved nearer to him and sat on a large log.

He must have sensed my presence and his eyes opened. Startled to see me there, he sat upright, pulling the earphones out of his ears and hurriedly pressing the music off. 'Sera, what are you doing here?' He reached out and grabbed his T-shirt, pulling it over his head.

I raised my eyebrows and pulled an apologetic face. 'Sorry,' I grimaced. 'I didn't mean to give you a fright.'

He looked past me. 'You are alone?'

I wasn't certain if he was referring to Leo, or Katie. I nodded. 'Yes, and I'm sorry I haven't been to visit you before now, but things have been a little chaotic at home recently.'

Henri shrugged. 'You and Katie are okay?'

'Yes, but I have house guests. They're harder work than I was expecting.'

'Leo?' he asked, his voice quieter.

'No, he's returned to London, but his sister and her daughter are staying with me for a few weeks.' I sighed. 'I hope you don't mind, but I wanted to escape for a while, so thought I'd come here.'

He gave that slow, lazy, one-shouldered shrug of his and I was grateful he didn't hold a grudge against me for not bothering with him for two weeks. 'Good.' He stood up, waving for me to follow him. 'I have something I wish to show you.'

Intrigued, I did as he asked and walked with him to his house. It was good to have something to take my mind of Dee and I was glad I'd made the effort to visit him. 'What is it?'

'No, you must wait.'

'Tell me?' I asked, impatiently.

He walked up the wooden steps to his porch and opened the front door, standing back, waiting for me to walk inside. 'To the kitchen,' he said, his dark eyes shining with uncontained amusement.

Fascinated by this unusually light mood and unable to wait another second, I hurried in stopping suddenly when I spotted his beautiful Collie bitch, Patti, lying in her basket with five adorable bundles of fluff suckling frantically at her.

'Puppies,' I whispered, clasping my hands together. 'Katie will be desperate for one of these.' Me too, I thought. 'They are so cute.'

'Yes, they are,' he smiled. 'She was being strange when I went to bed some days ago. The next morning, I find these little ones. I don't know where I'll find homes for them. I hope maybe you will help me and ask people you might know if they want one.'

I crouched down slowly so as not to frighten Patti and stroked her glossy head. 'You're such a clever girl.' She looked up at me and then nuzzled the pup closest to her as if to tell me to take note of her achievement. I stroked the pups in turn. 'They're adorable.'

'Will you allow me to gift one to Katie?'

'When she sees these, I'll have little choice but to take one home, so yes. Thank you. She'll be thrilled.' It would be wonderful to have a dog around the house again. I checked my watch and stood up. 'I have half an hour before I need to leave and collect her from school.'

'Tea?' he asked, in a mock English accent.

I nodded. 'I thought you'd never ask, but I'd rather something cooler, like standing under an ice-cold shower for ten minutes to try and cool off. I'm melting today.'

'Melting?' He pulled a face. 'Yes, it is too hot for a body.'

I laughed again. 'It is; far too hot.'

He walked over to his large fridge and pulled back the door.

I hurried over to stand slightly back from him, lifting my top a few inches and relishing the cold air as it hit my perspiring stomach. 'This is bliss.'

He took out two icy cold beers and turned before I expected him to, stopping motionless, beers held in the air when he spotted what I was doing.

'Beer?' he asked eventually, without moving to give me one.

'Um, please.' Embarrassed, I dropped my top, wondering what I must have been thinking to act in such an abandoned way with someone I'd only recently met.

He cleared his throat and looked me in the eye. 'Do you wish to sit outside?'

Glad of the change of subject, I agreed. 'That would be great.' We went to sit at the back of the house and I was hoping to entice him to tell me what he'd been about to share when Leo had interrupted us that day by the pool. After half an hour of small talk and many silences I realised Henri wasn't in the best of moods and also wasn't about to be rushed to speak about anything other than what he chose to say.

—

I arrived at Katie's pre-school on time. Usually she was one of the first to race out to hug me, but today I had to wait. Eventually she was escorted outside by her form teacher. I pulled a sympathetic face at Katie as she hobbled towards me, a large plaster stuck over her pudgy knee.

'What happened?' I asked, crouching down to touch the side of her leg lightly.

A large tear rolled down her rosy cheek. 'I tripped on my way outside just now,' she sniffed.

I gave her a bear hug and held her close, breathing in the hint of strawberry from her favourite shampoo that I used to wash her hair. 'Is it a bad cut?' I looked up at the teacher.

She shook her head and smiled. 'A little graze, nothing more,' she said, ruffling Katie's curls. 'She will be fine tomorrow.'

Katie ignored her teacher's reassurances. 'It hurts, Mummy.'

I knew my daughter well enough to realise that she was hoping for a day off school in case I took Dee and Ashley somewhere.

'We'll see how it is tomorrow, okay?'

'Yes,' she said, satisfied.

We arrived home a little later. I spotted Dee outside in the garden with Ashley. She was still reading while her daughter sat sucking her thumb next to her. Mum was in the kitchen making herself some tea.

'How was lunch?' I asked, giving her a quick hug and waiting for Katie to tell her about her knee before running upstairs to change into her shorts and T-shirt.

'Lunch was delicious and good fun, thank you,' she said. She put her finger up to her mouth and lowered her voice. 'I wish that girl would go out sometimes with Ashley, it's not good for them to be cooped up here every day. I've tried to chat to her, but never seem to get anywhere. I'm running out of ideas.'

'I did offer to take them out earlier, but Dee refused.'

'She's driving me mad, always here. I'm just not used to it, I suppose.'

The front door slammed shut and Leo bellowed as he marched down the hallway to the kitchen. 'Guess who?'

Mum pulled a face and turned back to finish making her tea.

'You're here,' I said, stating the obvious. 'It's good to see you.'

Leo kissed me on both cheeks. 'It's great to be back.' He looked over my shoulder in the direction of the garden. 'How's Dee?' he whispered. I couldn't miss the strain on his face when he mentioned her. 'I hope it's not been too difficult for you.'

I struggled to find the right words to answer him without being mean.

Mum gave him a smile and took her tea into the living room. 'Better get learning my lines,' she said, by way of an excuse to leave us to it.

'It's okay,' he said. 'I know it's hard work being with her right now. She's sullen, and doesn't even try to interact most of the time.'

I could see he was under no illusion about Dee's mental state. 'We haven't seen each other for years. We've both changed so much,' I said miserably. 'I didn't think we'd be this distant, though.' I glanced down the hallway to the garden. 'I'm not even sure where Dee and Ashley have gone now?'

All Dee seemed to want to do during the day was sleep and read. She barely let Ashley out of her sight, fretting and needing to know where she was at all times. It stung me to think she didn't trust Mum or me with her daughter.

When Leo didn't say anything, I tried again. 'Is there something I can do to encourage Dee to chat more?' I asked. 'I wish I could persuade her to relax a bit where Ashley's concerned. I feel sorry for the little girl. Dee pretty much suffocates her with all that attention.'

'She's alright. She might take herself off for a little walk to clear her head sometimes, that's all.'

'I have to admit I'm a little concerned about Ashley.'

He studied me for a few seconds, his earlier cheerfulness evaporating. 'Don't be, she's fine. Look, if you'd rather we go elsewhere, you only have to say.'

'That wasn't what I meant,' I said, shocked by his defensiveness.

'Really, I don't want to cause you any problems.'

He had totally misunderstood what I was trying to say. It was as if he was determined to be insulted for some reason. I could see I wasn't going to get through to him today. 'It's okay,' I assured him, not wishing to make things worse.

'If you're sure?' he asked, frowning.

I nodded. I wasn't sure at all, but Dee was my oldest friend and the least I could do was offer them somewhere to stay, at least for the time being.

–

Later that night, Leo barbecued king prawns and scallops. He had placed them in a marinade of oil with a little crushed garlic and lemon for a couple of hours and was in much better spirits.

'That was delicious,' I said honestly. 'You're a fantastic cook.' I pushed away my plate, leaving nothing but a couple of scraps of lettuce. I watched as he concentrated on opening a second bottle of wine before topping up my glass.

'Thanks,' he said, smiling at me. 'I wanted to impress you. I'm glad that I did.'

I wasn't sure, but suspected he might be flirting with me. It was an odd sensation, but not an altogether unpleasant one. He was very handsome, after all.

I cleared my throat. 'There's somewhere I want to take you tomorrow morning,' I said. If we had to spend time together I wanted us to go out occasionally. There was so much beautiful countryside to see around Oakwold and the New Forest, it seemed a waste to spend most of our time at the house.

'I'm intrigued,' he laughed.

'You used to go there years ago,' I said, giving him a clue. 'I thought it would be fun to revisit.'

'I'm not going to the farm,' Dee snapped, standing up and knocking over an empty bottle of wine. It was the first time all evening that she'd interacted with us in any way.

'I didn't mean that,' I said, horrified. 'I'd never expect you to do something that made you uncomfortable.' I shook my head. 'It's somewhere else. We'll need to leave straight after breakfast and I promise you'll enjoy it there.'

'We'd love to,' Leo said quickly before Dee had time to argue.

He went to pour wine into Dee's glass. 'No,' she said, placing her hand over the top. 'I'm going to go to bed.' Her mouth drew back in a tight, forced smile. 'I need an early night if we're going out early tomorrow.' She hesitated. 'Thank you for a lovely meal.'

She sounded so formal. I stood to give her frail body a hug and watched as she walked silently into the house to join her daughter in their room.

Sitting down, I lifted my glass and took a sip. 'I don't want you to make her come tomorrow if she doesn't want to.'

'It'll do her good to get out.' He looked up at Dee's bedroom window. 'She'll come around soon,' he said.

I doubted it. 'I hate seeing her troubled.'

'So do I. She'll be much better for staying here, I'm sure.' He looked at me. 'Thank you for being such a good friend, Sera, it means a lot. I've enjoyed meeting up with you and getting to know the adult you.' He lowered his voice. 'I know I'm only three years younger than you and Dee, but you two were way above me in the maturity stakes when we lived here in the nineties. I always secretly liked you.'

I couldn't help grinning at the idea of Dee's little brother having a crush on me all those years ago. I felt guilty that we'd been so mean to him. 'Really? I never suspected a thing.'

He raised an eyebrow. 'You weren't supposed to.'

Enjoying the moment, I settled back into my chair, my heart rate calming slightly. 'I like having you around, too,' I said, realising it for the first time. 'It's good to be able to reminisce about when we were young messing around at your mum's farm. I've missed not being able to do that.'

'Dee doesn't like to talk about it.'

I couldn't understand why. 'That's a shame,' I said. 'I wished many times we could go back to how it was then. I had a fantastic life until your family disappeared.' I didn't add that I'd battled for the following decade trying to find them; willing Dee to come back.

'Yes, well sometimes things happen that you'd rather forget.' He took a large gulp of his wine and stared out towards the woods at the back of the garden.

'What things?' I said, eagerly.

He closed his eyes. 'Leave it, Sera.' Then opening them, he gazed at me as if lost in thought. 'Some things are best left in the past.'

'But…'

His expression changed. 'What's the story with Henri?'

'What do you mean?' I asked, taken aback by the sudden change in topic.

'He seems a little intense, that's all.'

'Mysterious, maybe,' I said, trying not to sound defensive.

'You seemed close to him when I met him that time in the woods.'

I wasn't used to being questioned by anyone apart from Mum. I could feel my hackles rising. 'I haven't known him long at all.'

'Look, it's nothing to do with me, but how well do you know him?' he asked.

I didn't like being interrogated in this way. 'Henri is a friend.' I looked away from him. 'I don't know everything about him, that's true. In fact, I know very little,' I admitted to myself as much as Leo. 'But I go by my instinct and he's been kind to me and Katie, and I'm happy with that.'

'I didn't mean to offend you.' He smiled apologetically. 'I suppose I just want to look out for you.'

'I'm not your sister, Leo.' I could tell he meant well. 'It's very gentlemanly of you, but I'm used to looking after myself. Just be my friend, I don't need a protector.' I smiled to soften my words. I didn't want us to fall out. 'Let's talk about what we're doing tomorrow instead, shall we?'

—

That night I lay in my bed mesmerised by the shadows swaying gently on the ceiling. The large pine tree outside my window was barely moving, but it lulled me and allowed my mind to wander back to being with Marcus. I had missed him for so long that I wasn't sure if I could ever truly feel deep love for anyone else. Leo was familiar to me; it was easy to trust him. I could hardly believe I was even contemplating how it might feel to become close to a man again. I pulled the covers over my shoulders and closed my eyes. When sleep evaded me yet again, I let my mind wander.

Could I finally be reaching the end of my grieving process for Marcus? Was that possible? I would always miss him and what might have been, but I was beginning to think that it might be time to take a chance and see how it felt to share experiences with someone else.

I thought of Henri at the pool and wondered again what he had been about to tell me. He was so mysterious and very different to Marcus, who had been very sociable, always wanting everyone to have fun. Leo, on the other hand, was familiar and I liked the way he linked me to a past that I still yearned for. I sighed. Henri intrigued me, though. He was unlike anyone I'd ever known before and I couldn't help being fascinated by him.

Chapter Twelve

2018 – Oakwold, New Forest

Sera

'Mummy,' Katie chirped from the end of my bed. I pushed myself up onto my elbows, squinting when a shard of light streaming through a gap in my curtains blinded me. How long had she been sitting there playing with her dolls? I must have slept deeply not to have noticed her earlier. 'You didn't wake up,' she said, frowning, her fair hair sticking out all around her face like a halo.

I smiled at the golden-haired child, so precious to me, and wished for the umpteenth time that her father was here to enjoy her funny ways and strong personality.

'Yes, poppet, I was very tired.' I glanced at my bedside clock and gasped, throwing back my duvet and jumping out of bed almost in one movement. 'Come on, Katie,' I said, pulling on my dressing gown over my bed shorts and vest. 'You're going to be late for pre-school if we don't get a wriggle on.' I lifted her up, tickling her under her ribs and making her giggle.

Pushing my feet into my flip-flops, I carried her downstairs and sat her at the kitchen table. 'What do you want today? Toast with an egg on top, or porridge?'

She stuck her tongue out and shook her head. 'Yuck. I hate porridge. Want egg and soldiers.'

I put a couple of eggs in a pan of water and poured her a glass of milk and made myself a cup of coffee. 'Do you think you'll finish the rabbit painting at school today?'

'You've been painting a rabbit?' Leo asked from the doorway.

'Yes.' Katie smiled at him, proud of her accomplishment. Her smile faltered when she noticed Ashley standing silently behind him. Katie glanced up at me. 'Ashley wants an egg?'

'Would you? Un, um, *oeuf*?' I asked the silent child. She nodded slowly. She barely seemed to eat anything, so I was happy she was joining Katie for breakfast. I walked over to her and took her hand. 'Come and sit down with Katie and I'll make you both a lovely runny egg with soldiers.'

Katie watched Ashley take a seat and lowering her voice, explained. 'I don't go to school, it's pre-school and they're not really soldiers,' Katie told the confused child. 'They're pieces of toast and butter that we dip in our eggs.' She acted out what she was saying. 'It's yummy.'

'You slept well?' Leo asked, coming to stand next to me by the range.

'Eventually,' I said, checking the eggs. 'Then rather too well, I'm now running a bit late.'

'This is such a peaceful house. Even though it's on the edge of the town and cars drive past most of the time, I go into a deep sleep as soon as my head touches those pillows.'

I was happy to hear he was so relaxed. 'Good, and Dee? Have you seen her yet this morning?' I did my best to sound upbeat.

'Not yet, but I'm sure we will do soon. She's not one to get up late usually, but I think she's struggling to settle in here. I'm afraid us all being together again feels a little foreign to her, too.'

I served the little girls their breakfast and then, leaving Leo to watch over them, I ran upstairs to have a quick shower and change, giving Dee a reminder that we would have to leave soon.

–

I asked Katie if she would like a day off from pre-school to come out with Ashley, Dee, Leo and me.

'No, thank you, Mummy,' she whispered, I presumed not to offend Ashley. 'My knee is much better.'

I was hoping to ask Dee to let me take Ashley to drop Katie off at pre-school. She was still in bed though, so I took Ashley with me into town to buy some fruit and pastries. It was another sweltering day, so I treated her to a cool drink. We were walking out of the supermarket hand in hand, when one of the bags broke and several tins of tuna rolled away from me towards the parking area. I bent to salvage a bag of oranges and some tea, but it was difficult doing it with only one free hand. 'Damn.'

'I will bring them to you,' I heard Henri say when I struggled to put what I had retrieved into the other bag, hoping that wouldn't break too. I did my best but ended up dropping other bits. 'For pity's sake.'

I could hear his deep laugh as he grabbed the shopping I kept dropping. 'Stop,' he said, smiling broadly at me. 'One minute.'

I watched him limp into the shop and come out seconds later with two new bags. 'These are better.'

'Thank you,' I said, relieved to be able to stop making an idiot of myself. I helped him finish packing everything with Ashley clasping tightly onto my hand. 'I didn't think you shopped here?'

'On occasion.' He gave Ashley a crooked smile. He raised the bags and indicated my car. 'I will carry these. You are well?'

I walked next to him towards the car. 'Yes, thanks. I'm taking my guests to a market today, to have a look around.' He waited for me to open the boot of my car, and lowered the shopping into it, closing it for me. He checked his watch. 'I will leave you to your day.'

'I'll bring Katie to see the puppies soon.'

—

Back home to collect the others, I walked into the house to hear screaming and crying coming from the kitchen. I had barely closed the door, when Dee raced through the hall and skidded on the hard tiles, grabbing Ashley and clinging on to her. The child looked terrified.

'Where have you been?' she screamed at me, spittle at the sides of her mouth. 'How dare you take her without asking my permission first?'

I couldn't believe her reaction. 'We only popped out to the shops. We can't have been gone more than half an hour.'

'Don't do it again, do you hear me?' Her wide eyes blazed with fury. I nodded, not daring to upset her further by arguing.

I left her to take Ashley to their room. Frustrated with Dee's dramatics, I went to find Mum, confiding in her about my plans for the day and hoping she'd join us.

'I've got lines to learn today.'

I looked at her out of the corner of my eye and suspected she was fibbing. I didn't blame her; she must be desperate for time alone in her own house, especially after this latest bout of hysteria. Making the most of the others being out of the way, we sat down to enjoy a cup of tea.

Mum looked at me. 'You do know she's insane, don't you?'

'That's a little harsh, Mum,' I whispered.

'We're ready now,' Leo shouted from the upstairs landing. He came down the stairs with Ashley in his arms, I saw Dee following close behind them, her face puffy from crying. I couldn't help feeling a little guilty about instigating her upset but kept quiet. 'We're going on an adventure,' he said, smiling at Ashley.

The child didn't react, but looked at him as if she might cry. I couldn't understand it. Katie would have been jumping up and down and giggling. She wouldn't mind what we were doing; the anticipation of going out in the car to do anything remotely fun would be enough.

Leo saw me watching Ashley and frowned. 'We're all different, I suppose.'

It saddened me to see so little joy in the child's face. 'Come on, let's go.'

Leo made small talk during the journey. We wound the windows right down, but the heat in the air did little to cool us. The roads were dusty, which added to our discomfort, but I hoped that once we arrived at the market they would agree that it had been worthwhile.

Dee and Ashley sat in silence in the back of the car for the entire time, while Leo and I made small talk about how the usually lush plantation on either side of the road looked dull due to the coating of dust.

'We need some rain desperately,' I said, thinking of the farmers and growers who were contending with this unprecedented heat.

Ashley started to cough and I reached back to the basket I'd placed behind my seat until I felt the neck of a bottle of water. Lifting it, I said, 'Dee, can you give this to Ashley.' She took it from my hand and undid the top, passing it to the little girl. 'Sorry, Ashley,' I said, wishing I had decent air-con in my car and could close the windows. 'We'll be there very soon.'

Moments later I spotted several ponies ambling by the side of the road and slowed the car right down. I pointed them out to Ashley. 'Look, ponies. Aren't they pretty?'

Ashley watched them walking, the hint of a smile on her drawn face.

Finally, we arrived at the old country estate where we were headed.

'It doesn't look very inviting,' Dee said as I slowed before the ivy-clad entrance.

I checked that there wasn't a car behind me in my rear-view mirror and stopped. 'They do wonderful cakes,' I said, determined to remain cheerful and make the best of the day. 'Imagine how incredible this place used to be decades ago.'

The ornate gates were now rusted open and the enamelled family crest above the metal archway mostly worn away. I put the car in gear and drove through the tall gateposts. Some of the stones were missing and I wondered how long it would be until they completely collapsed.

Leo smiled thoughtfully. 'This place looks familiar,' he said, as the chatter and shouts from the stallholders trying to grab the attention of passing shoppers became louder the closer we got to the marketplace.

'It should do. We occasionally came here as children,' I said, relieved one of them was being positive. 'It wasn't as run-down then but they still held summer fêtes and folk festivals.'

I turned right and took the short bumpy lane, past old tenants' cottages, and turned into a stony car park. We eventually spotted a space between two other cars under the shelter of a gnarled oak tree.

'This is the market,' Dee said, hurriedly stepping out of the car, forgetting about Ashley. It was so out of character I wasn't sure how to react.

Leo followed her. I went to Ashley, taking her hand in mine. 'Here, you'd better put this on,' I said, picking up the peaked cap from the car seat and putting it on the little girl's head. 'We don't want you to get sunburnt, do we?'

I slipped on my sunglasses, grabbed my purse and locked the car. At least Dee seemed cheerful, for once. 'Okay?' I bent to ask the little girl. She stared up at me and gave a little shrug. It was a reaction of sorts, I supposed.

Leo stopped to let us catch up with him by the entrance of the yard where two rows of tightly packed stalls were set up.

'You're right. I remember Mum bringing us here when we were small.' He stepped back to avoid two elderly ladies who were marching towards a nearby second-hand clothes stall. 'You take your life in your hands coming here, don't you?' he said, watching them shuffling on their way.

'You do. There are a lot of determined people,' I said quietly when we were next to him. 'I couldn't wait to come again when I returned from the north.'

He nodded towards my favourite stall that had also been one of his mother's chosen shopping spots. 'I can almost picture Mum standing over there,' he said, his voice catching.

'She loved the skirts and tops that girl used to bring from her buying trips to India. Do you remember?'

He nodded. 'I do. I seem to recall you always banging on about this place, too.'

I breathed in the heady scents of the market. A mixture of lavender and geraniums took me back to when I was small at this very spot. In fact, the wizened little man serving at the stall was the same one from my childhood. I watched him deftly counting change for a customer. He didn't look all that different to when I'd first come here.

We walked through the crowds looking at everything from brightly painted pottery to straw baskets with colourful ribbons threaded through the weaving. I breathed in the patchouli and sandalwood from the clothes I liked to buy and was about to pick a fabric bag to check it, when Ashley pulled me towards the second-hand book store.

Happy to see her enjoying her visit to the market, I willingly went with her and watched her looking through the books. She moved several. Picking them up, she breathed in the familiar smell of an old book, closing her eyes in recognition; it was a strange thing for someone as young as her to do. She checked the front and back covers of other books, unsatisfied with them, putting them down again. Eventually, she found one I recognised from my own childhood and held it up to me. I took it from her and smiled.

'*What Katy Did* by Susan Coolidge. I remember my mum reading this to me many times.' I couldn't picture Dee taking the time to do the same and wondered if maybe it had been a book she'd enjoyed at school. 'Do you want this?'

Her lips drew back slightly giving the hint of a smile. I was so delighted to see her reaction that I hugged her. 'All right then.' I was finally getting somewhere with this child and it thrilled me.

I left her slowly turning the pages and looked for one I might want to read. I chose a battered copy of *Jane Eyre* and a couple of Georgette Heyer books I recalled reading when I was younger. After haggling briefly with the stall-holder, I paid him and gratefully accepted the plastic bag with my books inside. I looked forward to reading those over the next couple of weeks. I couldn't see Leo or Dee anywhere, so took Ashley's hand and went to look at the next stall.

'Having fun?' he asked about fifteen minutes later. 'That's new, isn't it?' He lifted the bottom of the striped material shoulder bag I'd treated myself to. 'It's already filled with stuff,' he teased. 'It weighs a ton.'

'Rubbish, we've only bought a few things,' I joked. 'Anyway, I've wanted one similar to this for ages.'

'And it suits you,' he said. 'You're a bit of a hippy at heart, aren't you?'

Thinking about it, he had a point. 'Come on, we'd better see where Dee's got to.'

We found her holding up a thirties vase with a yellow-and-black geometrical pattern on the front. 'That's gorgeous,' I said.

She stared at me and, handing the vase to Leo, took Ashley's hand from mine.

'Dee,' Leo didn't bother to hide the determination in his voice. 'Sera bought Ashley a lovely book.'

Dee closed her eyes in irritation for a few seconds, then opened them and smiled at him. She pointed at the vase. 'Will you buy this for me?'

I couldn't help being taken aback by her odd reaction, and that she didn't have money of her own. There was no point in arguing with her, so I moved away and focused my attention on a delicate, silver-plated toast rack. Ashley picked up an elephant-shaped egg cup with her free hand.

'That would be perfect for your breakfast egg and soldiers,' I said. She frowned and I wished I could speak French. 'Shall we ask Mummy if you can have it?'

She glanced at Dee out of the corner of her eye, seeing her deep in conversation with Leo. Ashley shook her head.

'I don't think she'd mind,' I whispered, not very convinced by my assurances.

'*Non.*'

I was so unused to hearing her voice that I hesitated before replying. 'Um, okay, then,' I said, saddened by her refusal. 'If you're sure?'

We looked at a few more stalls, but the intensity of the heat was becoming overbearing. I noticed Ashley wiping her forehead and becoming fretful. I was more concerned about the child than offending Dee, so asked if I could take Ashley to buy a drink.

Dee nodded and let go of the child's hand. 'Don't go far, will you?'

'No,' I assured her and quickly led Ashley to the shade under a tree at the other end of the market. 'Drink?' I asked, raising my cupped hand to my mouth. She needed to keep hydrated on such a hot day. She gave me a vacant stare. 'I'll get us some water.'

I took her to a stall and bought us a bottle of chilled water each. 'Make sure you drink all of that today,' I said, pulling the top off and downing half my own bottle. I poured a little into my hand and wiped my face and the back of my neck.

I checked my watch. I needed to start for home soon. I was hoping to spend a few hours working on several signs that I was holding on consignment at my studio. I caught Leo's eye and held up my car keys. He nodded and scanned the market for Dee. Eventually, they came over to us, Dee smiling and holding up two bags.

'That's a beautiful vase,' I said, happy that she had enjoyed our outing.

'I've also found a couple of cushions for our beds,' she said, indicating the larger bag. 'They're a wonderful burnt orange colour.'

We had been there nearly an hour and were all hot and sticky. I didn't relish the uncomfortable drive home again, but hoped they had all enjoyed their outing.

'Ready to go?' I asked, fanning my face with my hand. She didn't argue so we loaded the car and got in. The sun had moved, and the car was no longer in the shade. 'Sorry about the car,' I winced, sitting on my hot seat.

–

The drive home seemed to take much longer in the strong heat of the midday sun. None of us spoke and Dee and Ashley dozed off as I drove. I was relieved Katie hadn't wanted to come too because she would have had to cram in the back seat along with the other two.

Leo and I each had an arm out of our respective windows, doing our best to cool down as much as possible. 'It's at times like these I wouldn't mind having a pool in the garden.'

'A paddling pool would do for me right now,' Leo said, turning my paltry air-conditioning up full blast.

'Or a bottle of water.'

'Anything at all,' he laughed.

'We'll have to settle for a cold shower and a glass of something.'

Freshly showered and changed into a thin cotton top and shorts, I left them with Mum at home and drove to my studio. The concrete walls kept the temperature low. It could be too cold at times, especially in the winter. Today, though, the space gave a welcome relief from the heat of the market earlier. Seeing all the stalls had inspired me and I couldn't wait for the next time I was at my stall in the village square later that week.

I completed a small job and then collected Katie from pre-school, going home to join the others who were enjoying a drink with Mum in the shade in the garden.

Dee seemed a little more focused tonight and was beginning to relax. Even her demeanour seemed calmer. I hoped she'd enjoyed our trip to the market and was feeling a little more at home.

'I was wondering if we could arrange to take the girls out somewhere together this weekend,' she suggested, taking me by surprise.

'I'd love that,' I said enthused. 'We could maybe go for a walk in the wood near your old farm. If it's still this hot, we could swim in the pool there. Do you remember it?' I asked hopefully, recalling Dee's vehement objection about visiting the farm.

She frowned, her eyes glazing over. Then, after a moment's hesitation Dee smiled. 'I do. I was going to buy it and live there with my husband.'

'Yes,' I shrieked, unable to contain my excitement that she was finally reminiscing with me. 'And I was going to be the only person you invited to visit.'

She giggled. 'I remember.' She stared down at the space in front of her. 'I remember,' she whispered, lost in her own world again.

I could see Leo tense as he watched her mood changing. 'It's lovely and shady,' I said, not wishing the atmosphere to drop yet again. 'So we won't get sunburnt.'

'Would you like that, Ashley?' Dee asked, with enthusiasm. The little girl stared at her, her expression uncertain. Dee turned back to me and smiled tightly. 'She'd love to, but she'll probably have to borrow a swimming costume from Katie.'

I willed Dee to be a little less intense with her daughter, but at least she was happy now. I didn't know what had brought about her unexpected change of mood, but I wasn't going to chance ruining it by asking her. I was relieved to experience a hint of how my old friend used to be.

'We could make some sandwiches and take a little picnic,' she suggested. 'You'd like that, girls, wouldn't you?'

Katie nodded enthusiastically. Ashley sucked her thumb and gave Katie a sideways glance.

'I've bought some ice creams if you girls want one,' I said.

Katie jumped up and down. 'Yes, please, Mummy. Can me and Ashley go and get them?'

I laughed. 'You can't reach the freezer compartment, you know that.' I tickled her. I smiled at Ashley. 'Do you like ice cream?' For a second I thought she was about to cry, but was relieved when she simply nodded. 'Good, I'll get you both one.'

I could hear Katie's excited voice. 'You'll love them, Ashley. Mummy buys strawberry and chocolate ice creams and they taste yummy.'

I couldn't help thinking that Dee and Leo's strange demeanour was beginning to crack. I had spotted the occasional hint of the old Dee. Now that she was thawing would I finally be about to get to the bottom of why they had left so abruptly?

Chapter Thirteen

Mimi

My meeting in the dingy Soho backstreet office went well. At least I hoped it had. Mr Collins, or Gerald, as he'd insisted I call him, assured me he could find me work.

'It won't be as exciting as you might think,' he said, eyeing me up and down after I'd finished my brief audition. 'And I want you to have a few photos taken to, you know, show off different aspects of your, um, personality. Then I'm certain I'll find you something.' He hesitated. 'In the meantime, you'll need to find a job to tide you over.'

'Oh.' I couldn't hide my disappointment. I'd expected him to send me off to one of the impressive theatres in London with a note in my hand to start work immediately. Fool. I recalled my mother's high-pitched voice mocking me about the lacklustre future she swore would be mine.

'You'll end up back here within a month,' she'd warned, a spiteful gleam in her eyes. 'Then you can get yourself down to the leather factory, like your sister and me, and forget about all this nonsense.'

Gerald shook his head. 'You girls, you're all the same; dreamers, the lot of you.' He wrote a few notes on the pad on his large oak desk. Picking up a business card from a small holder, he turned it over and scribbled a name and address. Handing it to me, he said, 'A friend of mine runs this club, she'll give you work, but she'll expect you to turn up looking immaculate at all times.'

I forced a smile, relieved not to have to resort to waitressing in the grubby café where Hazel spent so much of her time working for a pittance. 'Thank you.'

He picked up a fat cigar, clipped one end off and rolled it between his index finger and thumb as he held it up to his ear. Satisfied, he placed it in his mouth and flicked a gold lighter, puffing away on the cigar to light it. I wasn't sure if I was supposed to leave, so waited for him to speak.

'You haven't seen the place yet.' He laughed. 'I'll get word to you if anything comes up, but if you don't hear from me before, pop back next Monday morning. We'll chat again then.'

'Yes, Mr Collins,' I said, hypnotised by the swirling thick smoke above his desk. 'I mean, Gerald.'

He rubbed his jowly chin. 'If I do get you some acting work, you're going to have to change your name. Mimi just doesn't sound professional enough.'

'My real name is Maureen,' I said. 'Will that do? I'm willing to change it to anything you like.'

'I'll give it some thought.' He looked me up and down. 'How tall are you?'

'Five feet seven.'

He made a note on the pad in front of him. 'You could certainly play the cool blonde to perfection, if your acting skills are as good as I hope. You'll be great playing the all-American girl. Since Michelle Pfeiffer and Heather Locklear became famous, there's been a liking for others with those blonde, sporty looks. You'll fit the part well.'

I couldn't hide my delight. 'I'd love that.'

'Fine.' He waved me away. 'I'll do my best.'

I thanked him, yet again, and hurried out. Relieved to be away from the smoky atmosphere, I leant against the office door to inspect his scrawl. I vaguely recognised the name of the club and wondered if I'd read about it in one of the society magazines.

Whatever this job was, it would be better than dragging myself back home. These might be small steps, I decided, but it was infinitely better than working in the factory. Whatever my mother predicted about my future, I had no intention of ever going back, however desperate things got in London.

'He must really like you,' Hazel said, when I called in quickly for a cup of tea during her short break. 'Vince never even introduced me to Mr Collins.' She stuck out her lower lip. 'I can't help being a teeny bit jealous of you. You've only just arrived and already you're on your way.'

'I am, aren't I?' I said, not feeling as positive as I was making out. 'And it's all down to you, Hazel. If you hadn't taken me with you to meet Vince I wouldn't be about to go and get a job in a glamorous club.'

She gave me a smile that bordered on a grimace. 'Yeah, cool.'

—

'But that's nothing more than a bathing suit,' moaned a tall girl next to me in the scruffy room that only had one mirror and a couple of working bulbs either side of it that was supposedly our dressing room. She glowered at me when I didn't back her up to the blousy manageress. 'We're supposed to be cocktail waitresses.'

'Some of you are.' The manageress studied the prospective employees lined up in front of her, the black-painted sweep above her large eyes adding to her menacing gaze. It was hard to know what she really looked like under all her make-up. She was terrifying, but I was certain her elaborate dress must have cost a fortune. However much this wasn't what I'd hoped for, I decided I couldn't afford to knock back the only job I'd been offered.

I smiled at her. 'Do we all have to wear the costumes?' I asked, indicating two other girls in bright cocktail dresses.

'Not everyone,' she said, sizing me up. 'Everyone starts the same way, as a waitress. If I see something in you I like, a spark, you'll soon be promoted.' She nodded sagely. 'You'll be allowed to mix with the clientele if that happens, and yes, you'll be given a cocktail dress to wear.'

I would simply have to ensure I was promoted then, and soon. I'd heard about Hollywood producers coming to these nightspots and meeting waitresses they then turned into the 'next big thing'. If I wanted to look the part when I met this miraculous person, I was going to need the right dress. This was the only way I could think of where I'd get the chance to do both. Hazel would be so envious.

After two nights doing my best to be sparkly and glamorous at the club, I wasn't sure if Hazel could ever be persuaded to swap places with me. The hours were long, and it was a constant battle to avoid the sweaty hands that grabbed whatever part of me they could reach as I passed or stop to serve drinks. I was beginning to think that maybe I wasn't going to stick it out. On the third night, just as I was giving a particularly revolting customer a pinch on his flabby hand, I looked up and saw

Vince leaning against the bar watching me. He smiled, his amusement at my retaliation to the hand obvious on his handsome face.

Determined not to reveal my delight at seeing him there, I stuck my nose in the air and walked up to the bar. I placed my tray down near to him ready for the barman to reload it with fresh cocktails.

'I didn't know you frequented this place,' I said, trying my best to sound as mature as possible.

'I don't very often, but I thought I'd better check up on my protégée.'

I couldn't help beaming at him, all thoughts of acting cool in front of him vanishing at his words. It felt good to belong even in a tiny way to someone other than my family. I was about to say something, when I noticed his attention being drawn away from me. Jealous, I turned to see who it could be. It was a man. I couldn't miss the dark shadows under his eyes, his expression wretched. He averted his gaze and stared at the floor.

I glanced at Vince. He was still, like a cat deciding whether to pounce on its prey. His eyes narrowed. A chill ran down my spine at the force of his stare. Sobered by his reaction, I realised then that Vince wasn't a man to cross. Which was just as well, because I would be heartbroken to be on the receiving end of such cold disdain. I determined never to give him cause to be angry with me.

The power Vince exuded that made people revere him somehow increased his appeal to me. I've no idea why. I imagined being on his arm, the two of us posing for photos on a red carpet at my first movie premiere. Him with his muscular arm around my shoulders, me with a ten-carat diamond solitaire on my engagement finger. Flashbulbs exploding in front of us as they took our photo.

'You okay?' he asked, his attention back on me once more.

I realised I'd been daydreaming. 'Sorry.' I blushed, hoping he couldn't guess what had been going through my mind. 'Who was that man?'

'No one you need to worry about.' He raised his right hand and moved his thumb lightly over my heavily made-up cheek. 'You look much older with this slap on your face.'

'You don't approve?' I asked, panic surging through me.

'Of you looking older?' He scanned the room. 'I couldn't care.' My mood plummeted. I had angered him, and I wanted to cry. 'Of you wearing this gunk on your face?' He studied me briefly. 'You're far prettier without it.'

I was barely able to hide my relief. I beamed at him. 'Really?'

Soothed by his assurances, I put my shoulders back, standing proud. I wanted him to approve of me. I tilted my head in what I hoped was a coquettish way, and smiled at him.

He smiled. 'You're gorgeous, do you know that?'

'Yes,' I fibbed.

He lowered his voice and leaned closer to me. 'Good girl, not letting that creep touch you up. You look out for yourself. I wasn't sure if the clientele at this place might be a little too full on for you, but seeing you in action puts my mind at ease.'

'I'll be fine,' I insisted, loving his protectiveness over me.

'You get any problems,' he lifted my chin with his finger, 'you tell me, and I'll have a word with them.'

'Okay, Vince.'

'Promise me, Mimi,' he said, his beautiful eyes seemingly boring into my soul.

'I promise,' I said, my stomach contracting under his focus. My heart pounded when he leaned closer, grazing his lips against my cheek. At that moment I would have agreed to anything.

'Good girl. You're special and I've got big plans for your future. How about coming out with me tomorrow afternoon? I'm testing out my new Ferrari. Have you ever been in one?'

I shook my head.

'Good, then you can come with me to the country. Maybe I can buy you a little treat of some kind.'

I couldn't believe someone as handsome as Vince was taking me out. I imagined us together in his flash sports car, a silk scarf tied around my hair as we raced along the lanes. I didn't own a scarf, but it was enough to dream. Maybe I could ask him to buy one for me.

My heart pounded with excitement, but before I could think of a response the manageress came over. She gave me a withering look before kissing him firmly on the lips. She made her point only too clearly. I took a breath to speak, when I saw him watching me over her shoulder. He winked at me, soothing my irritation with her slightly.

When she stepped back from him, he said, 'Greta, you're looking glorious as ever. I was just telling your waitress here how you make all the difference to this place.'

She ignored me, but pouted at him. 'You're a liar, Vincent Black, but a charming one.' Then giving me a sideways glance, she added, 'If my waitress doesn't get a bloody move on, she's going to be looking for another job tomorrow morning.'

123

'Sorry, Miss,' I said, trying to keep the sarcasm out of my voice. I bobbed a curtsey. Vince widened his eyes, but I could see the amusement in them. 'I was waiting for my tray to be filled.'

She glared at me through her thick false eyelashes. 'Remember, you don't mix with the clientele until you're one of my hostesses.'

Vince took her by the arm. 'Come on, Greta, stop worrying about your girls, for once. Join me for a drink. We haven't caught up with each other for months. I've missed you.'

I watched them walk away, her rounded hips swaying from side to side as Vince whispered something in her ear. She threw her head back and shrieked with laughter. My chest constricted. It was all I could do not to grab a nearby glass and aim it at her head. Her hand stroked his lower back and rested on his buttocks. I wondered if they had ever been lovers. If they were lovers now.

'You can cut that crap out for a start.'

I immediately turned my attention to the middle-aged barman. 'What did you say?'

Wiping a glass with his tea towel, he motioned towards Vince and Greta. 'You shouldn't get on the wrong side of either of those two,' he whispered, shaking his head. 'You'll live to regret it if you do.'

I looked back at the pair of them deep in conversation in a burgundy velvet booth to one side of the club. I was sick of everyone treating me like some country kid who barely knew how to tie her own shoelaces. I was tougher than I looked and one day I would prove it to them all. I glowered at the barman in silence, watching him make a couple of cocktails. He pulled the lid off the cocktail shaker and poured the pink liquid into two glasses.

'Just be careful.' He wiped the bottom of one of the glasses where he'd spilt a few drops before loading them onto my tray. 'You're new around here. You don't know the ropes. Take it a little easy until you do.' He held up a glass to one of the mounted optic dispensers at the side of the bar. 'Don't look now, but Greta's watching you,' he warned, his lips barely moving. 'Get a bloody move on, or she'll have you out that door. I mean it, kid. Watch out for yourself. Do your job, bugger off straight home afterwards, and you'll be okay.'

I picked up my tray carefully. I might be irritated, but I didn't fancy having to pay for a round of expensive, spilt cocktails. 'I'm not as soft as I look,' I said, glaring at him briefly before walking away. 'That old cow doesn't scare me.'

'Well, she bloody well should, and what's more, so should he.'

Chapter Fourteen

2018 – Oakwold, New Forest

Sera

'Maybe Dee is starting to feel a little better,' I whispered, when Mum and I were on our way up to bed later. 'She was less uptight today.'

She didn't look convinced. 'Well, I haven't noticed any improvement. I still think something's amiss between them if you ask me. And what about Hazel, they don't seem to be in contact with her at all? Don't you find that odd?'

I had the same suspicions, but I didn't want to add to the tension between them so kept my thoughts to myself. 'You've never been interested in what Hazel was doing before. Why would you want to know now?'

'Before, she was nearby on that damn farm, now she's gone. I can't help being curious to know what's become of her.'

That didn't make sense. The mother I knew would have been only too pleased that Hazel wasn't about to come and visit her son and daughter. 'You're not happy Dee's come to stay here, are you?'

She put a finger up to her lips and pulled me into her bathroom, closing the door quietly behind us. 'There's something about that girl.' She shook her head slowly. 'She was always such a bubbly young thing; I can't make her out at all now. It's as if she's a completely different person, although we know she's not. What could have possibly happened to change her so radically?' She glanced at herself in the mirror, as if she was expecting her reflection to have the answer. 'How long will she be staying here, do you think?'

I would have liked an answer to that question myself. All I knew was that she'd had an especially difficult time of it lately, whatever 'it' was. 'No idea.'

'I know you were a little lonely before they came here, darling,' my mother said. 'But I think I preferred it that way.'

I couldn't blame her. It was her house and it did feel a bit like Dee's life was taking over our once peaceful home. I agreed. 'I think I did, too, but Leo's a good man and he's doing his best to keep everyone happy. Even if I could turn Dee away, I couldn't do that to her little girl, or Leo. I feel sorry for them both. I think they're struggling as much as Dee is, in their own way.'

'You're probably right,' she mused. 'Leo's turned into a delicious-looking young chap, especially when you think how gawky he used to be. It's a shame he couldn't stay here without them.' She raised a perfectly waxed eyebrow. 'I remember when he was younger and came here with his sister, he was always mooning about over you then.'

Her comment surprised me. 'I never noticed.'

'No, because you were oblivious to the poor boy's feelings,' she said. 'And always day-dreaming about some pop star or other.'

'He's three years younger than me, Mum. When you're almost a teenager, three years is a big difference in age.'

'True.' She smiled. 'Thank heavens those couple of years don't matter when we're grown-ups.'

I couldn't help smiling. 'You're impossible, do you know that?' I teased, pecking her on the cheek before leaving the bathroom, only to find Leo outside on the landing, staring out of the window across the fields behind the house. I hoped he hadn't overheard Mum and me chatting.

'I love this house,' he said, his hands pushed into his pockets.

As he turned, he stared at me with a look of such intensity it almost took my breath away.

'Sera,' he said, his voice barely above a whisper. 'I enjoy being with you very much.'

This wasn't what I wanted to hear and I hoped Mum would not choose this moment to come out of the bathroom. I struggled to come up with a fitting reply.

He crossed his arms in front of his chest looking awkward. 'You know what I mean.'

I didn't know how to react but not wishing to cause further problems in the house, I replied, 'I'm glad you're feeling at home here.' I was aware it wasn't what he'd been hoping I'd say. He was such a caring guy and I didn't want to drag his embarrassment out any further, but I couldn't lie to him. 'I've really enjoyed getting to know you again.'

He went to say something then seemed to think better of it. 'Thank you. I know being in the New Forest is doing Dee, Ashley and me the power of good.'

'I'm glad being here is helping you all.'

–

'Wake up, Sera.' Mum knocked quietly on my bedroom door, early the following morning. Her voice was just above a whisper, but the shrill tone of it woke me. 'Hurry up, I need you to come and see something.'

'I'm coming,' I groaned, flinging back the duvet and getting out of bed. 'What...' I started to shout as I opened the door, but she put her hand over my mouth to shut me up.

'Shhh.' She motioned over her shoulder to the attic stairs. 'Let me in.'

I did as she asked, not that I had much choice. 'What's the matter?' I asked as soon as she closed the door, leaning against it and rolling her eyes heavenward. Mum had a tendency towards the melodramatic, she was an actress after all, but this was a little over the top even for her.

'This really has to stop, Sera,' she said in a way that didn't invite argument. 'That mad girl was ranting outside in the garden first thing this morning. I'm amazed it didn't wake you; it bloody well woke me up. I've got lines to learn and it doesn't get easier as I'm getting a tiny bit older. I need my sleep, darling.'

My mother never swore. 'Mum, my room overlooks the road at the front; I wouldn't hear anything happening in the garden from here. Did you work out what was upsetting her?'

She shook her head. 'No, but Leo manhandled her out of the back gate pretty soon afterwards. I think the child is still sleeping upstairs, though I can't imagine how. What do you think happened?'

I rubbed my eyes. 'How would I know? I was sleeping when it all kicked off, remember?'

'Get showered and dressed, so you're ready for when they come back – if they come back.' I could hear by the tone of her voice she would rather they didn't.

Unimpressed with my reaction, she flounced off before I could say another word.

I went into the bathroom and undressed, stepping into the shower cubicle. I turned on the water, not caring that it was freezing cold after the initial shock of it hitting my skin. The water slowly warmed and my brain cleared. Another drama with Dee, this was becoming a habit. I poured a little shampoo into the palm of my hand, lathered it up and washed my hair. What was happening to my once peaceful life? I washed and stepped out of the shower, drying myself hurriedly before, still damp, dressing in fresh underwear, shorts and a T-shirt.

I could hear voices and a commotion outside the back of the house. I didn't want Katie to get a fright so kicked my damp towel out of the way and ran onto the landing. 'Katie?' I called. 'Where are you?'

'Mummy, Mummy,' she shouted from downstairs. She was up earlier than usual. I hoped my mother was down there with her, but could tell by the panic in Katie's voice that she was frightened.

'I'm coming now.' I ran down to find her. She was waiting by the kitchen door, sucking her thumb. She'd picked that up from Ashley, I thought with irritation, not for the first time wondering why I'd seen fit to invite them into our home to cause so much disruption. I bent and lifted Katie.

'It's all right,' I whispered, kissing her tanned cheek. 'Let's go and see what's going on, shall we?'

Leo was holding Dee by the shoulder and shaking her. 'That's enough. You have to stop this. Getting hysterical isn't going to help anyone, is it?'

'What's happened?' I asked, not sure I wanted to hear the answer. He tilted his head and smiled at Katie.

'I'm sorry if we scared you.' He bent down so his face was level with hers. She immediately turned away from him, burying her face in my shoulder. 'Silly Dee found a lizard in the garden,' he said, stroking her arm.

I frowned at him in confusion. It was a silly comment and obviously not the reason behind her hysterics, but it had the desired effect with Katie.

She looked at him, eyes wide with curiosity. 'Was it big, or small?'

He held his index fingers about four inches apart. 'I don't know, but it was about this size.'

She didn't seem very impressed. 'That's only small,' she said with disdain.

'Yes,' he replied. 'But Ashley hasn't ever seen a lizard, so if you go and find her, we can show her one together.'

Katie smiled and wriggled to get down. 'Okay.' She ran off up the stairs and when I was confident that she wasn't within earshot, I turned to him and Dee. She was hugging herself tightly and sniffing noisily in between sobs by the back door.

'What the hell happened?' I demanded. I wasn't going to let the atmosphere in my home be ruined. 'Quickly, tell me before Katie and Ashley come down.'

Leo rubbed his face with both hands. 'They've found a body.'

What did he say? I stared at him, stunned. 'Who has? Where?'

Dee cried out. Leo glared at her and she blew her nose on a soggy tissue. 'Our old farm, that's where,' he said.

'A body at the farm?' I repeated like an idiot. I couldn't focus for a second. 'Henri?' I asked, terrified of Leo's reply.

He shook his head. 'No. He's the one who found the body.'

I closed my eyes, relief flowing through me. For a moment there I'd assumed the arsonist had returned. I tried to gather myself. 'How do you know all this?'

Dee sobbed again, and Leo pulled her into a hug. I suspected he was trying to shut her up. 'You've got to get a grip on your emotions, Dee.' He looked over her head at me. 'I went to the bakery in the village to buy us croissants for breakfast. The woman serving in there told me. There were a few people in the queue gossiping about the chap – you know, Henri.'

'I can imagine,' I said, unable to keep the irritation from my voice. If any of those miseries had bothered to try and get to know him, I was certain they wouldn't be so quick to judge.

He shook his head slowly. 'They don't like him much around here, do they?'

No, they didn't. 'I think they're only suspicious about him because he doesn't mix with them.'

'Silly bugger. He should make the effort if he hopes to settle here permanently.'

He was right. It wasn't the best way to integrate in any town. This was a tight-knit community and a stranger – especially one who had obviously encountered a traumatic past and now kept to himself – was asking for interest, if not suspicion. Even Leo was already back in the fold, having made an effort to shop locally and chat to people. He always bought meat from the butcher rather than driving a little way to the supermarket and it was noted and appreciated by the locals.

'It's easier for us,' I said, wanting to defend Henri's actions. 'We lived here years ago. Some people still remember us from when we were kids.' Although, I had to admit Henri didn't seem to care how the town people were towards him, as long as they left him well alone.

'True.'

'Does anyone know who the dead person is?' I asked.

'No,' Leo said, raking his right hand through his hair. 'No one can work out who it could be.'

I tried to imagine how horrifying it must have been for Henri to make such a grim discovery at his farm. Dee sniffed and I turned my attention back to her. What possible reason could she have for being so upset?

'I need to make sure Henri is coping with all the attention this must be bringing him,' I said, ignoring Leo's disapproving glare at me. Not wishing to discuss the matter with Mum and add fuel to her suspicions about Henri, I added, 'Can I leave you to look after Katie while I pay him a visit?'

For a moment, I thought he might refuse. 'Of course,' he said eventually. 'Please ask him to let me know if there's anything I can do to help.'

Not wishing to give him an opportunity to change his mind, I hurried away. 'I will,' I said, feeling mean for snapping at him earlier. 'I'm sure he'll be grateful to have your support.'

'I wouldn't be so sure,' Leo laughed, his arm still around Dee's shaking shoulders.

'You're probably right,' I shouted, running up the stairs to the kitchen door, grabbing my keys as I ran through the hallway.

—

I hurried to the farm, racing through the stone pillars and pulled up in front of the lilac and apple trees causing a small dust cloud to rise around my car. There were voices coming from the direction of the barn. As I neared the ruins I noticed a white van parked on the other side of the hedge with two people dressed in white paper suits. I presumed they must be the forensics team, so stopped and watched them for a few minutes hoping Henri was about somewhere and would come over and speak to me.

When he didn't appear, I decided to go and find him. I checked around the back of his house, spotting the old weathered tree trunk that I realised had probably acted as a makeshift seat since Hazel's time. Then, retracing my steps to the front, I hurried up the porch stairs. I knocked a couple of times on the frame of the open doorway and called his name. Nothing.

Determined not to leave without checking he was okay, I went through to the kitchen giving Patti and the puppies a quick cuddle, and hurried down the long dark passageway to the back of the house where I remembered Hazel used to have a small snug room. I pulled open the door.

My breath caught in my throat at the sight of him standing by a bookcase wearing nothing but shorts, as he flicked through the pages of an open book. Livid red welts covered the right side of his muscled back, down his flank and over most of his right leg. I had assumed the damage to his leg that I'd seen when we'd gone swimming was the only scarring apart from the slightly puckered skin on his right cheek. I had no idea his body had been this badly damaged.

He turned, horror in his eyes to discover me standing there. Neither of us spoke. I tried not to react, but didn't know whether to state the obvious, or not. 'I came to see if you were all right,' I stammered.

He sighed and held his hands out as if to say, *this is me*. He looked away from me, slamming the book closed and replacing it onto the bookcase shelf.

I stepped back to let him pass, unable to help staring at his retreating figure. The broad, muscular back so cruelly damaged. Why the hell hadn't I thought to knock on this door before barging in? Stupid, stupid idiot.

I went outside to wait for him in the shade of the porch, recalling how pretty the area had always been with Hazel's beloved geraniums lining the steps up to the porch. He was back downstairs before I had time to clear my head and figure out what to say next. I chewed the skin around one of my thumbnails.

Furious with myself for being so tongue-tied, I grimaced. 'Sorry.' How could I have made him feel so awkward? 'It was rude of me to barge in without knocking.'

'It is okay,' he said, but it clearly wasn't.

I struggled to think of something else to say then remembered why I'd hurried over here in the first place. Relieved to have something to focus on, I said, 'I heard they've found a body.'

He looked troubled as he glanced in the direction of the barn. 'I don't know how no one saw it there before. How could I have missed it?'

He sounded so guilty, as if it was his fault somehow. 'How were you to know there was a body in there? Could it have been the person who started the fire, do you think?'

He shook his head. 'No, this poor soul has been there for a long time. It was in a shallow grave and barely covered.'

'You spotted it?'

'Yes,' he sighed. 'This morning.' He lowered himself painfully to sit on a low wall next to me. 'The insurance assessors confirmed this morning that they have now finished working at the barn. I wanted to tidy up and began moving charred planks of wood that fell from the walls and ceiling.' He shook his head. 'I put my hand into the soil to pull up what I thought was a piece of wood; it was a charred bone from a finger.'

I shivered. 'How horrible.'

'I have seen much worse, but not at my own home, of course.'

I couldn't imagine where. I was about to ask when it occurred to me that maybe he was referring to the incident where he had received his scars, so said nothing.

He stared over at the remains of the collapsed barn. 'I admit I was shocked. I called the police and the forensics team have been here for hours.'

'I wonder who it could be?' I sat next to him and thought back to the elderly couple who took on the farm after Hazel's departure. 'I can't imagine it would have anything to do with the old people who lived here for the past fifteen years,' I said. 'I never took much notice of them, but they seemed very ordinary and not the sort of people you'd imagine burying a body on their farm.' Then again, what did murderers look like? 'This place lay empty for about a year after Leo and Dee's family disappeared. Maybe it happened when the house was empty?'

'They don't know yet,' he said, his voice weary. 'I hope they discover the person's identity soon.'

'Hmm, me too.' I imagined he had a family somewhere who must be waiting for news of him.

He turned to look at me. 'How did you hear about this? In the village?'

I nodded. 'Naturally. Leo went in to town buy break-fast and they were gossiping about the body.'

He shook his head slowly. After a few seconds he asked, 'What did they waste their time discussing before I moved here?'

'No idea.' I rocked to one side and nudged him lightly. 'Don't take any notice, it's only because you're new and rather mysterious.'

He pulled a puzzled expression. 'I cannot imagine what is so mysterious about me.'

I could see he was lying, but didn't push the point. I was as curious as the villagers about him, but now was not the time for answers about his past. It was none of my business where he'd come from and why he was so determined to guard his privacy.

'If you want company, you're more than welcome to join the rest of us for dinner at Mum's house. Katie would love to see you again.'

He smiled. 'She is a sweet child. Thank you, but I'll stay here at the farm. The animals remain nervous after the fire. I still don't know how it started...'

'That's fine, I understand.' I wished I could stay with him and be some sort of support. It must be hard to be so alone, especially at an uncertain time like this. I checked my watch. 'I should get home. Leo said to offer his support to you, though.'

'That is kind,' he said quietly, his tone sounding suspicious.

I sighed, wanting to keep him company for a little longer. 'I left Katie with Leo. I think they've had enough of Dee's hysteria, so I'd better get back.'

'She is upset? Why?' He frowned. I imagined he must think my friends very odd and over-emotional.

'I'm not sure. It could be because they grew up here, maybe?'

'Perhaps she is sickened at the thought of playing in the barn as a child when a body could have been lying below her feet. Some people have a problem with death that way. Spirits worry them.'

I hadn't considered that. Dee and I had spent hours terrifying each other at night by telling ghost stories, when all the while a real grisly event had taken place here.

I studied his face. I might have only met him a few times, but I could sense that we both needed someone to confide in. Being here with Henri was a welcome respite from all the secrets and hysteria I'd been coping with at home.

'Maybe, but I think there's more to it where Dee's concerned. Something happened to her recently to make her this frail, but I can't seem to discover exactly what.'

'She has her child and her family,' he scowled. 'To me she's self-indulgent.'

To me, too, I thought. 'We don't know what's happened to her. Maybe she's got a good reason to be like this?'

And maybe she is being self-indulgent, I reasoned, but refrained from agreeing. I thought back to what I'd learned about him just before. 'Everyone is different. Some people cope with tragedy better than others.'

He stared at me silently for a moment weighing up whether to say something. 'And you, Sera?'

'Sorry?' My heart pounded in anticipation of what he was about to say next.

'Your husband's death – how did you cope with it?'

I blinked, shocked by his comment. 'Badly,' I admitted. 'For a long time, it was as if my life had ended, which the life I'd enjoyed with him certainly had.'

He moved to place his hand on my wrist but lowered his hand instead. 'I should not ask. It is cruel.'

'It's okay. You have your own demons, I assume,' I said averting my gaze from him and staring up at the apple tree.

'You mean after my accident.' He stared at the barn. 'I wish you hadn't seen my scars.'

I wasn't sure whether or not to continue the conversation, but decided I had nothing to lose by not asking him. 'The only thing that bothers me about them is thinking how you suffered when you got them.'

'You have seen them though.' He sounded utterly miserable. 'I worry that to some people these scars define who I am.'

'Do you want to tell me what happened? You don't have to.'

He raked his hands back through his short black hair. 'I hate it, it's true. These… burns have ruined my life.'

'It must have been incredibly painful.'

He swallowed. 'Agony, for a time. The hardest part was no longer being able to do the job I loved.' He stood up and began walking up the stairs back into the house.

'Which was?' I followed him into the kitchen where he took two bottles of cider from the fridge and held them up. I took one and opened it. 'I shouldn't, I really do have to get back.'

'This, and that.' He opened one bottle, lifting it to his lips and taking a mouthful of the cool liquid. 'I lived in Paris.'

I noticed he had avoided answering my question. 'But why couldn't you carry on doing your job?'

'Because my leg was so badly burnt it pulled the skin and I now limp. You've seen how slowly I move sometimes.' He stared at me. 'Do not feel pity for me. That gives me more pain than my damaged skin.'

'I don't pity you,' I lied. 'I'm just sad it happened, that's all.'

He shrugged nonchalantly. 'Thank you, so am I.'

We stood in silence, both drinking every now and then from our bottles, enjoying the refreshing cider and the fact that he seemed to be relaxing a little. I stared out of the back window in the direction of the wood.

'You want to know how it happened,' he said. It was a statement rather than a question, his matter-of-fact tone filling the silence.

I chewed my lower lip sensing that this was probably the only time he'd offer the information. 'Only if you want to tell me,' I said, not wanting him to feel forced into confiding in me despite my desperation to learn the facts.

'I will tell you.' His embarrassment forgotten, or at least well hidden, he said, 'It was Bastille Day and the people in Paris were celebrating.' He glanced up at the kitchen clock and frowned. 'You said you needed to hurry home.'

'Bugger,' I said noticing the time, the responsibility of returning to Katie tugging at my need to know his story.

He gave me a crooked smile that, just for a moment, lit up his scarred face. 'You must wait then.'

I frowned, not bothering to hide my irritation. 'You did that on purpose.' I didn't blame him, I supposed. I understood his reluctance to share with me. He wasn't the only one with secrets.

Chapter Fifteen

2018 – Oakwold, New Forest

Sera

I wasn't looking forward to going home and wondered if Leo had managed to calm Dee. It would have been nice to be able to tell her something more definite about the body.

I found them out in the garden drinking coffee.

'Did you find anything out at the farm?'

'Not really.'

She burst into tears. 'Oh, Leo.'

He put his arm around her narrow shoulders. 'Shush, calm down.' He pulled an apologetic face at me. 'Sorry, Sera. It's upsetting for Dee right now.'

I could understand why. The discovery of the dead body had unsettled us all. 'I thought the same thing. It's a little unnerving, isn't it?'

'I'm just finding this a bit much, I'm afraid,' Dee said sniffing. Leo handed her a tissue and she blew her nose. 'Sorry.'

It was enough having to deal with Mum's annoyance having them in the house, but I wasn't prepared to worry about mentioning the farm in front of them.

'Maybe you should go back to France,' I suggested, willing her to agree. 'The gossip and intrigue is only going to get worse over the coming days and probably weeks. The investigation might not be solved for some time.' I could only guess, but it made sense to me. 'I think it might be traumatic for you to be so close at hand.'

She pushed Leo roughly away and glared at me. 'You. It's always all about you and what you think, isn't it, Sera? It always has been.'

I couldn't believe the viciousness of her accusations. 'What do you mean?' As far as I could remember, Dee had always been the bossy, dramatic one out of us two. Had I remembered things so differently to her?

'Hey, that's enough,' Leo snapped. 'Cut it out. Sera has been a good friend to you. To us both.'

She stood up, knocking her coffee all over her flowered skirt. 'Now look what you made me do.' She marched over to me, stopping almost nose to nose with me. 'We all know why he's so fucking defensive of you, don't we, Sera?' Her right shoulder crashed into mine as she slammed past me and stormed into the house.

Shocked by what had just happened, I rubbed the point of impact, trying to make sense of her reaction. 'I didn't realise she resented me like that.' I turned to Leo. 'Is it why she's been so surly since she arrived? Have you forced her to come and stay here?'

'Not at all,' he said, looking mortified at the suggestion. 'I'm sorry. It's not your fault. You've only done as I've asked. You've been a good friend. Please don't take any notice of her outbursts.'

It was easier in theory, but by the look on her face she really had an issue with me. I knew she relied heavily on him for most of her emotional support. But I couldn't understand her feeling threatened by me. Could it be because she and I had always been the inseparable ones and now the balance of our relationship had altered? I decided I needed to be careful to stay out of her odd relationship with Leo and remember that I was an outsider here, not her.

'It's fine,' I said, wanting to make him feel better. 'I'll try to be more sensitive towards her.' I lowered my voice, conscious that if I didn't she would be able to hear me from her attic bedroom. 'We both should.'

He stood up and came over to me. 'No. I won't have her ruining our friendship.' He faltered momentarily. 'Meeting up with you has been the best thing that's happened to me in a long time. As much as I love my sister, I'm not going to allow her insecurities to come between us.'

'However things seem now, Leo,' I said, 'ultimately my loyalty, and yours, has always been to Dee. Now isn't the time to change that. It's pretty obvious she needs us both. We can't let her feel pushed out, it would be cruel.'

He didn't reply, but stared into space, looking at something only he could see. I checked over my shoulder to ensure she wasn't nearby, before carrying on talking, willing him to understand.

'I don't think she can take much more right now.' Was he even listening to me? I tapped him on the shoulder. 'Leo, did you hear what I said?'

He snapped out of his reverie, looking stunned as if he hadn't even realised I was there, never mind speaking to him. 'What? Sorry.'

I closed my eyes to concentrate all my efforts on not losing my temper. 'I don't want to have to face the consequences of what Dee might do in her present emotional state.'

I hoped he was getting the message that if he did harbour feelings for me that they couldn't go any further. I had realised that day at the pool that there was something about Henri that attracted me to him. I didn't like the thought of having to admit my feelings to Leo and chance hurting his feelings. Having Dee upset with me was bad enough.

'I'm going to talk to her,' he said. Without waiting for me to answer, he went inside the house.

'Bugger.' Sitting on the wooden seat, I closed my eyes. I really should think before speaking. Mum was always telling me not to react instantly to things but to consider what I wanted to say before opening my mouth. It was about time I started following this particular nugget of advice, I mused.

Mum poked her head out of the back door. 'They're leaving,' she shouted, looking rather pleased about it. She went back in and immediately after, I heard the front door slamming. 'They've gone,' Mum said, rubbing her hands together.

'I wonder if they're coming back?' I said, almost to myself.

'More than likely,' Mum shouted from inside the kitchen. My mother had incredible hearing, when it suited her.

I took Katie into the kitchen, gave her a biscuit and poured her a cool drink before running upstairs to the attic room where Dee had been sleeping. Stopping at the doorway, it wasn't necessary to check if their clothes had been taken, every drawer was open, as were the wardrobe doors.

'Bloody hell.'

'Well?' my mother shouted from the lower landing.

I went to lean over the banisters to speak to her. 'They've moved out.'

'Thank heavens for that.' I heard her walk into the bathroom and lock the door.

I couldn't help agreeing with her. Their sudden departure was a relief, unlike fifteen years before. I wondered if they would stay away as long this time, or if it was the last time I'd see any of them. A part of me hoped they wouldn't return.

Chapter Sixteen

2018 – Oakwold, New Forest

Sera

The following morning, I sat down at the worn pine table and wiped crumbs from Katie's cheek before watching her go back outside.

'Do you think I've become hard since Marcus died?' I asked Mum when she came in to join me.

She inspected her scarlet nail polish for a moment. 'I think you lost the love of your life and it almost destroyed you. You needed to toughen up and become independent, but maybe now it's time to let someone else do things for you for a change.'

'You do things for me,' I said, taking her hand and giving it a gentle squeeze.

She bent forward and kissed me on the forehead. 'Not really. You live here, but you look after the house for me, especially when I'm away. You earn your own money by running your small business and you do everything for Katie. What does anyone else ever really do for you, Sera?'

I thought for a couple of seconds. 'I like being independent.'

'Aren't you ready for another relationship yet?'

I was, but I wasn't sure how she would react if I told her that I was becoming more attracted to Henri. 'Marcus controlled everything when we were together. I'm not quite ready to give up my independence to someone else.'

'It doesn't have to be like that with Leo.' She studied me. 'He's used to taking charge of his sister and, knowing Hazel as I did, needs to keep her organised too. He'd probably relish a relationship with a woman who doesn't need too much pampering.'

I hadn't been thinking of Leo, but didn't say so. 'It all seems a bit quick.'

'What do you want to do?' She reached out and took my hands in hers. 'I can't bear seeing you looking so lost, especially as I'm going away with Paul tomorrow.' She raised an eyebrow when I went to argue. 'Yes, I'm seeing him again and I hate leaving you in the middle of this mess.'

'Then don't,' I said, frowning. When had she and Paul been in touch? 'I thought it was over for good between you two?'

She shrugged. 'So did I. You have so much time ahead of you.' She picked up a loose strand of my hair and in an uncharacteristic gesture, tucked it behind my ear. 'You're so young and fresh and, well, gorgeous.'

I wasn't fooled by her act. 'Mum, you know you look stunning, so stop trying to kid me. If you want to spend time with Paul, that's fine by me. I just think you could do far better, that's all.'

I didn't want to think about Paul any more. 'Go on. I'll be fine, I always am.'

She gave me a brief hug. 'No, darling, you just pretend to be fine.'

Did I? 'Maybe I'll pop over and visit Henri for a bit. He needs cheering up too.'

Mum walked over to the window, staring out at the back garden and across to the woods. 'Why do you insist on ignoring my concerns about that man?'

'Mum, you don't even know Henri, how can you say such a thing?'

'Why don't you phone Leo instead? He's your friend and you need to make amends. Maybe it's time we stopped being annoyed by Dee and tried to work out why she's behaving so appallingly?'

That was a bit of a turnaround, even for Mum. It made me wonder how strong her dislike of Henri was. 'Honestly? You don't mind her coming back here?'

She shook her head. 'Not really. She's obviously upset. Even you must be a little spooked by this body business at the farm? I know I am.'

'It is a bit unnerving,' I admitted.

'Well, imagine how that poor girl feels. She's been through something lately and this is probably the thing that could tip her over the edge. I don't think we have much of a choice, not if we consider ourselves to be decent human beings.'

She'd unsettled me more about Henri than the body at the farm, but she did have a point about supporting my old friend. 'I'll call Leo then, but I'm going to want some answers this time.'

'Good, me too.'

I picked up the phone.

-

'You went without me,' Katie said, reproaching Leo as he entered the house the following morning.

He bent down to her level. 'We needed to go somewhere for a night, but we bought you these.' He handed her a bag of donuts then, opening the bag, pointed to a bottle of red wine.

She giggled. 'I can't drink wine, Mummy said.'

'Okay then,' he smiled. 'What about this?' He lifted out a wheel of Brie.

'Eugh, that smells.' She shook her head. Taking one side of the bag, Katie peered inside. Putting her hand in, she pulled out a punnet of strawberries. 'I can have these.'

'Katie,' I said, not pleased to see her delving into someone else's bag. 'You mustn't do that, it's very rude.'

He smiled down the hallway to me. 'It's fine.' He gave me an apologetic smile. 'I thought we could all go on a picnic today.'

'A picnic, a picnic!' Katie cheered, jumping up and down, dropping the punnet and spilling the strawberries on to the tiles.

I bent to pick them up, ruffling her hair. 'You take Ashley to unpack her things in her bedroom and I'll speak with Leo and Dee about this afternoon.'

Happy with this suggestion, she took hold of Ashley's hand, forcing her thumb from her mouth and dragged her upstairs.

I watched the two walk up the stairs. Katie, and the silent child complying with whatever anyone wanted from her.

Dee came in behind them looking rather pink-cheeked. 'Leo said I was unforgivably rude to you yesterday and I'm sorry.'

Recalling Mum's words, I walked over and gave her a hug. 'It's forgotten. Why don't you take your things up to your room and unpack? There's a regatta nearby. We could stop for a picnic and then it might be fun to take the girls to have a look at the boats racing on the river near Beaulieu.' I smiled at Leo.

'We might be able to find a few bits for the girls and maybe ourselves,' Dee said.

I was delighted she was agreeing to go. Maybe yesterday was the catalyst that would snap us all out of our awkwardness with each other so that we could finally move forward to build up our friendships again.

'Give me an hour to unpack and have a bit of a lie down,' she said. 'It's so hot out there, I'm feeling a little nauseous. I'll be fine in a bit.' She looked up at Leo and some unspoken message passed between them. 'I'll be here to watch the kids. Why don't the two of you go for a bit of a walk?'

I didn't answer. Her question seemed rather loaded, but I wanted a chance to speak to him, so led the way out of the back door. We walked through the garden and, pulling hard at the warped garden gate, opened it with a little difficulty.

'Shall we go to the woods?' I asked without waiting for an answer – first, we needed to be away from earshot of everyone in the house.

–

We walked silently through the long, dried grasses in the field behind the house. As usual, I stepped this way and that to miss the poppies, their blood-red petals so delicate and bright. The heat of the morning sunshine bore down on my neck, warming my body further and relaxing me. I loved walking to the woods, with Katie, or by myself. It always soothed me to come this way.

'So where did you go when you left here?' I asked, unable to resist a moment longer.

'The Lake District. I thought it was far enough away for Dee and I to have a bit of thinking time.'

'Right, and what would you have done if I hadn't phoned you to apologise and invite you back to stay here with us again?'

He didn't speak for a while and I was beginning to think it might be his way of telling me to mind my own business.

'This mess. It's all my fault,' he said eventually, the sudden sound of his voice startling me.

I stopped and stared at him. I doubted that. 'Go on.'

'She'd tried to hint about her difficulties, but I didn't want to face that she was in trouble.'

We carried on walking, not looking at each other as he spoke. 'She's never coped well since leaving here. Dee hated that Mum insisted we keep to ourselves and became very introverted.'

'I can't imagine Hazel not being surrounded with lots of friends and having parties.'

'No, it was very strange for us to cope with such a dramatic change in our lifestyle.' He sighed. 'I think part of the reason Dee struggled so much was the sudden isolation Mum forced on us. It was such a complete contrast to the life we'd known in Hampshire.'

'Yes, I can see why she would find it difficult,' I said, feeling sorry for them both.

He stopped walking and looked at me. 'She missed you very much. I know it probably doesn't seem like it because she's being impossible, but I think she was grieving for you and our lives here for years.'

I sighed heavily, I understood that pain. 'It must have been difficult leaving her life so abruptly.' I wanted to ask what made them disappear so suddenly, but didn't feel it was the right time to do so.

'It was. We went from the freedom of living in the countryside to a small flat on a council estate in the north. We didn't know anyone, spoke differently to the locals and it didn't help that Mum was paranoid about our safety and refused to let us out much at first. By then our neighbours thought us very odd and never really took to us.'

He began walking again, picking a piece of lavender and sniffing it. 'Eventually, I went to university and made friends and a new life for myself. No one cared how I spoke, or where I was from; they accepted me as I was. Dee, on the other hand, was left behind with Mum, who was drinking more and more.'

He rubbed his face with the palms of his hands and I noticed how exhausted he seemed. 'Dee got married on a whim. They went to live in France and her life seemed to spiral downwards after that. Each time I saw her she had disintegrated a little further.'

'Poor Dee.' I reflected on all the dreams she used to share with me about a magical future. It was upsetting to think none of her hopes had amounted to anything.

'She rallied when she discovered she was pregnant and had the baby...'

'Ashley.'

'What?' He looked confused and I could have kicked myself for interrupting. 'Yes, Ashley.' He appeared to be mulling over his words before continuing. 'She's damaged, Sera. Something dreadful happened.' He cleared his throat. 'I discovered her trying to hide a bruise on her cheek and another time on her wrists. I tried to help her—' he puffed out his cheeks and shook his head, '—she lied to me. She was ashamed that her louse of a husband was doing this and worse to her. I had no idea how bad things were and by the time I figured it out, Dee was in a hospital bed.'

I gasped. It was hard to imagine Dee's life being so troubled. 'That's horrendous.'

He nodded. 'She swore she was finished with her ex, but a few nights after she came home from hospital I was staying with her to look after her, because she hadn't wanted Mum to know the state she was in, and I spotted the bastard hanging around her cottage. I couldn't leave them there. So, after a lot of persuasion I snuck them out the back door and drove through the night to catch the ferry. We didn't have any plans. I was just determined to get them as far away from that life as possible.'

'It sounds like you've all been through hell.' I knew how difficult it was to be alone. The very least I could do was extend some kindness towards Dee and Ashley. I felt compelled to add, 'Didn't you want to take Dee and Ashley to stay with you in London though?' I asked, assuming it would be much easier for Leo to have them at his home so he would be near to his work.

'Yes, but her ex knew where I lived and I couldn't chance him coming to find her when I was out working.'

It made sense. 'You must feel free to stay here for as long as you both need,' I said, wishing I had phrased that differently and not given them an open invitation.

He squeezed my hand. 'I'm relieved to hear you say that, Sera. I don't know what we'd do otherwise.'

I wasn't sure either. They would have to move on at some point. I hoped I hadn't just got myself into a predicament that I would have difficulty resolving.

Chapter Seventeen

2018 – Oakwold, New Forest

Sera

Now I had a better understanding about why Dee and Ashley had so few belongings, I was even more determined to get them to come with me to buy some clothes. A few days later, I drove to one of the nearby towns to the weekly market. The town square was filled with stalls covered with bright colours like a chaotic rainbow. If this didn't lift their spirits, nothing would.

'This takes me back,' Leo said, marching over to the nearest book stall.

'Come on, girls,' I said. 'Let's go and find some treats.'

I led them to a favourite stall of mine where two sisters sold their beautifully hand-made children's clothes. 'Hello, ladies.' I kissed them both several times on each cheek. 'We're looking for a few things for this little girl.' I raised Ashley's hand slightly.

'They are your guests?' one of them asked.

'They've come to spend some time with us over the summer.'

'What is your favourite colour?' she asked Ashley, obviously taken aback when the child didn't seem to know how to answer this simple question.

I knew that if anyone had asked Katie the same thing she'd have bellowed 'pink' back at them without hesitation. 'She's shy,' I explained. 'Show us a few things and Ashley can tell us if she likes them, or not.'

I was expecting Dee to involve herself in this bit of shopping, but she walked off towards a nearby pottery stall. Maybe she was trying to show me that she trusted me with her daughter. I briefly watched her studying the vases and plates displayed chaotically on the stall and wondered where she was thinking of keeping them.

Realising one of the sisters was waiting for me to answer, I took my cue from Katie's taste and chose two skirts, T-shirts and a jacket I thought would suit Ashley. Katie had similar clothes in her wardrobe and loved them. I then bought three brightly coloured towels for them. If they were going to stay, then I was determined to get them out of the house and swimming a few times each week. Maybe I could even change Dee's mind about going to the farm if I reminded her how heavenly it was to cool off in the pool. Who knew how long this heatwave was going to last, or when they would decide to return to France? I wanted Ashley to have happy memories of her stay with us.

I spotted Dee and Leo through the throngs of shoppers. They were talking in the shadows behind one of the stalls. They seemed to be disagreeing about something, so I focused on keeping Katie and Ashley busy. I loved seeing families making the most of their Sunday together milling around us, chattering as they bartered for produce. As we stopped at each stall, Katie chattered to Ashley, oblivious that their conversation was one-sided.

Seeing Leo by himself, I waved him over. 'Take these, will you?' I handed him the basket and two bags I'd been carrying. 'We still need to buy fruit and veg.'

He pulled a face. 'Great.' He grimaced theatrically. 'What's in these, logs?'

I giggled and went to inspect some melons I'd seen. I pressed the top lightly and gave them both a sniff. I didn't need to gauge their freshness, I'd never picked up anything here that hadn't come straight from the fields either that morning or the day before. Breathing in their cool sweetness, I handed them to the stallholder and studied the grapes. Having bought enough fruit to complete our picnic, I sought out the vegetables we needed and paid for everything, refusing Leo's attempts to do so.

Dee ambled ahead of us. I walked up to her when I saw she was checking some pottery. 'That would look perfect in your bedroom at your new home,' I said.

She frowned. I imagined she was trying to work out if I was hinting at them leaving. 'The attic has so few pieces in it,' she murmured. 'It could do with brightening up.'

I held back a snappy retort. Then, noticing brightly coloured bowls like the ones Katie and I enjoyed eating our cereal or soup from, I decided to buy one as a gift for Ashley.

'Look,' I said, lifting a white bowl in front of her, characteristically decorated with a dark red and blue banding around the rim. 'Would you like one?'

'Say yes,' Katie squealed. 'It's like mine.'

Ashley treated us to a half-smile and nodded. Delighted with my progress with her, I bought it.

'Hey, you lot, look what I've found,' Leo shouted from the other side of the square. I hadn't notice him leaving us and peered over to see what he was so excited about.

'Come on, girls. You, too, Dee,' I said, urging them to join him. After a slight hesitation even Dee's curiosity was roused. 'What have you found?' I asked when we reached him.

'Donuts,' Leo said, holding up a large cream donut. He closed his eyes and took a large bite. 'Delicious,' he mumbled, his mouth full.

'Please can I have one?' Katie asked, her eyes wide with anticipation. 'Ashley wants the same.'

I wasn't certain she did. 'Do you?'

She nodded, taking her cue from Katie. I placed our order.

'Dee?' I indicated the tempting food. She was painfully thin. I willed her to want one. She'd always loved the cakes when we were teenagers. We had occasionally been treated to them by Hazel from this very market. Unable to hide my delight when she agreed, I put my arm around her shoulders and gave her a hug.

'I wonder if they're as good as when we were young,' I whispered.

'I doubt it,' she said, amusement shining through her eyes for once.

It was such a joy to have her acting more like the Dee I remembered.

We held on to our donuts, munching them as we made our way back to the car. It had been a fraught start to the day, but the afternoon was more enjoyable than I could have hoped.

-

Back at the house, I left the girls playing in the garden and unwrapped our packages with Leo in the kitchen.

'You've spoilt Ashley with all these gifts,' he said, sounding happy.

'It's my pleasure. She has so little of her own here. I thought it might help her feel more at home to have a few personal bits in the house.'

'That's very kind of you.'

We put away the shopping. 'Now, for the picnic,' I said, washing the grapes and strawberries, before adding them with the melon to Mum's well-used wicker hamper. Mum had taken me on so many picnics in her old car on afternoons when she had collected me from school. I recalled my excitement at the sight of her old wicker hamper sitting on the back seat, knowing we were off on a 'mystery tour'. I wouldn't tell them where we were going because I wanted it to be a surprise.

Next, I rolled up the new towels and took two from the airing cupboard for Katie and me. Finally, we were ready.

'I know exactly where I'm taking you,' I said, excited at the thought of our outing. 'If you don't have costumes, you can borrow one that Paul left behind. Dee and Ashley can use spares from Katie and me.'

We loaded the car and set off, stopping first at the local baker's on the edge of Oakwold where Leo bought rolls, then driving out past Beaulieu and into the surrounding hilly countryside. He watched the scenery and pointed out a run-down house, the bright sunshine glowing against the small imperfections in the stone façade and making it glow as if it was on fire.

I slowed down, spotting a roadside stall with an untidy sign letting us know that they had bottles of elderflower juice for sale. I'd stopped here many times over the years and the taste of the sweet drink was like nectar.

'We must take some of this with us,' I insisted, when Dee groaned as I stopped the car and got out.

I dropped several coins into a plastic tub and took two bottles. These would make the perfect accompaniment for the food. I handed the bottles across to Leo and set off again.

'How could I have forgotten the beauty of this place?' Leo continued, 'I can't believe my memories about it are so vague?'

I wasn't sure. I turned off the main road onto a sloping lane that would lead us down to a quiet spot near the river, perfect for setting up our picnic. The tarmac ended and we continued our lazy drive down a dusty dirt track passing bees and butterflies flitting about the heads of the poppies and cornflowers. Last of all, I took one sharp turn and there was the river.

'Thank heavens for that,' Dee groaned from the back of the car. 'I thought we'd never get here.'

'It's lovely,' Katie said. 'Do you love it, Ashley?'

I glanced in the rear-view mirror and smiled when I saw Ashley looking at Dee out of the corner of her eye.

'We'll have to come here by ourselves, one day,' Dee said, stroking Ashley's hair. The young girl looked up at her shyly.

What was it with those two? I couldn't understand why she was so timid around her mother. I hated to see her fearful of her own mother. Maybe she had witnessed things that caused her to moderate her reactions around Dee. I remembered what Leo had told me and was relieved to be giving Ashley a respite from her life in France.

'Come on,' I said, parking the car and getting out. 'Help me with this hamper and these swimming things.'

Leo went and lifted the hamper out of the small boot. I handed the bags to Dee before unclipping the girls from their car seats and gave each of them a towel to carry.

'It's almost two o'clock, we want to make the most of the afternoon,' I said, catching sight of several sunflowers randomly dotted around the parking area.

'It's so hot,' Dee said, closing the boot of the car and following. There was no need to lock the car, I couldn't see anyone else in the area.

'We'll need to sit in the shade, or we'll fry in no time.'

I agreed and, spotting a large oak tree, pointed to it. 'Over there looks shady enough for us and it's close enough to the water.'

I followed Leo to the patch under the tree and helped him set out the rug and unpack the hamper. Realising I'd forgotten our bag of rolls, I walked back to the car to retrieve them.

After helping Katie change, we walked back to join Leo and Dee. I could see them whispering.

He noticed me coming towards them and cleared his throat. 'Ready for that swim?'

I was happy to bathe in my T-shirt and shorts, so didn't bother to put on my swimming costume. I picked Katie up and carefully stepped into the cool water. There had been so little rainfall for the previous few months and such heat that the water level was very low and the current light. It was a shame for the farmers having to water their animals further downstream, but for us it was perfect for swimming and paddling about.

'This is bliss,' Dee said, closing her eyes while clasping tightly hold of Ashley's hand.

'Why haven't you brought us here before?' Leo asked, lying back and resting one arm on the bank. 'I could have done with this every day of our stay.'

Dee laughed. 'I'm quite happy not to have to drive all this way every day, thank you.'

'It isn't far.' He glared at her as if daring her to argue. 'And it's worth the drive.'

Katie giggled as Leo splashed water in our direction. I held her around her waist, lifting her and swinging her out of the way of the drops of water and then back again for his next gentle onslaught. We enjoyed the coolness of the water against our hot skin for almost an hour.

'Right, that's enough now,' I said lifting her up towards the bank.

Katie wriggled and pleaded to stay in the water. 'More, Mummy.'

'Two minutes, Katie. No more,' I said as Leo and Dee got out and went to sit on their towels.

Eventually, our skin began wrinkling, so I lifted Katie out of the water and onto the bank, the sun glinting off her wet shoulders like diamonds on her golden skin. I ignored her insistence that she hadn't finished playing in the water.

'We need to eat something,' I said, aware that Leo and Dee were whispering again. She glanced at me out of the corner of her eye, said something else and then both focused their attention on me. It was unnerving. 'Is something the matter?'

'No, why?' Leo said, forcing a smile.

I draped a towel around Katie's shoulders, which she instantly shrugged off. Shaking my head, I started making up our rolls. 'Hand out the plates.' I told Katie to keep her out of mischief to give myself time to think about Leo and Dee's odd behaviour.

'This is just what I needed,' Dee said, coming over with Ashley to join us under the shade of the leafy tree. 'Thanks, Sera.'

Seeing her so relaxed made me wonder if I was being a little over-sensitive. I handed her two plates.

'The fillings for the rolls are in there.' I pointed to the small cool box in the hamper, sitting back on my haunches and watching as she caringly put together a small plate of food for herself and Ashley. Maybe all she needed was the peace and quiet of the English countryside, days out with nothing to think about but relishing the sunshine. I hoped so, because these were things I could give her.

I wished I'd brought a camera with me. I watched Katie eating and lay back, closing my eyes, listening as she laughed, chattering away to Ashley who surprised me by speaking a little in a mixture of French and broken English.

Dee hummed tunelessly to herself. I opened one eye and watched Ashley picking at her food. Leo lay back on the rug, closed his eyes and dozed off, snoring lightly. For once, being in their company was relaxing.

'I don't mean to be as snappy as I am, Sera,' Dee said quietly, breaking the silence. 'I've had a difficult time and I think I need to work on myself a bit.'

I knew how it felt to be forced into a situation you hadn't chosen. 'Then you're in the perfect place,' I said, patting her arm. 'You take all the time you need.'

We all had another swim to cool down, and wash off the stickiness of the melons from the girls' faces, before piling back into the car and setting off for home. Both girls fell asleep during the journey. I was happy. Today had gone better than I had hoped. I even felt as if I'd made a breakthrough with my childhood friend.

'Can we stop for a moment?' Leo asked, not very far into the journey. 'I want to take in this view.'

I was happy to oblige.

'You're lucky to live here, Sera,' he said as we stood side by side looking down through different coloured fields to the church steeple standing proudly in the middle of the next town.

I murmured an agreement, enjoying the scene ahead; the sun shining on the river like a silvery ribbon cutting through the countryside. 'I am,' I admitted. 'This is the perfect place for me to bring up Katie. It was a bit awkward moving back in with Mum initially, but I'm glad she insisted we return to live with her.'

'Maybe Dee and I should buy a small place near here. Then we could be neighbours.'

I wasn't sure if it was the notion of seeing Dee more, or the thought of them moving from Mum's and getting their own place, that appealed most.

I noticed the lowering sun reflect off the roof of a house and felt pretty sure it was Henri's. I wondered why I hadn't seen him for a while. I had popped to the farm a couple of times earlier in the week to say hi, but he had been out. The last time I pushed a note through his letterbox saying to give me a call if he wanted a chat, but hadn't heard from him. I hoped he was okay.

Leo nudged me. 'You okay?'

'Yes,' I said, dragging myself back to the present. 'You should come here when the town is shrouded in mist some mornings. It's magical.'

He looked at me, went to say something and then changed his mind. 'We'd better get those two sleepyheads home to bed, they're exhausted.'

Dee smiled at him when we joined her in the car. 'It was a good day,' she said before resting a hand on each of our shoulders. 'Thanks, Sera.'

I looked at Ashley and Katie, two little girls with such different experiences in life and my heart squeezed in pain. Whatever Dee's difficulties and however she saw fit to treat Ashley, I needed to support her for the little girl's sake. For now, I needed to hold my tongue and put Ashley's feelings before my own. Let her enjoy some of the things Katie took for granted. Let her be as carefree as she could be. While she had the chance.

Chapter Eighteen

2003 – Oakwold, New Forest

Young Sera

'You take this note to Hazel, you hear me?' my mum said on yet another stinking hot day.

I was glad of the excuse to get out of the house. I was sick of being there with no one to talk to while Mum lay in the shade and learnt her lines. I didn't mind getting clammy and sweaty on my walk to the farm, even if the heat did make my hair go frizzy.

'Sera, are you listening to me?' She gave me a disapproving look and tapped the envelope in my hand.

'What does it say?' I asked, before she had the chance to give me a deadline for my return home. I held it up to the living-room window to try and see through the thick cream envelope she'd sealed shut.

'Never you mind,' she snapped. 'Just make sure you don't forget to hand it to her personally. I want to be certain she's read it.'

Intrigued by this out-of-character approach to Dee's mum, I stared at her open-mouthed. 'But Mum, you hate Hazel,' I said, confused. 'Why are you writing to her?'

'I don't hate her.' She frowned, something she didn't often do as the thought of wrinkles horrified her. 'And stop looking gormless, the wind will change if you're not careful and you'll end up looking like that for the rest of your life.'

I stared at her suspiciously. 'Why won't you tell me what it says?'

She narrowed her eyes. 'Stop being nosy. Do as I ask, or you can stay here and I'll take it to her. You can do chores while I'm gone.' She knew her threat would work. I pushed a strand of hair away from my face and hurried to the door. 'I'll be expecting a reply too,' she shouted before I managed to escape unscathed. 'So don't think you can go and read it with that daughter of hers.'

I stopped and turned to her, my hackles rising at her nastiness towards my best friend. 'Why don't you like her?'

She rubbed her temples with her fingertips. 'I do. It's this heat, it's getting me down. Now stop answering me back and get a move on. Make sure you give it to her.'

I crammed the envelope into my denim shorts pocket and ran out of the house, through the garden and out of the heavy wooden gate. Sometimes she really got on my nerves. I didn't understand why she was so horrible about that family. What had they ever done to her?

Hazel and Mum were so different, I mused as I walked into the field. I never would have found a collection of Angelique books in Mum's bookshelves. Hazel never seemed to work. I was sure Mum would be more relaxed if she didn't have to travel away on location so often. She was never carefree enough to dance through the wildflowers, like I'd spotted Hazel doing many times in the small field closest to her farmhouse.

Everything about Hazel was light and fun; she even smelt amazing. In fact, the scent of patchouli and sandalwood emanated throughout her untidy farmhouse. With her wild curly hair, she was like a gypsy princess from one of my childhood fairy tales.

She'd never choke me with hairspray, or spend hours making sure everything in her house was exactly in its place. No one cared at the farm if the furniture was a bit dusty, or the beds were left unmade for a day. Nothing was ever done on the spur of the moment at my house. Hazel's farm was fun. She seemed to conjure up a party seamlessly, her guests dancing and laughing in the field, or in the barn where candles standing in makeshift holders nailed onto the walls flickered their light in the old building. Mum's idea of a party was dull people standing around our living room holding cocktails, with me doing circuits of the room offering canapés.

Dee must have been waiting for me to come out of our garden, because as soon as I'd gone several yards, I saw her in the field.

'We're going to the pool in the woods,' she shouted, waving me over to her.

Irritated with Mum, I was in no rush to deliver her letter. I waded through the long grasses to join Dee. I noticed Leo ambling along behind her as if he was trying not to be noticed.

'Hi, Leo,' I said guiltily when I saw his scabbed knee through his worn jeans. 'Sorry again for pulling you out of the tree the other day.'

'It's okay,' he mumbled, shuffling his feet in the dusty ground.

Dee glanced at her brother. 'Come on, ignore him. He's just weird. Do you like my hair?'

'It's great,' I said, envious that she always managed to get her hair to look better than mine. 'You're so lucky having curly hair, mine's so flat with just a bit of frizz.' I stared enviously at the colourful silk scarf tied around her head. 'Is that one of your mum's you've nicked?'

'Yeah.' She giggled and punched me playfully on the arm.

'Maybe you could come to my house the next time Mum's away and we can try bleaching our hair?' I said bravely.

Remembering the letter I was supposed to deliver, I added, 'I need to take something to Hazel.'

'Can't it wait?' Dee asked, waving a fly away from her face.

'Do you think your mum might have another party soon?' I asked Dee, as we ran through the field.

'Tonight maybe,' she said, stopping for breath. 'You know what she's like.'

I pictured the sixty or seventy people at her most recent party. Someone had lit a bonfire in one of the nearby fields and everyone carried a chair, or old piece of tree trunk to sit on.

'Do you have that cigarette on you?'

Dee glanced back to make sure Leo wasn't near enough to hear us. 'I don't want him splitting on us and telling Jack I've nicked this,' she said, stopping right next to me. She slowly pushed her hand inside her front pocket, carefully extracting the rolled-up cigarette we'd pinched from him the night before when he wasn't looking.

'Do you think we should?' I giggled. I liked Hazel's boyfriend, he was fine with us as long as we didn't bug him and Hazel at the parties.

'We'll lose Leo and smoke it in the woods,' she whispered.

I'd once heard my mum commenting that Hazel spent her life surrounded by noise to block out her past. I couldn't imagine it being true, however.

I touched my pocket lightly, feeling the letter underneath the material. 'I really should give this to your mum,' I admitted reluctantly.

'Mum's writing songs again and wants some peace,' Dee said. 'We have to stay away from the farm for a bit.'

'You must be excited that she's writing songs again?'

'None of her other songs have ever done anything,' Dee pouted. 'She gets really down when something doesn't work out. I wish she wouldn't have these bouts of trying.'

'What does Jack think?'

'He thinks it's a good thing,' Leo said. 'He says she's got a beautiful voice and should make the most of it.'

'Why don't you bugger off,' Dee shouted, pushing him roughly on his shoulder. 'Sera and I've got stuff to talk about.' When he didn't change direction, she added, 'Private things.'

'You bugger off.' He glowered at her and stomped off on a different path.

'Good,' she said. 'Now we can smoke this and see what it's like.'

We ran towards the shade of the wood, jumping over stinging nettles and flowers. I was a bit nervous to see what would happen when we smoked Jack's odd-smelling roll-up, but ran through the trees enjoying being cool for a change.

'I really need to deliver this to your mum,' I said, unable to forget the letter as I guiltily pulled it from my back pocket and waved it in front of Dee's face.

'What's in it?' she asked.

'No idea.'

She snatched it from me and studied it. 'Your mum sealed it. Come on, let's sneak into the house and steam it open.'

'We can't,' I snapped, reaching to take it. Dee swung away from me and held it high before tugging gently at the top to try and peak inside.

'Typical of your mum to use a fancy thick envelope we can't see through,' Dee moaned.

It was. I squinted up through the trees at the cornflower blue sky. 'I don't care if Hazel's writing, my mum will kill me if I don't deliver this letter today.'

'Fine. We'll smoke this tomorrow then.' She sighed heavily and got up.

We hurried to the farm. Leo was just arriving at the edge of the wood, waving a stick to knock the blood-red petals from the poppies standing in his path.

'Don't do that, you moron,' Dee shouted, pushing his shoulder, grabbing the stick and throwing it away from him.

'Hey, that's mine.'

'Tough,' I shouted. Poppies were my favourite flower and he'd annoyed me by being destructive.

—

We ran as fast as we could to the farm, then up the front steps and into the house. The front door banged loudly against the hall wall to signify our arrival.

'What the hell are you lot doing?' Hazel shouted. 'You were supposed to leave me in peace for a few hours.'

'It's not her fault.' I held the envelope out towards her. 'Mum said I had to bring you this. She's waiting for your reply.'

'Your mum?' Hazel said, eyes narrowing as she stared at the envelope in my hand. It was as if I was trying to hand her a lit firework. 'What's it about?'

I shook my head, wondering why she was acting so odd. 'No idea.'

She finally took it from me, slowly turning the envelope over and studying it ominously. 'It says, "*Hazel*".'

I'm not sure what else she expected to see written on an envelope, it was for her after all. I knew Mum could be a bit of a control freak, but she wasn't that scary, surely.

Hazel took a deep breath and turned to go back into the living room. 'I'd better read it then.'

Dee and I followed her in silence, glancing at Jack who was staring out of the window.

'Hello, girls,' he said, turning to face us.

I spotted the packet with his nicked cigarette sticking out of Dee's shorts pocket and pulled a face at her.

'What?' she mouthed, frowning.

I looked pointedly at her pocket and she moved behind a chair out of Jack's line of vision and pushed the pack further inside.

'I thought you were told to stay away for a few hours,' he said, looking from us to Hazel.

Hazel explained about the letter. She pulled open a small drawer, retrieving a silver paperknife. We watched in anticipation as she slid the blade into the fold and ripped it open in one clean swipe. She carefully took out the single sheet of paper and opened it. She'd only just started reading when she gasped. Clamping a hand to her mouth, she reached for the back of the sofa and sat down, clutching the note in her hand.

Jack rushed to her side and crouched down in front of her, trying and failing to take the letter from her grasp.

'Mum, what's the matter?' Dee asked. 'What did Maureen say?' She glanced up at me accusatorily and I widened my eyes trying to show that I was innocent of any wrongdoing. I was as ignorant as she about the contents.

'Are you okay?' I asked, my voice shaky from fright.

She didn't react.

'Of course she's not, you idiot,' Dee shouted.

'Girls, stop.' Hazel put her hand out to take mine and gave it a little squeeze. 'It's not Sera's fault.' She hesitated. 'I've just had a bit of a fright. I'll be fine.'

I watched her for a bit, summoning up the courage before asking, 'What should I tell Mum?'

'Tell her?' She averted her gaze. I could see her chest rising and falling as she breathed heavily. What could have given her such a fright? 'Let me think for a minute.'

We stood watching her. Jack stroked her legs and I waited for her to reply. I'd never seen Hazel like this before. I couldn't imagine what Mum must have told her. I wasn't sure I wanted to know either, not if this was how much it upset people.

Eventually, she sat upright and forced a smile. 'I'm fine,' she said, raising her chin defiantly. 'Sera, please tell your mum I've received her note. I feel the same way she does, and I'll be sure to do as she asked.'

What the hell did that mean? I frowned, disappointed not to be any the wiser.

'I'm scared,' I heard Leo say quietly from the doorway.

'No, baby, it's nothing for you to worry about.' She hugged Jack tightly, then let go, waving Leo over to ruffle his hair. 'I just have to think things through for a bit.' She looked up at me. 'If Mimi...' she hesitated. 'Your mum needs to speak to me again about this, she can give me a call. She has my number.' She smiled at Jack and stood up. 'Tell her I'll meet her, if she thinks it would be better.' She waved me away. 'You'd better go home now, Sera. Let Mimi know what I've said. She'll be waiting to hear from you.'

I hesitated and glanced at Dee. Hazel rarely referred to Mum at all and when she did she didn't mention her by name. To hear her use a shortened version was odd to say the least. She made it sound as if they were real friends. They certainly shared some sort of history, even if it was something neither of them seemed to want to extend to the rest of us.

I sensed that something terrible had happened, or was about to. I couldn't work out what. I struggled not to panic.

'What's wrong, Hazel?' I asked, my voice quivering with fear. Were we in danger? 'I don't understand what's happening,' I admitted, too frightened to keep quiet. 'What has Mum told you?'

'Tell us, Mum,' Dee demanded, starting to cry.

I looked at my friend and then to Hazel. She was staring at her hands, a haunted look in her eyes. There must be something badly wrong. Why else would she react this way and why would our mums, who never bothered with each other, make contact now?

'It's not for me to say,' Hazel replied eventually, her voice calm, controlled. She grabbed me, holding me tightly in a hug for longer than seemed necessary. Then she kissed the top of my head before taking my wrist and pulling me to the front door, then she pushed me outside.

'Go. Now. Hurry home and don't stop for anything along the way.'

I ran home as fast as I could, not stopping until I found Mum in the kitchen, wiping down the worktops.

'Well?' she said, turning to me. 'What did she say?'

I was out of breath, so it took me a moment to gather myself. 'She said to say she's got your message, that she feels the same way you do and will do as you ask.' I tried to calm my breathing. 'And that if you want to speak to her about this again, you can phone her,' I panted. 'Or, if you'd prefer, she's happy to meet up with you.' I waited for her to say something and when she didn't, I added, 'Do you want me to phone her now and arrange a time for you two to meet up?'

She shook her head slowly. 'No. Not just yet.'

Chapter Nineteen

2018 – Oakwold, New Forest

Sera

Mum went away on a shoot for a week. Usually the times she was away passed quickly, but this time Katie went down with a sore throat, so I was tied to the house more than normal. The heat added to Katie's misery and she cried if I left her even for a short time. I bought several electric fans and plugged them around the house in a vain attempt to circulate some air. Placing bowls of ice in front of the fans helped, but only slightly. I would have given a lot for air-conditioning, but it wasn't something we could afford to have installed. I had to stop feeling sorry for myself and Katie, and do the best I could. Poor Katie had only wanted to eat ice cream and drink orange juice for several days and all of us were thoroughly sick of the heat.

When she was feeling a little better, I rummaged around in the basement and found an old blow-up paddling pool. Leo cleaned it, setting it up for me in the shadiest part of the garden under the large pear tree. After a little encouragement, Ashley nervously stepped into the water and eventually, having watched Katie pretending to swim for a few minutes, joined her.

Both girls spent hours staying cool despite the heat of the day, by wallowing in the water and it was a relief that Katie had cheered up.

Apart from the occasional topping up from buckets filled at the outside tap to keep the water cool, all we had to do was watch them and fan ourselves and I looked forward to her returning to pre-school, so that I could get on with my work at the studio.

'This heat is exhausting,' Dee moaned one morning. 'If we don't get some rain soon I'm going to go mad with this hay fever, it's getting worse every day.' She sneezed as she reached the kitchen door, as if to make her point.

Later that day, I left Katie with Dee and Ashley and walked to the small corner shop at the end of our road to buy some sweets for the girls. I hadn't been back since losing my temper about Henri, but wasn't in the mood to walk far in the oppressive heat.

'Ahh, Sera,' said the shopkeeper, as if nothing had ever happened. 'You've heard the news?'

'No,' I said, not sure to what news she was referring.

'About the tenant. The one at the farm?'

I nodded eager for her to continue, not wishing her to see how anxious her comment made me, but realising she hadn't forgotten my last visit to her shop. I picked up two paper bags and using the small plastic scoop, half-filled them with a mixture of sweets for the girls.

'He was taken by the police for questioning at the station.'

'When?' I asked, unable to hide my panic.

She smirked. 'Yesterday morning.' Her delight at my reaction exhausted, she eventually added. 'They released him in the afternoon.'

Old crone, looking so self-satisfied. Why anyone could glean enjoyment from someone else's misery I couldn't imagine. She weighed the sweets I'd selected and twisting the tops of the paper bags, handed them to me, holding out her other wrinkled hand for payment.

'He's a good man, you know,' I said, counting my coins and handing her a couple. 'Whatever you all might think.'

She closed her fingers over the metal and shook her head, pressing the drawer release on the old till and dropping them inside. She took out my change, checked it and handed to me. 'Too many changes and too many strangers; everything is different around here now.'

She turned her attention to the ancient fan above her head and switched it to a higher speed. 'There have been fires reported south of here, too. Did you know that?' she added.

'Hopefully we'll have rain soon, then we won't have to worry about them here,' I answered as cheerily as I could manage, desperate to cut short this depressing conversation and leave.

I hurried home to deliver the sweets. Having received Dee's assurance that I could give Ashley some, I called both girls into the kitchen.

'Here you go,' I said, handing out a bag to each of the delighted little girls. They ran to play upstairs.

–

I went to find Mum, who'd got back the night before, to ask her to look after Katie while I paid Henri a visit to find out why he had been arrested. The doorbell rang.

'Dammit. I'll get that,' I shouted, hurrying to the front door and pulling it open. Two policemen stood, grim-faced on the doorstep. Recovering from my shock at seeing them there, I opened my mouth to speak. 'Can I help you?' They explained that they wished to ask Leo and Dee some questions. 'Why? What about?' This was ridiculous, first Henri getting questioned and now Leo and Dee? Surely the two enquiries couldn't be connected? Could they?

'We're unable to discuss this with anyone but the people involved,' one informed me. 'Now, if you'd take us to them?'

'Yes,' I said, stepping back to give them space to enter the hallway. 'Please, come this way.'

I showed them to the living room. It was stifling in there. For some reason neither Mum nor I had remembered to open the double doors onto the balcony overlooking the garden. As I did so, I heard something drop behind me and noticed Dee standing at the doorway an open book at her feet.

'What are they doing here?' she murmured, the colour disappearing from her face.

I wished I could have given her warning. 'They want to speak to you and Leo. Is he in?'

She stared at the policemen. 'What? Um, outside maybe?' She stepped towards the door. 'I'll go and look for him.'

'No.' The taller of the two men stepped in front of her. He nodded in my direction. 'You. Please go and fetch him.'

I gave Dee a reassuring smile. She had been slightly calmer and more relaxed lately and it irked me that these visitors could change that. 'I'll be as quick as I can,' I promised her. 'I'm sure this won't take long.'

She sat, her back straight as she picked at the skin on the side of her thumb.

I rushed out of the room, aware that I could have no idea how long their questions would take, or even why they wished to ask Leo and Dee anything. Reaching the back door, I ran down the stairs to the garden.

'Where's Leo?' I asked Mum, who was standing by the peach tree with Paul. She had a script in one hand with the other in the air, her fist clasped as if holding a dagger. Paul was holding his own script and grabbed her by the throat with his free hand. 'Two policemen are here,' I shouted as I neared them. Paul dropped his hand immediately. It would have been funny on another occasion. 'They want to speak to him and Dee about something.'

Mum turned to me, her legs almost giving way. Paul caught her and led her to a nearby seat. 'You okay, Mimi?' he asked. 'Blimey, it's not as if they want to speak to you.'

I did my best not to give him a mouthful. Why was he so useless in a crisis? Mum wasn't someone who liked to cause a scene, or show any weakness, so her reaction confused me. I walked over to her seat and knelt on the grass next to it. 'You okay, Mum?'

'Yes, yes,' she snapped. 'It's the heat. We've been out here too long, and it's got to me. Stop making a fuss.' She waved me away like an annoying wasp.

I stood up, knowing to leave her alone. 'Do you know where I can find Leo?' I asked, picturing Dee's anxiety at being left alone with the police.

The sound of the front door slamming against the hall wall made me and Mum jump. 'What the—?'

'Dee,' I heard Leo shout. 'Where the hell are you?'

I ran up the back steps and into the house.

'Why are the police here?' he demanded, his face red with fury. 'And where's my sister and niece?'

'Dee's in the living room,' I said, assuming he must have seen the police car parked outside the front of the house to be so annoyed. I noticed the living-room door was closed, certain I'd left it open earlier. 'They're only here to ask you both a few questions, though I've no idea what about. Do you know?'

He shook his head.

'I think Ashley's upstairs with Katie. I'll keep her away, don't worry.'

He took a deep breath. 'I don't mean to act like a lunatic, but Dee's too fragile to be left alone with them.'

I agreed and watched him go. When he'd closed the door I leant in closer, but was only able to hear muffled voices and the occasional snippet about the dead body at the farm. Why would they be asking Dee and Leo about that? I lived nearby and would have more reason to be involved in any questioning than two people who hadn't lived here for fifteen years.

I heard crying and Leo was, as usual, doing his best to comfort his sister. I remembered Ashley and went up to her room to check on her.

Opening the door quietly, I watched as she hummed to the teddy Katie had given her. She seemed fine, so I crept back out and closed the door after me, not wishing her to hear the commotion downstairs. I wanted to find out if the police were intending staying much longer. I didn't think the strained atmosphere was healthy for the little girl.

I went to check on Katie. She was lying on top of her bed brushing her doll's hair. 'Ashley wants her mummy,' she said when I crouched down to straighten her doll's skirt.

I stroked her face. 'She'll be fine, sweetheart, you mustn't worry. Why don't you ask her to come and play in your room?'

Satisfied they hadn't been disturbed by the latest goings-on in the house, I went back outside to see if Mum was feeling better. She and Paul were continuing with their rehearsal as if nothing had happened. It was as if I'd imagined her reaction minutes earlier.

I wished she didn't feel the need to always appear strong in front of me. She had once told me when I had asked where my father was, that she was both mother and father to me. I presumed that she felt it was her duty, therefore, to always hide her fears from me. Unfortunately, it also meant that she kept her innermost thoughts and emotions from me, too. I knew she found my openness difficult to cope with at times and must question why I hadn't absorbed more of the reserved side of her nature. It occurred to me that she might have a more secretive side that I hadn't noticed before. I pushed the thought away and instead tried to picture what my father must have been like for me to be so different to her.

I noticed her looking reflective. 'You okay, Mum?' I asked, trying not to let her see how much it had upset me to see her get such a fright. 'Do you need me to do anything for you?'

She gave me her best actress smile. 'Darling, don't I look perfectly fine?'

'That's the point of my question, how do I know when I'm looking at the real you?' I teased.

'That's not funny, Seraphina,' she glared at me. Her large eyes darkened. I couldn't think why she was taking my silly joke so badly.

'Hey, relax. I was only messing about,' I said. When she didn't look like she was going to calm down, I added. 'You know that, surely?'

She stared at me for a little longer. I could almost see her thoughts clambering through her mind. She glanced up at the living-room window where Leo and Dee were still ensconced with the two police officers and then back at me.

'What can the police want with those two?'

'I've no idea. I did ask Leo, but he didn't know either.'

I made sure Mum was settled and went back into the house, stopping in the hallway. I tried to make out what was being said in the living room, but could only pick up hushed voices.

Impatient to discover the cause behind the visit, I checked on Katie and Ashley again.

'Hey, girls.' I opened Katie's door to her completely pink bedroom. 'Everything okay?'

Katie held up a ragdoll that Mum had bought her when she was very small and said, 'Ashley doesn't have any dolls.' When I looked concerned at this snippet of information, she nudged Ashley. 'Do you, Ashley?'

The little girl stared silently at me for a second and then shook her head slowly. She almost seemed guilty, as if she was betraying a secret.

'Are the police speaking with Leo and Ashley's mummy?'

I crouched down next to Katie. 'Have you been downstairs?'

Ashley looked terrified. Sorry to have frightened her, I cupped her chin and smiled. 'It's okay,' I said in what I hoped was a soothing voice. 'I won't tell anyone.' I looked down at Katie. 'You should probably keep this a secret, too. Okay?'

She nodded her head vigorously. 'Yes, Mummy.' She put an arm around Ashley's skinny shoulders. 'Are they telling them off?'

'Don't be silly, Katie.'

The contrast in these children was remarkable. Katie with her bubbly character, golden-tanned skin and pudgy arm, next to Ashley's almost translucent skin. I would have hugged Ashley if I didn't suspect doing so would terrify her. I wondered when her birthday might be, and if maybe Katie and I could buy her a doll then without offending Dee.

Not knowing what to do with myself, I walked slowly from room to room checking all the windows were open. The lack of breeze through the house, despite the fans and all the downstairs windows being open, left the place with an oppressive air about it.

The sun streamed into my bedroom. I ran my hand over the thick layers of white paint on the wooden shutters and pulled them closed to keep in as much shade as possible before crossing the landing to go up the stairs to the attic to Dee's and Leo's bedrooms.

Entering Leo's room at the front of the house, I opened his window and pulled the small single shutter closed. Nothing was out of place. I could see his rucksack on top of the wardrobe. There wasn't a crease on his bed sheets or pillow. Next to his bed a single book lay beside a carafe of water, its lid a clean glass resting upside down, both of them joined by a plain lamp on the oak bedside table. I smiled at the simplicity of the room and turned to leave. Leo's beige linen jacket was placed neatly on a wooden hanger on the back of the door. It moved slowly side to side from the jolting of me opening the door.

Where had he been all these years? I wondered where the rest of his things must be and where his home had been. In France like Dee? He must miss his personal effects; I know I would if I had to be away from everything for long. I didn't own much, but my photos and books were precious to me, as were an overnight case crammed with Katie's baby clothes, and drawings she had done for me at pre-school.

I entered the larger attic room. This was another sight entirely. Clothes were strewn on every surface, including the floor. I hadn't realised Dee had managed to fit so many items in her bag. Ashley's bed, on the other hand, was roughly made, but tidy. It seemed odd for such a little girl to take pride in her bed. The teddy Katie had given her was resting against her pillow. Tears welled in my eyes, blurring the vision in front of me. I wanted to look after her. Teach her to be a little girl and not spend her time worrying so much.

Remembering what I'd come up here for, I hurried over to the two square windows and opened them, pushing them as far out as I could before closing the shutters. This room above all the others needed fresh, clean air to waft through it, blowing away the tension. Even though it wasn't my room, I couldn't help hanging up and folding away Dee's T-shirts and straightening her bedclothes. I heard the front door slam.

Leaving the bedroom, I ran down the stairs as Dee ran up them. 'She's in Katie's room,' I said before she had time to ask her daughter's whereabouts.

'Thanks,' she said, giving me a smile. 'I need to give her a cuddle. She always makes me feel better when she hugs me.'

I smiled, understanding her sentiment. I followed her.

'What did the police want with you both?'

She hugged the silent child tightly without speaking for a few seconds. I was about to repeat my question, when she answered. 'They've been questioning Henri, did you know that?'

'I was told earlier at the shop.' I was surprised that she seemed more self-assured after being questioned than she had before. 'The police told you that?'

'No,' she said. 'Leo was told by someone in the village. The police wanted to know anything he and I could tell them about the farm.' She lowered her voice, which was pointless as she was still holding Ashley. 'They're trying to identify the burnt body.'

'But what could you possibly tell them?' It didn't make sense.

She let go of Ashley, stroked her hair and followed me downstairs. 'That's what Leo repeatedly said to them. We haven't lived there for years. How the hell could we know who it was?'

She had a point.

I decided to spend some time by myself and met Leo in the kitchen on my way to the cellar.

'How are you?' I asked although he seemed perfectly fine as he poured himself a coffee.

'Bloody cops. I don't know why they don't focus on the job in hand rather than picking on innocent people.'

'They're probably just following a line of enquiry,' I said, repeating something I'd heard on one of the detective shows on television, not really sure what it meant. 'You both did live there, so maybe they're speaking to you to be certain they haven't missed anything?'

'It did seem that way. I heard them mention Henri on their way out.'

I stiffened, not wishing to show him my concern. 'What did they say?'

'I have no idea, they wouldn't elaborate when I asked them.'

I shivered, crossing my arms in front of my chest. 'I doubt Henri has anything to do with it.'

He stared at me silently for a few seconds before shaking his head. 'You don't know that, Sera. For all you know, the three of us could be involved in some way.'

My mouth opened as I tried to find an answer to his shocking statement.

Leo laughed and nudged me. 'Don't look so horrified. I was joking. Of course none of us are involved. How could we be?'

Leo could be bloody annoying sometimes. Irritated, I left him to go to the cellar and lose myself in my work. I reached up and, lifting the small hook I'd fixed onto the door out of Katie's reach, went inside and turned on the Bakelite light switch. I walked into the huge cavernous room.

I began sorting through the signs. My arms ached in the dim, room after moving so many of them into two rows. It didn't matter how I tried to focus on what I was doing, I couldn't stop thinking about how my small family's lives had changed since Dee and Leo's arrival. I rested my hands on my waist and arched my back to try and ease it. Spotting the plait of garlic hanging from the hook nearby, I was reminded of Henri. At least the police had released him. I hoped he was okay. I wasn't sure if he avoiding me, though? And if he was, why? I realised nothing made sense any more. It hadn't made sense for some time.

Chapter Twenty

1990 – London

Mimi

It was hard to imagine I hadn't known Vince two months ago and now, here I was, relaxing against red leather seats in the back of an immaculate Jaguar on my way to Scotland. The leather was cool against my skin. I could barely contain my excitement. I still couldn't quite believe we were travelling with Gerald, Vince, and a group of their friends to a private country house party. When Vince suggested taking Hazel and me with him to Scotland two days previously, neither of us could believe our luck and had been ecstatic.

To be attending an event such as this one was something I couldn't have dreamt about when we had been introduced to Vince that night. So much had changed for me since meeting Hazel and Vince. I was living the life I'd imagined. Well, not quite, but I was getting there and seeing glamour and wealth that I could never have imagined before leaving home.

I half listened to Vince chatting to Callum, our driver for the journey, about some phone calls he needed to make. I gazed out of the window as we passed vibrant fields that looked as if an artist had got carried away with the abundant greens and yellows on his palette. There were so few buildings in the Highlands, compared to driving in the lush English countryside and the tiny villages were pretty, with many of their village houses' windowsills graced with tubs of petunias and bamboo structures supporting colourful sweet peas.

I pushed away a guilty pang at the notion that Alice had been called back to her family's estate in Hereford for her grandfather's funeral. It was easy to do; I knew Vince's glamorous girlfriend wouldn't give me a second thought if the tables were turned and I'd been the one having to miss out on this trip.

Gerald was travelling with his mistress and a couple of his and Vince's other friends in the car behind us. Mistress. What would my mother think if she knew I was mixing with people who openly flaunted their lover in front of friends? The idea thrilled me. I loved my new life. I was eager to make the most of any opportunity that presented itself to me and this had to be the most exciting experience so far.

'Pull over here, Callum,' Vince said as we entered a tiny village which didn't seem to consist of much more than a café and a tobacconist. 'If you girls need to use the bathroom, now's the time,' Vince said, getting out of the car and holding the doors open for us.

Hazel and I stepped out. I stretched, watching her staring after Vince as he walked with Gerald to the tiny shop.

'We'd better get a move on,' Hazel said. 'We don't want to keep him waiting.'

I bit back a retort. I didn't like her assumption she knew best how we should behave around Vince. He had been sitting next to me in the back of the car, insisting she sat in the front. To be seen with someone as charismatic and handsome as Vince was a dream come true, I mused as we walked towards the café and asked to use the bathroom. I loved that he made me feel like I was special to him.

'You don't know him nearly as well as you think,' I whispered as we washed our hands in the small cracked basin fixed to the wall, studying my eyeshadow and mascara to check it still looked immaculate. I didn't mean to sound superior, but I couldn't help it.

She gave me a knowing smile. 'Maybe you're the deluded one, Mimi. Have you ever considered that?'

I straightened the bodice on my crimson dress that Vince had treated me to before coming away. 'No,' I said, simply satisfied with my reflection.

'What are you both doing in there?' Vince bellowed from outside.

We both hurriedly retouched our lipstick and ran out to join him. 'Sorry, Vince,' we said in unison, glaring at each other for a split second.

'Get in, and let's go.'

We had been driving for a few minutes when Vince's hand moved slightly up my thigh. 'Glad you came?' he asked, a twinkle in his eyes.

I giggled. 'What do you think?' I said, enjoying this attention and understanding why he'd insisted Hazel sat in the front with Callum. 'I've never been to Scotland before. It's very different, isn't it?' I asked, still amazed to have been asked to accompany him. I would have been heartbroken if he had left me behind and only taken Hazel.

'Different to London?' Hazel sniggered. 'Er, yes.'

I tensed, disliking the prospect of her needing to emphasise my limited geographical experience.

'We're not back in some country village now, Mimi.'

I hoped I would have hidden my jealousy of her if she'd been the one Vince chose to sit next to. She'd never shown this side of her character before. Maybe she wasn't the sweet, innocent girl we all took her for?

'Now, that's not very friendly, is it?' Vince said, resting a large hand heavily on her bare tanned shoulder, while giving my thigh a little squeeze with his other hand.

I snuggled a little closer to him, relishing the closeness between us. 'It's okay,' I said, enjoying her ignorance of his flirtation. I loved it when he stood up for me. One of these days he would be telling people I was his girlfriend, if I had my way. 'I'm sure Hazel didn't mean to sound so nasty.'

She laughed. I could hear the embarrassment in her voice and couldn't help feeling a little sorry for her. 'I wasn't intentionally mean,' she admitted. 'But you forget, Mimi, it was only a few months ago that you came to London and you've still got a lot to learn about how everything works in the big city.'

'Maybe not as much as you think,' I said as sweetly as I could manage. Vince nudged me lightly with his elbow and mouthed, 'Naughty girl' to me. If only she knew about our secret meetings when she was working at the café or away at auditions. I pushed away the image of Hazel's disappointment if she ever discovered that some of my auditions had in fact been assignations with the man who filled both of our daydreams.

'I want you girls to enjoy yourselves,' he said, his voice a little louder than usual. 'I didn't bring you on this trip for you to snipe at each other.'

'Sorry, Vince,' we said in unison.

'Good. Now, Hazel, I want you to get a sense of how the entertainment works. Learn as much as you can from the way they conduct themselves.'

'I understand,' she said.

'And me?' I asked, unable to hide my envy. 'Why have you brought me along?'

He laughed a deep, sexy laugh that brightened everything around him. His beautiful lips drew back in a wide smile; he was so handsome my heart contracted painfully. 'I brought you, beautiful Mimi, because I thought you might enjoy something like this.'

Hazel turned and glared at me.

'It's a long drive to Scotland and we've got a late night ahead. I'm going to grab forty winks while I have the chance and it'll be easier if you two stop sniping at each other and give me a bit of peace to have a kip.' He tapped Callum on his shoulder. 'Put on some music, will you, mate?'

For a moment I felt disappointed, believing he meant what he'd said. I saw Hazel relax, closing her eyes, doing exactly as she was told. Callum twiddled around with the radio until he found something by Sting. As the first strains of 'Englishman in New York' began to play, Vince gave me a wink. He was certainly my Englishman of choice.

He bent his head and kissed my shoulder lightly. 'You're so perfect,' he whispered.

I caught Callum's gaze through the rear-view mirror. I could tell he was smiling. He gave me the creeps and I was relieved when he looked away and focused on the road.

I glanced at Vince and nodded towards Callum. He shrugged. 'Don't worry about him.'

He kissed the side of my neck and my resolve vanished. Vince smelt so good. He was nothing like the pasty-faced, spotty boys at home. He spoilt me by treating me like a princess and buying me unexpected gifts, my favourite being the beautiful crimson dress that I was wearing with matching shoes and bag. I smoothed the skirt down to try and eradicate the slight creases that had formed during the journey. I sighed, relieved I'd saved myself for a real man. I closed my eyes.

–

The next thing I knew, the car was stopping.

'Oh, look,' Hazel squealed from the front seat. I woke with a start. Desperate to rub my eyes, I remembered just in time that I was wearing make-up. 'There's the road sign for Scotland.'

A couple of hours later she shouted again. I wished she would calm down; she wasn't the only excited person in the car. Typical of Hazel to demand all the attention.

'Hurry up, you two,' her sing-song voice pierced through my half-asleep brain. 'Look at that.'

I peered out of the window and saw two large stone pillars of what I presumed was the country house where the party was to be held. Fuelled with delight, I wound down the window.

'Look, Vince,' I said. When he didn't reply, I turned to look at him over my shoulder. 'If that's the entrance, what's the house going to be like?' I reached back to grab his hand.

He took my hand in one of his and gently pushed my cheek so that I was once again looking away from him out of the window. 'We're not going there just yet,' he said. 'But when we do, we're going to have a memorable time.'

I could feel his warm breath on my shoulders, and shivered. I sensed Hazel glaring at us. When she didn't look away, I frowned. 'What's the matter with you?'

She stared at me for a bit and then turned her attention to Vince, her face softening almost instantly as she forced a smile back onto her face. 'Nothing,' she said sweetly.

Callum, satisfied we had seen the view, started the car and we drove on again. Suddenly, I couldn't help feeling a little guilty towards Hazel. After all, she had met Vince before me and never made any secret about her crush on him. I pretended to stare at the beautiful scene in front of us, the cottages and tea rooms. The wind rushed through my sleep-mussed hair and I tried to fix everything I was feeling at that moment into my mind to remember forever. My anticipation of the next few days gave me a buzz I wanted to savour.

Hazel had told me the night before in our tiny shared room to make the most of every experience that came our way and that's what I intended doing. We both wanted success, and both wanted Vince. We had little money and only one chance to make our new life in London work.

'Which way, boss?' Callum asked, breaking the tense silence that had taken over the car.

'We can drive into the countryside a bit more and check out some of the small hamlets,' Vince said. 'I know you've mentioned you'd like that, Hazel.' He gave her one of his winning smiles. She beamed, giving me a sideways glance that contained all the smugness I would have felt if I'd been on the receiving end of his attention. I knew we were acting like children, but the stakes were high, as far as we were concerned.

He squeezed me gently to him. 'And as for you, beautiful girl, what can I show you?' He winked at me and my jealousy seeped away.

'I'm sure Mimi doesn't know anything about the Highlands,' Hazel said, once again staring out of the window. 'Let alone the best places to visit.'

'Then maybe we should educate her,' he said. 'What do you think, Mimi?'

I tried to keep the excitement out of my voice. I was surrounded by mountainous scenery, it was glorious, and I was in love. Could life be any better?

'Callum,' Vince said. 'Drop us off and leave us for an hour.'

'Yes, boss.'

Vince directed his attention at me. 'Take Hazel to find a little tea room somewhere while I take Mimi for a walk.' He winked at me.

'Thanks, Vince,' I said, not taking my eyes off Hazel.

'Stop calling me Vince. Call me Vinnie, we're close friends now.'

Without any warning Hazel's arm shot out at me, her fingers stretching towards my face. I flinched just in time for her to miss clawing my eyes. She grabbed hold of my hair and yanked. 'You bitch,' she screamed.

I could feel her tearing my hair out by the roots and snatched her fist with both hands and pinched, digging my nails as deep into her skin as I could manage. 'Let go, you cow.'

'Hey, what the hell is this all about?' Vinnie yelled.

Callum grabbed her as Hazel's other arm flayed towards me in an attempted punch.

'Right, that's enough,' Vinnie shouted, his voice cold, not inviting argument. 'Let go of her hair,' he said slowly. 'Now.'

She locked eyes with him, opened her mouth to say something, then closed it. Letting go, she grimaced at the sight of my blonde strands entangled in her long fingers. Reaching out of the window, Hazel brushed her hands together to rid them of my hairs.

I rubbed my head vigorously. 'That bloody hurt,' I whined, mortified.

'I said, that's enough,' Vinnie said, his tone quiet, yet menacing. He moved slightly away from me, the coolness of the space between us devastating me.

'Callum, pull over,' Vinnie ordered.

I chewed my lower lip to stop from arguing. The car slowed and slid over to the side of the road.

'Right, you get out and sit in the front,' he said, pushing my bottom away from him. 'Hazel, you slide in the back with me. We'll have no more cat fights. I've got business to attend to tonight and I don't need you two acting like a couple of spoilt kids.'

I couldn't believe how quickly she launched herself out of the car. Hazel pulled open my door and held her arm out. 'Stop wasting time.' She winked at me as if she'd planned this to happen.

I slunk out of the car, miserable and wishing she was back at home. I was going to have to find another place to live, I decided. I couldn't spend time with someone who wanted the same things I did, it just wasn't working. I heard her giggle, hating the thought that he'd replaced me so easily. It was a stark reminder he didn't belong to me at all. He never really had. Why then couldn't I shift the sensation that I somehow belonged to him?

'This is beautiful,' Hazel cooed from the back seat. 'It's exactly how you described it to me the other day,' she murmured, letting me know they had spent time alone together.

I was determined not to show how upset I was. If he wanted to play games then that was fine, but I had a few games of my own to play.

Chapter Twenty-One

2018 – Oakwold, New Forest

Sera

After a day working on my stall at the village market, I finished packing the enamel signs I hadn't managed to sell and drank the rest of the bottled water I'd taken with me. Grateful to be shaded from the sun, I crouched down and carefully arranged the stock in the box, so none would be damaged on the way back to the studio. It was fine to have them artfully aged, but I didn't need them to be unsaleable. Satisfied with my efforts, I folded the tops of the box over and wove the four cardboard leaves together to hold the top closed.

'Good sales today?'

'Henri.' I smiled, not thinking to hide my delight at seeing him standing holding a large baguette and a full shopping bag at the other side of the stall.

He smiled, the damaged side of his face pulling back slightly more than the perfect side. 'You are happy to see me?'

I tilted my head to one side, pressing my lips together, hands on my hips and pretended to think. 'Yes, I am,' I said, having forgotten my annoyance with him. 'Where have you been the past few weeks? If you had a phone I could have called.'

'I am waiting for one to be set up at the farm, but the phone company, it takes many weeks.'

'I hope you're getting an answerphone like other people?'

He contemplated this idea briefly. 'No need. You are the only person who will telephone me.'

'Or not,' I teased.

'Pardon?'

My English sarcasm was lost on him. I studied him. Maybe it wasn't.

He walked around to join me. 'I do not understand.'

'Hmm, I'm not so sure about that,' I said enjoying the cool grassy smell of his clothes. 'How come you're out and away from your farm?'

He stepped back, pointing at his watch. 'I 'ave something I must do before I can go home. You will meet me at the farm in one hour, yes?'

I was too intrigued to argue, so nodded. 'Okay.'

He glanced down at the box of signs. 'I will put this into your car.'

'It's fine, I can do it,' I argued half-heartedly as he bent down and lifted it up and started to walk to my car. It wasn't such a big box, but it was heavy. 'Are you sure you can manage?' I asked before thinking.

He immediately stopped and turned to face me. 'I am capable of more than you suppose, Sera. Please, do not assume otherwise.'

I couldn't miss the hurt on his face. 'Idiot,' I mumbled, unable to believe my own thoughtlessness. 'Of course,' I said quickly. 'Sorry.' I raced ahead of him and opened the boot of the car, watching as he lowered the box into the awkward space, just about big enough to take it. 'Henri,' I said, embarrassed. 'I…'

He stood upright and stared at me, raising a hand to stop me saying anything further. 'Enough.' He began walking away, his footsteps laboured where only moments before his whole demeanour had been light.

I ran to catch up with him. Taking him by his arm I held on to him and when he didn't stop I stepped in front of him, so he would have to move around me to get past. 'Look, I know you're capable of whatever you put your mind to. I only asked because I care.'

His scowl softened. Then as if remembering why he was so cross, his expression darkened again. 'It's good to have a friend.' He held his hands out. 'I know how I look, but I do not need to be reminded how I am.'

I wanted to cry. I had offended him, deeply. 'Henri, please.'

Before I could utter another word, he put one hand at the back of my head and bending down, pressed his lips hard against mine in a kiss. The shock of what he was doing passed instantly as I forgot my surprise and surrendered to the exquisite sensation.

Eventually he stopped, leaving me wanting more. We stared at each other, both adjusting to what had just happened between us. 'Do not see me as an invalid,' he said, his voice catching slightly.

I hadn't expected this. Then again, I hadn't ever contemplated us kissing. 'Henri, I...'

He exhaled sharply. 'It is okay, we are friends?'

I nodded slowly. I wasn't sure I could be happy having him simply as a friend after that kiss. It had ignited something in me that I hadn't experienced since kissing Marcus for the first time. I couldn't find the right words and stared at him silently, thoughts racing through my head. I'd been single by choice since losing Marcus. I was almost used to not having him in my life. This kiss changed everything, especially the equilibrium of my long dormant emotions. First Leo, spending time at the house getting used to being a part of my small family. I enjoyed his company, more than I'd ever expected to, but Henri was different. He was a friend, but now I realised he could be more than that, to me at least.

'Shall I still meet you at the farm?' I said eventually.

'Yes.'

I sighed with relief. 'Good.'

He took me by both elbows and bent his head down towards me. 'I am sensitive, but I am not a fool. You ask me if I am okay because you have concern for me.' He kissed the tip of my nose. 'I will see you in one hour.'

He walked away, shaking his head. I wasn't sure if it was because of what I had said, or his reaction to it, but I did know at that moment I would rather he kissed my mouth. I touched my nose, as I watched Henri walk away. He was certainly complex. I wasn't sure if I'd ever be able to work him out.

–

Still shaky after my encounter with Henri, I drove to my studio to drop off the unsold signs. It had been another long hot day and I was relieved Mum had offered to look after Katie for me while she learnt her lines. She had yet again split up from Paul and I wondered if this time it would be for good.

I drew up alongside the studio and parked the car. Stepping out, I spotted someone through the window. My heart pounded as I cupped my hand either side of my face on the glass to block out the sun and try to get a better view. Squinting, I stared into the darkened room. The only light was through a small window at the back in the tiny kitchenette. I couldn't see anything. I watched for a little longer, feeling a little foolish for my paranoia.

Stepping back, I retrieved the front door key from my pocket and unlocked the door. I pulled both sides back to let out some of the dank air and freshen up the space a bit. Opening the boot of the car, I took a deep breath before reaching down to manoeuvre the box out, cursing the depth of the area.

'Need any help?' A familiar voice asked in an amused tone.

Startled to hear Dee's voice here in Southampton, I stood up too quickly and cracked my head on the edge of the opened boot.

'Ouch, shit.' I rubbed my scalp tentatively. 'What are you doing in town?' I looked around to see if she was alone.

'Leo dropped me off a while ago. He's taken Ashley to buy sandals. I thought I'd see how well I remembered the place and try to find your studio.'

Irritated to have my peace shattered, I couldn't tell if she was joking, or not. 'Help me with this and I'll show you around, if you like?'

We bent down and took a side each. 'Blimey, this is heavy,' she groaned, her face reddening as she walked backwards into the darkness of my studio.

'Let's put it on here,' I said, nodding towards the metal table where I carried out most of my work. 'I've only really popped in quickly to drop this off,' I said, not wanting her to get used to being here.

'I'm sick of this heat,' she said, fanning her face with one of my small posters. 'It's oppressive. I don't remember it being this bad when I was a kid.' She wrinkled her nose.

I wiped my forehead with the back of my hand. 'They say it's going to reach the mid-thirties tomorrow.'

Dee groaned. 'I wondered about offering to help at your stall today, but it was too hot.'

'It's fine,' I said, relieved she hadn't come. 'You did well to find this place.' I knew from the first few times I'd come here how confusing the back streets were to navigate.

'Not sure how really,' she laughed. 'In fact, you could give me a lift home. I'm shattered. Coming into town wasn't a clever move today, even some of the tarmac on the roads has shifted under the pressure of the heavier vehicles.'

I nodded, recalling seeing melting tarmac on my way here. I walked through to the kitchenette and poured a glass of water. 'Want one?'

She nodded. 'Yes, please.'

I handed her my drink and held a second glass under the running tap. I grimaced. 'The water's warm, I'm afraid.'

'No worries, I'm thirsty as hell, so anything will do.'

What had she been doing? I wondered. This wasn't the sort of place you simply walked by. There was nothing else around the area apart from smaller terraced houses and storage units. 'Won't Leo be expecting to pick you up from somewhere?'

She looked at me as if I'd asked her when she last exploded into millions of pieces of glass. 'I'm not a complete idiot.'

I sipped my drink. 'I didn't mean to insinuate you were. It's just that, well—' I wasn't exactly sure what to say next.

'Didn't he wonder what you wanted to come here for?' There, I'd said it.

She smiled at me. 'You want to know, you mean.' Without waiting for me to disagree, she shrugged. 'Is it so strange I might want to find out where my best friend spends so much of her time?'

Put like that, my curiosity did seem a little odd. 'No.' My head was starting to throb. I rubbed my temples lightly, willing the pain to ease.

'So, why ask then?'

I drained the last of the water in my glass. It was too hot for a confrontation. I couldn't wait to get her away from here. This was the only place I had left that she hadn't invaded. I needed her to go. I held out my hand to take her glass.

She passed it over slowly. 'You don't like me very much anymore, do you?'

Should I lie? I considered her question for a nano-second and something snapped. 'You haven't given me much reason to be fond of you.'

Dee's shoulders slumped. 'I suppose not.'

I rubbed my eyes before folding my arms across my chest. I was tired of the constant drama that Dee had brought to my home. This was my exclusive space that she had chosen to come into and it gave me the courage to confront her.

'Why did you leave fifteen years ago?' I asked, not caring that I was being blunt. 'And why have you come back now?' A shadow crossed her face, but she had asked for it. I wasn't ready to give up trying to discover the truth behind her extended visit. I still wasn't sure if any of Leo's tale was based on truth. 'What happened to you that was so bad? You left your home without packing any toys for your little girl?'

She didn't say anything for a bit, then when I was about to have another go at her, she gave me a pointed stare. 'Your marriage was perfect, or so your mother insists. Mine wasn't, so you're not in a position to judge me.'

'When exactly were you married?' I asked, trying to sound a little friendlier to hurry her along. I washed the glasses and put them away in the small cupboard, eager to finish this nonsense and go to be with Henri.

'I was eighteen; desperate to leave home and live my life my way.' She puffed out her cheeks and shook her head. 'He thought I was someone to vent his frustrations on. When I decided I'd had enough of his shit, he battered me. I was pregnant at the time.'

I closed my eyes at the picture in my head. 'Dee, that's horrendous.' I leant against the worktop, surprised by her bluntness and concentrated on hiding my shock. 'What about Leo?'

'He was away.' She looked relieved. 'I hate to think what would have happened if he'd come home sooner.' She stared at her feet. 'Or if he'd stayed away longer.'

I didn't quite understand what she meant, but didn't interrupt to delay leaving the studio.

'He came to me wanting to know why I hadn't answered any of his calls.' She sighed. 'He found me pretty messed up. We spent time by the coast while my bruises faded and then came here.'

I imagined Leo's horror at arriving at Dee's home and find his sister in such a state. It wasn't the same story he had told me, but the main gist I got from them both was that Dee had been physically as well as mentally abused by someone she'd been involved with. It wasn't surprising then that she seemed so different after all the things she must have suffered in the years since we'd last been together at the farm. I suspected her version was probably a little closer to what had really happened than Leo's.

'At least the baby was okay,' I said, hoping I didn't sound patronising.

'What?' Dee snapped, as if she didn't understand what I'd just said.

'Ashley,' I said. 'At least she was okay.'

She opened her mouth to speak, closing it again without answering. Crossing one ankle over the other, she studied the toes of her trainers. She slammed one hand down on the metal table.

I'd wasted enough time listening to her confusing stories; I grabbed my car keys. 'Come on, I thought you wanted to go home?'

She followed me to the door. A part of me was curious about Dee's lost years, but she had changed so utterly I wasn't sure how to be with her any more. I couldn't wait to deliver Dee back at the house, shower, change and go to see Henri. He was another mystery, but one I was determined to unravel.

Life must have been very dull here before these people came into my life, I decided. Dull, or simply peaceful? I wasn't certain which.

'Leo's got a soft spot for you, did you know that?' she asked, as if she could sense I was thinking about another man.

'Yes.'

Her face reddened. 'I think you should leave him alone.'

I wasn't sure why we were having this conversation. 'Why?'

'I don't want my brother getting hurt,' she said simply. 'He's a good man.'

I pulled the right sliding door closed. Then, standing back waiting for her to leave, I did the same with the other side, locking up. 'I think that's between me and Leo, don't you?'

'He's my younger brother, Sera,' she said, a barely concealed threat in her tone as she waited for me to unlock the car. I was seeing some of the old Dee back. She'd had balls when we were younger and annoyed as I was with her, it was good to see some fight in her again. 'He may seem like the one in charge of most situations, but not everything is as straightforward as it might appear.'

You can say that again, I thought.

Chapter Twenty-Two

2018 – Oakwold, New Forest

Sera

I needed someone sane to talk to.

I barely kept to the speed limit on my way to the farm, only slowing down as I entered Henri's dusty driveway. Parking the car, I got out and ran up his porch stairs. He pushed open the front door, concern on his tanned face as he grabbed my arms. 'You are okay?'

I smiled, relieved to see him. 'Sorry, I know we said one hour, but I had an unexpected visitor at my studio.' Unable to help myself, I leant forward and kissed him. He hesitated and then taking me in his arms, held me tightly.

Letting go, he stepped back. We stared at each other, both shocked by the recent turn of events.

Henri laughed. 'That was... unexpected. We will sit outside, where it is cooler.'

'Perfect,' I said, slightly dizzy from the kiss.

'I will get us a cold drink and then we can talk.'

He sounded a little odd, but I put it down to my kissing him. 'I hope it's more of that delicious cider,' I said. Hazel's cider had always been heavenly, too. I yearned to taste it again but also hoped that if he had something to drink he might be more forthcoming and confide in me about his past life in Paris.

'No. Today I have Calvados.' He widened his eyes. 'I brought it with me from France. You look tense in your shoulders and I prescribe at least two glasses, each.'

I grinned. I liked this friendlier version of Henri. 'Perfect. I need something to calm me down after spending the last half an hour with Dee.' I went to go with him into his kitchen.

'No,' he said, perhaps a little too harshly. 'I will bring your drink to you, outside.'

I went to do as he'd said, but first stopped to pet the puppies. Henri took two glasses from the shelf above the sink and caught my eye. I went to smile but he immediately glanced at the table. I followed his gaze, noticing the table was covered with papers. Some looked very old, but from my vantage point I couldn't make out what they were about.

'What's that?'

He picked up a tea towel and gave the clean glasses a cursory wipe before dropping the cloth over the papers on the table. 'My work. Come,' he said, grabbing a bottle of Calvados from the sideboard. He shook his head and smiled as he stood back to let me go in front of him, his determination that I leave obvious.

I was surrounded by too many secrets and didn't like the idea of him being party to more. I walked ahead of him when he didn't reply, not letting myself look back at the table, despite how much I wanted to.

We sat either side of the small rattan table and I recounted my visit to the studio and Dee's unexpected arrival. 'I know I sound like a whiny brat, but it's my private space where I go to get away from everyone.'

I watched as he poured us both a glass of the amber liquid. He handed me one, held his up and waited for me to do the same.

'*Santé*. To the whiny brat,' he teased.

'Do you even know what that means?'

He nodded head. 'We are drinking to our good health.'

I grinned at him. '*Santé*,' I echoed, staring at my glass, entranced. 'This is just what I need, thank you.'

He stared at me thoughtfully, reaching out and taking my nearest hand to him. 'Drink.'

I did as I was told this time, enjoying the heat of the apple-brandy drink as it wended its way down my throat and past my chest.

'I heard that the police interviewed you,' I admitted, wondering if he would tell me the same thing as Dee had. 'What did they want?'

'They were asking if I had seen anyone I didn't know... lurking? Is that the word?' I nodded. 'Any strangers here before the fire.'

'Had you?'

'No. I don't see anyone here.'

'Have they discovered who started the fire yet?'

'No, not yet. If they have found out more, they haven't told me.'

We sat lost in our own worlds for a moment. So, he had been questioned about the same thing as Dee and Leo. I was relieved for some reason.

'I've been trying to figure out what your job used to be,' I said, making the most of his openness.

He tapped the side of his nose. 'I will not tell you. You must guess.'

'Were you in the army?' I gasped, excited with my idea.

'No,' he laughed.

I enjoyed hearing the deep guttural sound. 'What did you do before coming here then?' I waved my hands in the air theatrically, accidentally knocking my full glass and sending my drink all over my shorts. 'Bugger.'

Henri went to stand. 'I will bring you a wet towel.'

Guiltily, I realised this could be my chance to see what he was hiding from me. I shook my head and motioned for him to sit. 'No. It was my clumsiness, and anyway, I might have to take these off to rinse them out. You refill my glass; I won't be long.'

I hurried inside and took off my shorts, running them under the tap and wringing them out. I glanced through the window to check he was still sitting out on the porch, probably too polite to come inside and disturb me. I hurried over to the table and lifted the tea towel to peek underneath, careful not to move anything. Peering at old newspaper cuttings I noted that they seemed to be about the disappearance of a man who hadn't been heard of for fifteen years. There was something familiar about him, but I couldn't think what.

'Sera?' Henri called.

'I'm on my way now,' I said, carefully lowering the cloth once again to cover the paperwork. I pulled my shorts back on and joined him outside. Sitting down I grimaced as my wet shorts connected with the wooden seat, relieved for once that it was such a hot day. Wracking my brains to work out why the missing man seemed so familiar, I said. 'You were about to tell me what you did before coming to live on this farm.'

'I want to be honest with you, Sera.' He looked down at his hands. 'I was a detective. I was, how you say, pensioned off, after I did something terrible and a woman was killed.'

'Tell me.' I felt disgusted with myself for nosing through his things. I needed to make amends and helping him share something that was an obvious burden to him would be a start. 'Please.'

'We knew each other for many years...' he hesitated. 'Her life had gone very badly. I tried to help her by paying for information on suspects and cases that I was working on.' He stopped. I took one of his hands in mine and waited silently for him to continue. 'I was warned by her brother not to involve her, but she insisted she wanted to keep helping me.' His voice cracked with emotion and he gave me a pleading look. I wasn't sure if he was trying to persuade me or himself. 'I should have known better.' He pulled his hand from my grasp.

'Was she the reason you were burnt?'

He nodded slowly. 'They set fire to her home. I went into her house to rescue her, but I was too late. She died on the way to hospital.' He cleared his throat. 'I failed her, Sera, I let her down.'

'You nearly killed yourself in the process, Henri. I can't see how you could have done more.'

He shook his head. 'I should have listened and left her out of it.'

'Well, I think you were very brave to put your life at risk.'

'No. I didn't listen, and a good woman died.'

Trying to take his focus away from the events that obviously traumatised him still, I asked, 'You're quite the *Jack of all trades*, aren't you?'

'Jack of what? Why would you say that?'

Unsure whether my attempt to distract him had misfired, I added. 'You know, you were a detective, now you're a farmer. You're capable of doing various jobs.'

'A *Jack of all trades*,' he mumbled staring at the burnt ruins of the barn for a while.

Jack... the words echoed in my head. Slowly, as if through an early morning mist, an image appeared in my memory.

'Oh my God,' I said, horrified at the prospect of what I was about to say. 'That newspaper cutting. The missing man.' I watched as his expression changed to one of shock as he realised what I must have done. 'He's Jack, isn't he? Hazel's boyfriend.'

Chapter Twenty-Three

2018 – Oakwold, New Forest

Sera

Henri clenched his teeth. I could see the muscle working on his jaw and that he was fighting the urge to be angry with me. 'I covered the table for a reason,' he snapped. 'If I wanted you to see, I'd have shown them to you.'

'I know,' I said, ashamed at my uncharacteristic behaviour. 'It was unforgivable of me, but, oh, I don't know… there are too many secrets in my life already. I wanted my relationship with you to be without any.'

He closed his eyes briefly and groaned. Lifting the bottle, he went to refill our glasses.

'No more Calvados for me, thanks,' I said. 'But I don't understand. Why hide them from me?' I asked, confused. 'Are they the reason you've come to live on this particular farm?'

He considered me carefully, then lifted his glass and downed his drink in one.

Intrigued, I leant back in my chair, crossing my legs thoughtfully. I was missing something, but what?

Henri sighed heavily. 'Jack was my father, Sera.'

'What?' I tried to make sense of it all. Henri was French. 'I hadn't realised he had a son.'

'His real name was Jacques. J-A-C-Q-U-E-S.' He spelled it out for me. 'He must have wanted to fit in with his British friends and anglicised his name.' He looked pensive.

I couldn't believe what I was hearing. 'Henri, no.'

'He left my mother when I was twelve,' he said quietly. 'Theirs was never a peaceful relationship, but he never forgot my birthday, or Christmas. On occasion he would turn up at Maman's house to see me, usually bearing a gift. They fought. He left. Always the same scenario.'

'So, you suspected something was wrong when he missed a birthday?' I recalled how upset Katie was when her birthday came around and her father wasn't there.

'When I didn't receive a birthday card or any contact from him on my eighteenth birthday, I suspected something was wrong.'

'That's heartbreaking.' I felt the urge to hug him, but didn't like to impose on his grief.

'The need to trace him built over the years. Even as a detective I never gave up searching for a trace of him. Keeping my eyes open for any information that I could find, or news reports.'

I tried to put this into the context of Hazel's life. 'What date is your birthday?' I asked, not sure how much I wanted to hear the answer. Perhaps I was about to open a Pandora's box of chaos that could change everything for me.

'Twenty-first of September.' He waited for me to take this in.

I could barely catch my breath. How I wished now that I hadn't looked at the newspaper cuttings. 'So, you turned eighteen a month after Hazel went missing with Dee and Leo?'

'Yes.' He sighed, staring across the yard at the remains of the barn again.

I followed his gaze and we sat watching the burnt-out shell of the building in silent contemplation. A horrific thought dawned on me. 'You think... the body in the barn was your father?'

He kept staring straight ahead. 'I know it.'

Stunned as if he'd slapped me, I followed his line of vision to the blackened ruins. I pictured Jack singing and swinging Hazel round in his arms at the last party she'd held. My heart pounded in shock as I struggled to absorb what he had told me. They were incredibly passionate about each other. Could that passion have led to murder? The notion was too dreadful to contemplate.

'But Hazel would never... I mean—' I couldn't imagine Hazel being capable of hurting anyone, least of all the man she loved. 'Not Hazel.'

I looked at him. There was something else. What was he so nervous to tell me?

'Henri?' I squeezed his arm when he didn't look at me. 'Look, I know Hazel could never have killed your father. She just couldn't, okay? She wouldn't have it in her to do something violent. She was all about love and fun.' He still didn't say anything. I could see he wasn't convinced. 'Maybe you've got this wrong.' Panic rose through me. 'Or it could have been someone else? Have you considered that?'

He glanced at his hands then back at me, a haunted look in his dark eyes. I sensed he hadn't finished confiding in me.

'Go on,' I said, terrified to hear what he was about to say, but needing to know everything.

He reached out and took one of my hands in his, resting them on the table in between us. His actions made me nervous. The tables had turned somehow.

'Promise me you'll listen to everything I have to tell you before making a judgement,' he pleaded, his eyes boring into me, willing me to agree.

I frowned. 'All right.'

He studied my face momentarily before speaking. 'My father used to write small notes in birthday cards. His last one mentioned that he was living with a singer called Hazel on a farm in the New Forest.' He hesitated and narrowed his eyes. He was waiting for me to react, but I wasn't sure why. He continued, 'I searched for her through a UK police contact over several years and tracked her down here. That was as far as her records went for many years – that I could find, anyway.'

'Go on.'

'A detective friend, an ex-police officer I'd met years ago in France, had been looking at a cold case in London for a woman who was trying to find out what had happened to her fiancé. I believe she was dying and wanted to resolve a mystery she'd lived with for many years.' I couldn't imagine why he would be nervous about telling me something this random, but waited for him to continue. 'She had told him that the man, a Vincent Black, had travelled to Scotland with two women back in '90.'

'Right,' I said, confused.

'A singer called Hazel and a cocktail waitress and wannabe actress called Mimi. They travelled together to a house party. She doesn't know where the party was and my friend has not been able to find out more about it. Apparently the two women had been sharing a flat.'

His words echoed in my head. I stared at him, but it was as if we were in a bubble and I was waiting for it to explode all around me.

'Mimi?' I felt sick. Was he about to fill in some of my mother's mysterious past? 'Go on,' I said, barely able to breathe, my heart was pounding so hard in my chest. I couldn't imagine Mum and Hazel being flatmates. How did I not know this? Did Dee know?

'Alice said that the three of them disappeared. Never returned to London.'

'Sorry, what?'

'She suspected Vincent had set up home with one of them, but wasn't sure which one.' He exhaled slowly. 'It seems that she didn't like the two women very much at all. Which I suppose is understandable if you think one of them has run off with your fiancé.'

'You are talking about Mum and Hazel, aren't you?' I knew it was a bloody stupid question, but I needed to be completely certain I'd heard right.

'I am.' He gave my hands a squeeze and let go of one of them to massage his temple with his free hand. 'I do not have to continue, if it upsets you.'

'You can't stop now,' I snapped. 'Not now you've told me this much.'

He rubbed his chin and took a deep breath.

'Was anyone else travelling with them to Scotland, do you know?'

'He had a driver. No one can recall his name, so my friend has been unable to trace him.'

I had always known my mother had worked in London for a short time before moving to the New Forest to have me. I'd always suspected she'd run away from something there, but had assumed my father had been married and

218

the wife had warned Mum off, or a similar scenario. But this seemed much darker than I had expected.

'I had no idea Mum and Hazel were ever close.' The revelation stunned me. 'Please, carry on.'

It was strange hearing him refer to her as Mimi. I'd only ever heard Mum referred to as Maureen, except for Katie calling her Nana Mimi, and that had been Mum's suggestion. I had assumed it was something she'd come up with as an affectionate name between herself and Katie, not a name she'd used in her past.

'What else do you know?'

'The trail went cold,' Henri added, raising a shoulder in a lazy shrug. 'I could not find anything further about these women. I did find the farm several years ago and enquired after her. The tenants told me she had disappeared with her family and, I assumed, my father, but they could tell me nothing more. I thought my search was over. I returned here a few months ago to try and look for Hazel again. In case she had returned here.' He hesitated.

'Go on.'

'I discovered that the elderly tenants who moved in after she left had died leaving the farm vacant for some years. I enquired about leasing it.' He looked concerned by my silence.

'Makes sense,' I said, forcing myself to appear calm. My stomach churned. I needed him to tell me every detail.

'I thought if I could move in to my father's last known address then maybe I might discover more about what happened to him.'

No wonder he kept himself and his business private. If anyone around here suspected he was investigating their lives, or those of their neighbours, he'd be even more unpopular than he was already.

I studied my nails as the enormity of what he'd confided in me took root. 'As sorry as I am about your father's disappearance, Henri...' I said, closing my eyes to try and regulate my rising temper. 'And I truly am... Why wait this long to tell me you've been investigating my mother's past?'

'Sera?' he began, closing his eyes and shaking his head. 'I am a fool. I should not have told you.'

I held my hand up to stop him. 'Rubbish. You should have told me before,' I said, hurt that he couldn't confide in me. 'I don't understand why it had to be a secret?'

He rose slowly, wincing as he straightened his leg. 'I had to know what happened to my father. I wanted to investigate without anyone becoming suspicious. People are rarely open if they suspect you are trying to find out information. You must surely understand this?'

I probably would have if one of the people he had been researching hadn't been Mum. 'You've been tracking my mum like she's some sort of villain. She's not. Are you implying that she had something to do with this man's disappearance?' I shivered despite the heat.

'Sera, I...'

I was furious at him. How dare he investigate my mother behind her back? Behind mine?

'She might have known Hazel in the eighties,' I said, still finding this nugget of information, that they were ever remotely close, a bit odd. I hesitated. Something niggled in my mind. I struggled to bring the memory forward. Yes. Hadn't Mum told me I didn't know Hazel as well as I thought when we'd argued once? Maybe if I hadn't been in such a mood with her I would have realised the signi-ficance of what she was saying. That they had been friends previously and fallen out over something big enough to stop them talking for years despite their daughters being best friends.

My fury returned. 'What exactly are you accusing my mother of doing? Shacking up with someone else's bloke? Seriously? Is that it?'

'Sera.' He went to comfort me.

'No,' I pushed him away. 'I'm going. My mother was right about you hiding things. I stupidly thought we could be friends.' He grabbed my arm as I turned to leave, holding me back. 'Let me go.'

'No. You will listen to me, or I will come to your house and tell you.'

'No. You won't.' I snatched my arm away from him. I ran to the car, aware he couldn't catch up with me before I got inside.

'Sera, please stop.'

I ignored his pleas. If anyone was going to tell me what happened, it was going to be Mum. I'd had enough of his revelations, and her secrets. I needed to confront her and find out what had happened all those years ago.

Chapter Twenty-Four

1990 – Scotland

Mimi

Changing his mind about taking us for a drive, Vinnie told Callum to drive straight to East Loch house. My disappointment was soon forgotten as we drove through the large stone pillars and up the long, curved driveway. Callum slowed down so we could see the imposing stone building where we would be house guests for the next couple of days.

'Wow,' I whispered in awe. It was a stunning place, with a large curved frontage three storeys high, vast arched windows either side, flanked by a sequence of smaller windows. The house was on a slight hill, with wide steps leading up from the front garden and huge trees either side. I could see it backed onto a wood, probably a forest, and couldn't help feeling that the place was rather spooky.

'Right, let's get going,' Vinnie said, impatiently. 'Now remember, you two, I want you to be on your best behaviour. You're staying at the home of Lord and Lady Panmoe. He's a bit of a letch and she's an old cow, but I have important business with him. If I have to reprimand you for anything, anything at all, mind, there'll be hell to pay.' Hazel and I nodded silently.

The car stopped at the back of the house where a high turret appeared atop the front door. Unnerved now that we had arrived, I could feel my stomach fluttering. I took a deep breath to try and calm down and followed the others out of the car.

'Here, take your cases,' Vinnie said, as Callum practically threw them at us. 'As soon as we're settled you can go back to London, Callum. I don't know how long I'm going to be staying here and the girls can make their own way back on the train if I need them to leave earlier than me.'

The door opened and two large lurchers bounded out to greet us. Hazel shrieked and stood behind me for protection. Brave, as ever, I thought sarcastically. They were followed by a florid-faced man, with wild grey hair and a skinny woman dragging on a long black cigarette holder. They came out to welcome us. He looked Hazel and me up and down and raising one of his bushy eyebrows, turned his attention to Vinnie, slapping him on his shoulder and grinning. 'Bought a couple of dolly birds with you, I see. Good man. We could do with some fresh blood here.'

'Old tosser,' Hazel mumbled. I couldn't help smiling.

Unfortunately the woman, who I presumed was his wife, saw me and narrowed her heavily made-up eyes. She walked up to us with a smile that that looked more threatening than friendly. 'Girls, welcome to East Loch House. Come, it's too hot out here and I'm sure you could do with a drink. We'll leave the men to their chatter.'

Despite the smile on her face, I sensed that she didn't like us, so wasn't surprised when, as soon as we were inside the tiled hallway and out of earshot from the men, she turned on us. 'Listen, you little tarts. If I catch either one of you giving my husband the eye again, I'll tell Vincent. And I'm sure you have the intelligence to know that he wouldn't be impressed.'

I realised she had confused my amusement at Hazel's comment for flirtation towards her revolting husband. 'You're mistaken,' I tried to explain, not wishing to make the wrong impression, however vile this woman seemed.

She took a deep drag from her cigarette holder and exhaled into my face. I instantly started coughing. 'I didn't come down with the last shower. I know a girl on the make when I see one.'

Furious, I opened my mouth to argue, when Vinnie and Lord Panmoe walked in, followed by Callum. I forced a smile and glanced at Lady Panmoe's expression, if I hadn't witnessed her reaction to us seconds before, I wouldn't have believed it possible.

A maid hurried into the hallway. 'Show these ladies to their room and take the gentleman's case up to his.' A butler appeared and instructed the maid to take us to the west wing. We followed her to a door, which we assumed was to be Vinnie's as she placed his case next to it.

'Your room is this way,' she said, leading us down the hall and opening a door. 'You're to be sharing.'

We thanked her and finally left alone, looked around the grand room. It has seen better days and I imagined that we weren't given one of the better suites in the house because of our lowly status.

'Not quite what I was expecting,' I admitted, walking over to the large sash window and looking out across a lawned area to the side of the house and over to the woods. 'What do you think of Lord and Lady Muck?'

'Horrible,' Hazel said. 'The novelty of being here has already worn off.'

I nodded. 'I know what you mean.' I unpacked my small case and hung up the cocktail dress Vinnie had bought me. It was emerald green chiffon and the most beautiful dress I'd ever seen.

'Vinnie seems different somehow,' I said to Hazel as she dressed.

'He's not as nice as we thought,' she whispered. 'His girlfriend hasn't really gone home, she's in a private clinic. I heard him telling Callum to phone up and check on her.'

'Why? What's wrong with her?'

'I heard Callum telling him after that her broken arm and ribs are healing slowly.'

I could see the pain on Hazel's face. 'Do you mean Vinnie hurt her?' Did she?

Hazel nodded. 'You mustn't breathe a word of this to anyone. And be careful around him. We shouldn't fight. We should look out for each other.'

That was a fine thing to suggest after her attacking me like she had, but I agreed. I wished I could have been more shocked, but there was something about the way I'd seen Vinnie behave to some women in the club that made me suspect he had a much darker side to him.

We freshened up and reapplied our make-up, before returning downstairs. Following the sound of laughter and music, we entered a large room. I guessed there must have been fifteen or twenty people there, some drunker than others.

'These lot must have been drinking all day,' Hazel said, changing the subject.

Vinnie broke off from his small group and came to join us. 'Looking gorgeous, girls. Right, I want you to be charming to your hosts. There's a lot riding on tonight, so don't let me down.'

I wasn't sure what I was supposed to be doing, but decided to use the event as practice and pretend I was acting a part in a play. I soon forgot my nerves when a couple came over to chat to Hazel and me.

—

A couple of hours later, one of the male guests went around the room holding two silver bowls. He held one out to each of the guests to take a piece of coloured paper.

Not wishing to stand out from everyone else, I dipped my hand in when it was my turn and pulled out an orange piece of paper. Not sure what to do with it, I waited with everyone else until they had each taken a turn. His lordship then picked up a spoon from a nearby table and tapped the side of his glass, calling for everyone to be silent.

'I believe the time has come for the evening's entertainment,' he said grinning widely and showing off a mouthful of discoloured teeth. 'Each of you now has a piece of coloured paper. You have to find your partner, who will be the person of the opposite sex with the same colour as you.'

Everyone began laughing. Hazel and I joined in the fun and milled around the room like the others until we located our partner. Partner for what, I couldn't imagine, but was intrigued to discover more.

I was joined by a tall, pale man, who seemed to be enjoying the evening less than the rest of us. 'Hello,' he said, reaching out to shake my hand. 'I'm Alastair, and you are?'

'Maureen,' I said, hoping to impress him.

'You look very pretty, Maureen.'

'Thank you,' I said, smiling at him. 'I wonder what we'll have to do now?'

He glanced around and lowered his voice. 'You don't know?'

'No.' I looked around me, noticing his lordship pinching Hazel's bottom and was holding up his yellow piece of paper next to hers. Vinnie was glaring at her, which was odd. Surely the person he should be giving looks to should be his host.

'Right,' his lordship bellowed. 'Off you go.'

I looked at Alastair for an answer. 'Where are we supposed to be going?'

He cleared his throat and putting a finger into his wing collar, pulled it slightly away from his neck. 'To a bedroom.'

I stared at him, confused. 'A—' I could see the others hand in hand, arm in arm, laughing at each other. Vinnie was accompanied by a woman who looked as if she'd won a prize, which, judging by the rest of the guests, she had. Hazel, on the other hand, looked as horrified as me to discover what we were in for. She was trying not to panic as she was dragged out of the room.

'We'd better go, too,' Alastair said quietly as he took my hand.

I snatched it away from him. 'Don't. I'm not taking part in this sordid game.'

He leant down and whispered, 'I promise I dislike this as much as you, but we need to go to a room and at least pretend we're taking part. Unless you want to upset that crook you came here with?'

I didn't have to think twice. He seemed genuine and I just had to hope that he was. 'Fine.' I took his hand and he led me upstairs.

'Which is the way to your room?'

'Why mine?' I was terrified and didn't like the idea of him knowing where I was supposed to be sleeping later.

'Because if we go straight to your room rather than to mine, then I can leave you there after we've spent some time together, so that they think we've, you know, slept together. At least then you won't have to wander the corridors alone trying to find your way to your room. Who knows what could happen with this drunken bunch around?'

'Okay.'

We went to mine and Hazel's room. I could hear her getting angry with his lordship and Vinnie saying something to her I couldn't quite catch.

Inside the bedroom, I sat on the dressing-table stool, whilst Alastair sat on the end of my single bed.

'I'm sorry you've been brought here tonight. It must be shocking for you.'

I nodded. He looked sad and I couldn't help wondering what he was doing here. He seemed decent enough. Then I remembered that he'd been talking to a woman earlier.

'Your wife is here, isn't she? Don't you mind her going off with someone else?'

He lowered his gaze and stared at his hands. 'I'm only here because she enjoys this sort of thing.'

I gasped. 'Why don't you refuse?'

'Because I love her and don't want to disappoint her.'

'That's ridiculous,' I said disgusted with his weakness. 'Why would you want to stay married to someone who sleeps with other men?'

He didn't answer. We sat in silence for about half an hour until we heard a commotion down the corridor. We stood up and rushed to the door to see what was going on.

'Hang on a second,' he said, unzipping the back of my dress.

'Hey, what the hell do you think you're doing?'

He untied his bow tie and unbuttoned his shirt. 'We can't go out there without at least looking as if we've been getting up to stuff in here. Mess up your hair a little. We need to be believable.'

I imagined Vinnie's anger, if he thought I hadn't done as he expected and did as Alastair suggested.

'Right, now we can go,' he said, opening the door.

Vinnie was outside alone with Lord Panmoe and Hazel. He had Hazel by the wrist and seemed to be apologising to the older man, who by the looks of things had raw claw marks on his cheek. He looked from me to Alastair and smiled. 'Nice to see one of my girls knows how to behave. Go to bed now, Mimi. Hazel will be along in a bit.'

I watched Alastair disappear into another of the rooms and went back inside.

Leaning against the closed bedroom door I tried to make sense of what had happened. This wasn't the party I'd been expecting. And Vinnie wasn't the man I thought him to be. He'd practically prostituted Hazel and me out to these revolting people, and all for a business deal.

I heard Lord Panmoe shout that he wanted someone, I presumed Vinnie, out by the following morning. Not wishing to be caught still dressed when he had told me to go to bed, I quickly undressed, washed and got into my bed.

I closed my eyes willing myself to sleep away my disappointment. Tonight had begun so well.

I must have dozed off eventually because when I opened my eyes it was pitch black. I kicked off the sheet in the hot, stuffy room and walked over to the window to open it further. I pulled back the curtains, allowing the moon's brightness to flood in, cutting the room in two, and turned to go back to bed. That's when I noticed Hazel's bed was empty.

Chapter Twenty-Five

Sera

'Sera,' Henri shouted from the doorway of the farmhouse. 'Let me explain.'

Ignoring Henri's pleas for me to listen to reason, I turned the key in the ignition and as soon as the engine spluttered into life, pressed my foot down on the accelerator and drove away as fast as I could towards home.

Unable to hold back any longer, I gave into the tears that almost choked me. Damn Henri. How could he expect me to react favourably after admitting he'd been tracking Mum for so many years? I reached out, unclipping the glovebox and rummaging around until my hand found a tissue. 'Bastard,' I sniffed, blowing my nose as well as I could manage with only one free hand.

I parked the car outside the house, not bothering to find somewhere shady. Wiping my eyes with my fingers, I composed myself as much as possible. I didn't want to scare Katie by letting her see me in a dishevelled state. Opening the front door, I walked through to the living room, but it was empty. I could hear Mum's voice in the kitchen. She must have recognised the echo of my footsteps in the hall because she began speaking to me before I'd even reached the door.

'I was listening to the news on the car radio, when I collected Katie earlier,' she said, washing her hands. 'They've given warnings about fires breaking out around here. You know how frightened I am of those things,' she said without waiting for me to reply. 'Apparently, the temperatures we're experiencing now are the hottest for nearly five hundred years. They're estimating that almost fourteen thousand people have died in France already due to the intensity of the heat and it's not much cooler here.'

I watched her drying her hands, waiting for her to stop talking so I could ask her to sit and listen to what I had to say.

'They're even having problems trying to find places cool enough to store the bod—' She stopped mid-sentence when she noticed me and frowned. 'What's the matter?' She waved for me to sit.

I peered out of the back door. Spotting Katie going down the steps to the garden I realised, with relief, that she mustn't have heard me come in. I sat down and blew my nose once again, lowering my head into my hands to try and gather my senses.

'It's fine,' Mum said. 'She can't hear us.' She pushed the back door until it was almost closed and sat facing me. 'What's happened? Tell me.'

I could see the concern on her beautifully made-up face and didn't want to worry her any longer than I had already. I explained about my visit to Henri's and repeated everything he'd told me. I expected, well, hoped mostly, that Mum would laugh it off. Tell me not to be so sensitive, which would have been her usual quip for something like this. Instead, she leant back in her chair, unblinking and silent. The colour in her face drained and for the second time in as many days she looked as if she was about to pass out.

I moved forward, resting my hands on her knees. 'Mum? What is it?'

Her breathing came in short bursts and she closed her eyes. I ran to the sink and poured her a glass of water. 'Take a sip of this,' I said, my voice quivering. I watched her do as I asked, and she seemed to calm down a little.

This reaction was completely different to the one I'd imagined.

'Mum,' I asked quietly, when she had regained a little colour in her cheeks. 'Who was Vincent?'

She stood up. Before she could take a step, she wavered, went to grab the table, missed, and dropped. I reached out to her, unable to stop her hitting her head against the table on her way down, but managing to catch her so she didn't land too heavily on the tiled floor.

'Mum?' I said, trying not to panic. My tough mother, always so cynical and ballsy, had collapsed. I struggled to recollect any first aid. Grabbing one of the cushions from the nearest chair, I lifted her head carefully to slide it underneath. Then, making sure she was on her side in the recovery position, I ran to the back door for help.

'Leo!' I couldn't find him and for a second wasn't sure what to do next. Grabbing a clean tea towel from a drawer, I wet it under the tap, squeezing out the excess water as I returned to sit next to her. At least the tiles were cool, which in the heat could only be a good thing.

'Mum?' I said, stroking her clammy forehead, dabbing the broken skin near her temple where her head had connected with the table. 'It's okay. Everything's fine.'

I tapped her cheek lightly. Relief poured through me when I noticed her lashes move slightly. Her eyes flickered

233

once and then opened wide. She went to sit up, so I held the damp tea towel against the side of her head with one hand and grabbed hold of her shoulder with the other to slow her down.

'What happened?'

'Take it easy,' I soothed. 'You've had a bit of a fall.'

I passed her the drink, watching her take a few sips. I could see she was trying to recall what had happened. She gasped, covering her mouth with her free hand. She looked at me, her face taut with fear.

I took the glass from her, placing it out of the way on the table. 'Let me help you up,' I suggested, taking her arm and wanting to get her sitting more comfortably.

She reached out and took hold of the side of the table and together we managed to get her to her feet. 'I don't want to be in here if Katie comes in,' she said.

'Okay, let's go through to the living room?'

I helped her walk down through the hallway. She sat down on one side of the large yellow sofa and I placed a cushion behind her back.

'Thank you, darling,' she said, her voice shaky.

I opened my mouth to speak, but before I managed to utter a word the doorbell rang. 'I hope it's not the police again,' I groaned, shocked when I noticed Mum tense and move to get up. 'No, you stay there. I'll tell them to come back another time.'

I walked down the hallway and pulled the front door open, a scowl on my face, ready to give them a mouthful for coming back again so soon.

'Sera,' Henri said. He looked devastated. For a second I almost forgot what he had done. 'I must speak with you.'

I glared at him. 'Seriously?' I shook my head. 'You can't honestly believe we've got anything to say to each other now.' I sighed heavily. 'You've been snooping in my mother's past, Henri.'

'You 'ave to listen to me.'

'No.' I held my hand up to stop him coming any closer. 'I've told Mum what you've been doing.' I could feel tears welling inside me. 'Hell, Henri, she bloody passed out. I don't know what you think you've discovered about her, but whatever it is, she's very frightened, and I'm not having anyone do that to her. Do you understand me?'

He looked as if he hated me at that second, or maybe it was my mother his anger was directed towards, I wasn't sure. 'I am French, Sera, not stupid, of course I understand you. But there are things I must tell you.'

'I said, no.' I had no intention of him coming to this house and causing more disruption.

He moved to leave, then stopped and looking at me over his shoulder said, 'If you wished to confide in me, I would always believe you. Why can you not trust me?'

I did trust him; that was the problem. How could I admit to him that my problem wasn't his honesty, but my shock at discovering my only parent had a secret that traumatised her so utterly? I stepped outside, holding the door closed behind me, so that Mum couldn't hear what I had to say.

'When I told my mother what you'd said, her reaction was far more intense than I expected. I've always suspected she had something in her past, but not something as big as this.' He looked forlorn. Every part of me wanted to forgive him and forget what I'd discovered. 'You have your quest to find out what happened to your father. I have to ensure Mum is okay.' I tried to sound reasonable. 'We might not like it, but we're linked by something horrifying from both our parents' pasts.'

He reached out and rested the palm of his hand against my cheek. 'I understand,' he hesitated. 'I will leave you to care for her.'

I watched him walk away, his shoulders stooped. I wanted to follow him. Henri disappeared around the corner at the end of the street and I went back inside to join Mum.

I crouched down in front of her. As I did so I spotted a cigarette end in the fireplace. Mum hated smoking and forbade anyone doing it in her house. I had never seen Dee or Leo smoking, so assumed it must have been someone else, but who? She squeezed my hand to get my attention. I looked at her, forcing a smile. 'What is it?'

She stared at me without speaking for a moment, looking if she was about to cry. I moved a little closer to her. It unnerved me that something I'd said caused such a drastic change in her usual calm persona.

She exhaled sharply. 'Sera, there's something I must tell you.'

'What is it?' I said, nervous to discover what it was.

'Years ago—' She cleared her throat. She seemed to reconsider how to tell me. 'There was this man.' She took her hand from mine and covered her eyes. 'I'm sorry, I can't think straight.'

I smiled to reassure her. 'It's fine. Whatever it is, you can tell me.'

She parted her hands, placing one hand either side of her face, trying to weigh up my reaction.

'I will always love you,' I said. 'I don't care what you tell me, nothing will ever change that.'

She winced, as if in physical pain. I wondered if the cut on her head was as painful as it looked. 'Will you, though, Seraphina? I'm not so sure.'

'Yes. I will.'

'You're such a kind, trusting girl. You have no idea how devious people can be, or how cruel.'

I was intrigued. 'So, tell me.' I wanted to know everything I could about her. 'Stop fretting and spit it out.'

'This man,' she said. 'Your father.'

I gasped. She had never mentioned my father before. Eventually, I gave up asking. This was the first time she had been the one to start a conversation about him.

'I should have told you about him years ago,' she said, sighing heavily. 'He died.'

I couldn't help being disappointed that I'd never get to meet him. 'That's it?'

She shook her head, taking the cloth from her head and inspecting the blood that had seeped into the pristine cloth. 'I was there when he died.'

I heard footsteps coming down the stairs, but was desperate for her to continue. 'And?'

'Hazel was, too.'

Before I could say anything further, Dee and Leo entered the room.

'Sorry,' Leo said frowning. 'I didn't realise you were in here.'

'Would you mind leaving us for a bit?' Mum said. 'We're having a chat.'

He looked concerned. 'Is everything okay?'

'Yes. Fine, thanks,' I said, willing him to go. I didn't want to give Mum a chance to change her mind about confiding in me. I watched him put his arm around Dee's shoulders and lead her out towards the garden.

'Right, Mum,' I said, as I as soon as they had left. 'Tell me everything.'

She smiled at me, back to her usual reserved demeanour that I was used to. 'No, darling, I was being silly. Really, it was nothing.'

'Too bad,' I said, irritated that she'd done exactly what I'd been afraid of. 'I'm sick of people fobbing me off. Something happened in the past with you and Hazel, and I want to know about it, now.'

I repeated everything Henri had said to me, watching the colour drain from her face once again, but this time not caring that she didn't like what she was hearing.

'So, he's a detective then. I always said there was something shady about him,' she sneered. 'And he's seen fit to poke his nose into my affairs?'

'Well, Hazel's affairs, if we're being precise.'

'How dare he come to you with gossip about me?' She sat up straighter, more like her old self, which I admit made me feel much better. 'He knows where to find me and come here to discuss this with me, not you.'

I didn't mind her getting angry, I'd probably react the same if I was in her place. I wanted to know what made her keep secrets from me for all these years. 'What have you been hiding from me, Mum?'

She stared at me and I could see tiredness wash over her. 'Your father.' She stuck her perfect chin out defiantly.

'Yes, who was he?' I concentrated on hiding my excitement.

'Hazel and I... Well, we killed him.'

It wasn't what I was expecting to hear. I stared open-mouthed at her, stunned by the brutal way she'd delivered her admission. Before I'd gathered my senses enough to process this mind-numbing information, Leo ran into the room, crashing the door back against the wall.

'Have you seen Dee? I only left her for a moment to get her a drink. She's gone.'

I was still staring at Mum, trying to take in what she'd told me in this latest drama.

'There have been updates on the radio about fires moving in this direction,' he added.

I recalled Mum mentioning the fires. This would have to wait until later. I listened to him telling us about the devastation the fires were leaving in their wake. I couldn't bear the idea of losing my home and the precious memories my belongings held for me.

'Have you checked Dee's room?' Mum asked, unable to keep her irritation in check.

'Yes,' he replied, his right hand clenched so tightly into a fist that the bones of his knuckles seemed about to burst through his skin. 'But that's not all. I can't find Ashley either.'

Chapter Twenty-Six

2003 – Oakwold, New Forest

Young Sera

When I woke the following morning the memory of Hazel insisting I leave her house the previous night still stung. I couldn't imagine what she needed to speak to Dee, Leo and Jack about that I couldn't hear. Hazel had never shut me out before. I felt nauseous and had a strong sense of foreboding that something was going to happen.

Before Mum was awake, I dressed and ran over to the farm, not caring that it was barely past seven in the morning and no one would probably be up yet. I'd sit on their porch and wait for one of them to stir. I couldn't stand the thought of pacing around my bedroom willing the hands on my alarm clock to move.

As expected, no one else was up, so I made myself comfortable on the shabby wooden armchair outside their back door. It had been there for as long as I could remember. The farm was peaceful. Too peaceful. Not wishing to annoy Hazel, I stayed where I was and stared at her terracotta pots filled with the scarlet geraniums she loved to display either side of the steps to her front door.

I must have dozed off, because when I checked my watch again it was almost ten o'clock. I listened for voices, but the only noise came from the chickens.

I opened the back door, which was never locked and nervously walked in through the hall to the kitchen. Plates and cups littered the sides. A box half-filled with plates wrapped in newspaper stood by an opened cupboard door. Strange, I couldn't understand why Hazel would pack away her plates. I returned to the hallway and stopped at the bottom of the stairs.

'Dee?' I called, wanting to be heard, but hoping not to disturb anyone. She was never this quiet; always up first and making some sort of racket somewhere at the farm.

When she didn't answer, I forgot about making a noise and ran up the stairs to her bedroom. The door was wide open, and her favourite jeans lay across her bed. She'd strung her new leather belt through the denim loops. I thought that she must have changed her mind about wearing them because of the uncharacteristic heat. Unusually, her bed was unmade.

I listened for any movement. Feeling uneasy, I decided to look in Leo's bedroom, this time knocking before I entered. I was met with another untidy room; his wardrobe doors open and the hangers empty. Unable to ignore the sense that something was terribly wrong, I hurried across to Hazel's room. Her bedclothes were half pulled onto the floor. Her open wardrobe doors displayed mostly empty hangers. Several scarves pooled on the floor nearby.

I tried not to panic and ran down the stairs, out to the barn. I pulled opened the heavy door to check if I'd made a mistake. Maybe they had held an impromptu party the night before and were still asleep in there. Painfully aware I was kidding myself, I pushed away the image of the empty wardrobes, certain there must be an alternative explanation. Just because I didn't know what had happened, didn't mean I should imagine the worst. Or so I told myself time and time again as I looked for any sign of the family.

Only the usual detritus from their day-to-day living was in the house. I spotted another half-packed box. They wouldn't have packed their things to leave them behind, surely? Bolstered by this thought, I shouted for Dee as loudly as I could. My heart pounded with the effort of waiting for the answer that I suspected by now would not be coming.

Where were they? I retraced my steps to Dee's room. Bracing myself for the inevitable, I discovered that she, too, had taken most of her clothes. They had gone. Left me behind. By the look of their home they had no intention of ever coming back. Why would they do such a thing?

Sobbing, I dried my eyes with the hem of my T-shirt. I desperately searched for anything precious to her that she might have left behind, and spotted a small photo album. I picked it up and put it on the bed, then opened her dressing-table drawer to check inside. I scooped up two bangles, a necklace with a daisy pendant and a silver ring with an enamel bluebird I recalled her mum buying her for a birthday. I threw everything down next to the album. The jeans were her favourites and she knew how much I loved them. I swallowed back tears when I realised her leaving them on the bed had been her goodbye message to me. So, she had considered me, after all.

I rolled up the jeans and pushed them into Dee's old school satchel lying at the bottom of her wardrobe. I lifted the leather strap over my head, so it lay across my chest and put the rest of Dee's possessions from her bed inside it. As an afterthought, I peeled several photos of us both taken on previous summers and Christmases off the walls, slipping them deep into the outside pocket.

Sun rays cast long golden shafts across the familiar room. How many lazy days had I spent in this house daydreaming that I was part of this family while Dee persuaded me to misbehave in some way? She was strong and the instigator of all our adventures. I didn't know how to pass a day without spending time with her.

I shivered as an eerie feeling seemed to invade the house. I needed to go, but unable to leave just yet, I took hold of several colourful silk scarves that reminded me so much of Hazel. I breathed in the familiar patchouli and sandalwood mixture and remembered how she used to joke about being my second mum. I scrunched the material in my hands and shoved them into the bag, pushing away memories of Dee holding my hands and swinging me round outside in the yard as we swore we would always be best friends. Then I grabbed Hazel's silver-backed hairbrush set from her walnut dressing table and packed that, too.

Why had they disappeared so suddenly? Something must have frightened them badly, otherwise they would never have left without saying goodbye, or leave such treasures. But what?

My heart ached as I looked at a small silver frame surrounding a picture of Jack hugging Hazel from behind. She was laughing, her head thrown back as she gazed up at him. The sheer joy of that moment captured forever behind glass made me sob. It was Dee who had taken the photo, whispering for me to stand behind them and make bunny ears over their heads. I didn't, of course, just as she had expected. I wasn't leaving this precious memento behind for some faceless auctioneer to hand over to the highest bidder. One of these days, I promised myself, I would give these possessions back to Hazel and Dee. If I ever discovered where they were.

Unable to think what else I could do, I began walking home. I was halfway across the hot, dusty field when it dawned on me that something my mother had written in her letter could have been the catalyst that set this unexpected exodus in motion.

The note.

Hope swelling through my veins, I ran back to the farm. I was out of breath, but determined to find my mother's note to Hazel. If she wouldn't tell me what was in it, I'd find out for myself.

I let myself into the house. Stopping in the hall, I tried to recall the events of the evening before when I'd delivered it to Hazel. I hadn't thought to go into the living room earlier, so went to see if I could find it in there.

I scanned the room. I couldn't see it anywhere. Then, noticing there had been a fire in the grate, I went over and crouched. I heard a distant rumble of thunder just as I spotted a corner of my mother's cream vellum paper. I picked it up, but there was only the first two letters of a word. The rest had been burnt. Now I'd never know what she'd written in it.

Desperate to get away from there, I ran as fast as I could across the fields, not keeping to my usual path, or caring that my legs were being stung by nettles. Finally, breathless and in the safety of my bedroom, I quietly locked the door and slumped onto my bed. My legs itched and burnt, but I barely felt the pain. I angrily brushed away tears and unbuckled the two straps holding the satchel closed, tipping the contents onto my eiderdown.

It dawned on me that this was all that was left of a precious period in my life.

I couldn't imagine a world without Dee's laughter, constant singing and bossiness. My life was going to be much greyer without her in it. I wondered how long it would take me to get used to coping without Hazel's family because it was obvious, even to me, that they weren't intending on coming back.

Chapter Twenty-Seven

2018 – Oakwold, New Forest

Sera

Dee had run away, again. Only this time, for a fleeting second, I was relieved.

'Where do you think she's gone?' Mum asked Leo.

I was distracted by whimpering coming from the landing and ran upstairs to find Katie sobbing. 'Ashley's gone. She took the teddy I gave her.' I picked her up and hugged her tightly as she gulped great sobs into my shoulder.

'It's okay, darling,' I soothed. 'Dee's a little upset, that's all. We'll find her and bring Ashley back home.'

I was following Leo and carrying Katie through the back gate to go and look for them when Mum bellowed from an upstairs window for us to stop.

'I can't wait for you, Sera,' Leo shouted over his shoulder as he broke into a run and hurtled across the field in the direction of the wood beyond Henri's farm.

'What, Mum?' I called, surprised to see she had gone upstairs and irritated with her for holding me back. 'I've got to help Leo find them.'

Seconds later she ran outside, bearing down on me, arms open wide. 'You're not taking that baby with you.

I've just heard a report on the radio of a huge fire on the other side of the hill. It's out of control and the wind is blowing it in this direction. We should stay here in case they come to evacuate everyone from their houses.'

I hesitated and stared at Mum. She never usually told me what to do with Katie, especially not with such force, and I knew she was right.

She tapped me on the shoulder and pointed towards the woods. 'I know the fires are a distance away, but it wouldn't take long for them to reach the village. What if we have to leave at a moment's notice?'

I understood her concerns. 'Mum, I have to go. You keep Katie here and pack a few essentials for us, just in case.'

The anguish on her face made me feel guilty about my determination to go.

'Sera, the foliage is tinder dry and this hot wind is aggravating conditions. You mustn't go into the woods, it isn't safe.'

I turned sharply, squinting through the open gate. I could see Leo almost at the edge of the wood, and darker skies in the distance I'd assumed to be the threat of rain. Now, as I concentrated a little harder, it was obvious that what I was looking at was smoke. I was terrified, but couldn't in all honesty stay at home and not go and look for Dee and her little girl.

'I'd rather stay here,' I admitted, pulling an apologetic face at her. 'I can't, though, not when Dee's oblivious to the danger and especially as she's got Ashley with her.' I handed Katie to my mum's outstretched arms.

Katie screamed in fury. 'Katie find Ashley!' She kicked out, throwing her teddy onto the ground.

'No, sweetheart,' Mum said, holding her tightly. 'Mummy won't be long. We'll stay here and look out for her.'

I lowered my voice. 'Mum, if you need to take her to a friend's in the next town, do. I'll find you later. I promise I won't do anything reckless. I know those woods better than Leo or Dee and I can't let them get lost out there and do nothing. I'll be fine.'

Her eyes welled up with unshed tears. 'You'd better be. Now go, if you must, but be back as soon as you can. We'll be waiting for you.' She immediately turned away from me and began carrying my screaming child towards the house.

–

I broke into a run. I wanted to get this over with. Dried grasses snapped underfoot as I stepped on them. It hadn't rained for so long I wasn't surprised a few fires had broken out. It was hot and I soon became breathless. I neared the woods and instead of the shade giving relief from the insistent heat, it struck me that the temperature here was warmer than in the direct sunlight. The fire must be getting closer.

I reasoned that they couldn't have got far and finding them wouldn't take too long. I certainly hoped I was right. Needing to stop for a few seconds, I bent down, resting my hands on my knees to help my breathing recover. I tilted my head, listening out for any familiar voices. There wasn't even the usual birdsong. I did my best to quell the panic seeping into my mind. I lifted the bottom of my T-shirt to wipe my damp forehead before running further into the woods calling for Dee and Ashley as loudly as I could manage.

I concentrated as I ran, narrowly avoiding a smaller branch hidden among the long brittle grass. Where were they? They couldn't have gone far. Dee was too frail to carry Ashley for long and Leo must be close behind them by now, surely. I slowed to a walk, the heat making me a little nauseous, but kept walking further into the woods, trying to stick to the usual track I took when going this way. I was so focused on finding them I hadn't noticed I'd been straying deeper than I would normally go. After a little while I stopped to get my bearings. I peered through the thicket and overgrown areas and heard a distinctive crackling of fire as it devastated the vegetation in the forest.

Fear shot through me and my heart pounded. The fire was closing in and I hadn't found them. I turned around, but in the smoky air I couldn't tell which way I'd come. I tried not to panic. Dare I keep looking for them for a bit longer, or should I do as Mum insisted and go home?

I rubbed my dry eyes and tried to think. Every instinct told me to get away from here as fast as possible, but I needed to find these people. However, I couldn't ignore Mum and Katie worrying about me at home. It was a relief when I heard the bells of distant fire engines. They sounded a little too distant for my liking, though it was hard to tell which direction they were coming from. It dawned on me that I was becoming so disorientated I wasn't even certain which way was home.

A loud crash shocked me as something heavy landed feet away. I cried out, trying not to become hysterical when I noticed a tongue of orange flames dancing an insane tango on the hillside, wending its way at speed towards the woods. I didn't care which way home happened to be now, my only thought was to get the hell out of here. I ran as fast as my legs would carry me. A sharp edge of bark tore at my shin as I passed a broken trunk, but nothing was going to stop me.

My legs got heavier. I began to cry. 'Keep going,' I whispered, focusing all my attention on placing one foot in front of the other. Breathless and trembling, I reached the edge of the wood. It was a long way from where I'd entered. I couldn't believe how far I had gone in my search for Dee. Where the hell had they got to? Maybe she had returned to the house. I hoped so. I heard the unmistakable creaking and screaming of falling trees as they gave in to the tremendous heat.

I turned towards the sound, light-headed with fear when I spotted how close the fire was to me. I needed to run, but my legs were like jelly and my muscles so strained, I couldn't get them to work properly. I was about to give in to my mounting hysterics when I heard a voice.

'Sera, where are you?' It was Henri calling for me. He sounded frantic and I didn't think I'd ever been so relieved to hear another person's voice.

I tried to answer him, but could only manage a pathetic sob. I needed him to find me. I took a deep breath and tried again. 'Henri,' I cried. 'I'm over here.' My voice sounded tinny and unnatural. I pleaded with God to let Henri hear me.

I heard him shout again, and spotted his red T-shirt moving quickly through the thick branches and trees. He called me again. 'Sera, where are you?'

'Henri,' I sobbed. I glanced over towards the cracking and spitting of the fire as it kept closing in. 'We're going the wrong way.'

I could hear the pounding of his footsteps as he came closer and the occasional swear word as he tripped, or bashed into something. 'Run this way,' he insisted.

I ran a few steps but the notion of running towards the fire seemed like madness, so I stopped.

'Now!'

I had to trust him. I had no choice. I broke into a run of sorts and as the shadows of the wood enveloped me, he almost bowled me over. Slamming into me, he grabbed hold of me, pulling me tight against his pounding chest. 'I thought I'd lost you.'

It didn't even occur to me to be taken aback by his words, I simply clung to him, my hands gripping the back of his damp top, relieved not to be alone any longer.

'I'm so scared. How did you know I was here?'

'I was on my way to warn you and saw you from across the field running into the woods.' Letting go of me, he then took hold of my shoulders. 'It will be okay. Be calm.' He scanned the area around us. Pointing towards a dip in the bank he shouted for me to take off my shoes.

'What for?'

'They are the closest thing you have for a spade.' He grabbed a large stick and clawed the ground.

He wasn't making any sense. 'What are you doing?' We needed to run, not mess about in this hell.

'Dig. Hurry.' He motioned for me to get on my knees and copy him. Needing to trust him, I did as he insisted. 'We cannot outrun this fire,' he panted, as we clawed away at the earth beneath us. 'We must dig a ditch and cover ourselves with earth.' He took a deep, laboured breath in the airless wood. 'I am hoping the fire will jump from this ledge and continue over there, missing us.'

Fires didn't jump, did they? It didn't seem very plausible, but I couldn't see an alternative. I knew I couldn't outrun a fire.

'I couldn't find them,' I cried, stabbing frantically at the earth, which thankfully was still a little moist from the shade of the trees. I don't know if it was sheer panic, or a will to live, or something else entirely, but I dug like a crazy woman. With his strength and perseverance, we soon had an area big enough for us both to lie back into the crevice under the bank.

'Lie down, as far back as possible,' he said, helping me push myself backwards. The cool damp earth soothed my overheated skin and made what was transpiring around me seem like I wasn't completely involved.

'Now you,' I said, arms outstretched to take hold of him. He bent down to come to me, when he stopped. Kneeling upright, his head turned slightly, alerted to something.

'What is it? Henri, get in,' I screamed, panic-stricken.

'Crying,' he said simply, holding up his hand to quieten me. 'Do not move. If I am not back in two minutes lift the material of your top over your face and cover yourself with the loose earth. Do not move until you are certain the fire has passed over you.'

I couldn't take in what he was saying. 'Henri, you're not leaving me here?'

He turned without another word and ran off into the woods. I lay petrified. He had left me. He was going to die. We both were.

I could feel the thundering crash of the burning trees as the fire fought its way towards me. This wasn't happening. It couldn't be. I strained my eyes to see him, the temptation to run towards the field taking hold of me. Did I still have time to make it? I was kidding myself. I had no choice but to lie here in this dip in the bank and trust him. So, giving one last look in the direction he'd gone, I grabbed a small branch and scooped a heap of earth towards my feet, my legs and upwards, slowly covering my body.

I heard cries and saw Henri making his way towards me. He was carrying Ashley, his arm clamping her to his chest. His other hand was gripped tightly around Dee's wrist. As he dragged her to my hiding place, she stumbled, tears coursing down her dusty face.

He put Ashley down next to me. 'Sera,' he said breathlessly. 'Kick away the earth, dig deeper.'

I did as he said. 'You too,' I shouted at Dee. 'Bloody help us.'

She glanced at me, then following my lead, took off her wooden sandal, handed me one and we both dug frantically. If this damn bank didn't collapse on us it would be nothing short of a miracle, I realised, glancing up at the roots of the tree arcing above us.

'Enough, no more time now. Get in,' Henri ordered, the panic obvious in his voice. 'You first,' he pushed Dee back to lie flat against the dugout wall then, handing Ashley to her, told her to lie still. 'Hold her, tight,' he said to Dee. He looked at me, his face taught with tension. 'Now you.'

I wriggled into the dip, getting as close to Dee as I could. 'Lift your tops to cover your faces,' I said, repeating what he'd told me to do earlier. Dee lifted Ashley's dirty top over the child's pinched face. 'It's going to be all right,' I said, giving her a promise, I knew I might not be able to keep. 'You'll lie between me and Mummy.'

We didn't have much choice. The dip in the bank was only really big enough for two of us, but at a push we should just about manage. I hoped so, anyway. I felt the weight of damp earth being dropped on my feet, my legs, over my hips and then the heat of Henri's hot, damp body against me. He slid one arm under my head and pressed tightly against me, somehow managing to pull earth over us. I covered my face with my top and hugged the trembling child, grateful to have him behind me.

He only just managed to cover us when a roar of heat, crashing debris and smoke rolled over on top of us in a thunderous fiery wave of destruction. We collectively held our breaths. I squeezed poor Ashley so tight against my chest I worried I might hurt her. Henri squashed against me, pushing me against the others and almost crushing Dee against the earth wall of the bank.

The heat and the deafening rage of the fire seemed like it was taking forever to pass over us. I reasoned that if I could be almost senseless with terror, we must at least still be alive. Henri's plan appeared to be working. I was beginning to hope we might survive this horror and pictured Katie's pretty face.

After an interminable period that probably only lasted a minute or two, Henri's body relaxed slightly. I waited for him to tell me what to do next, too afraid to move in case I uncovered our bodies.

He backed away slowly from me then pulled me out of the hole. 'It is okay. The fire jumped the bank. We can go.'

I took Ashley from Dee and lifted her back out of the dip, reaching a hand out to Dee to help her. She lowered her top from her face and I uncovered Ashley's face and forced a smile. 'You see, we're fine,' I said, my voice husky from the dry air.

Dee stared at me, then at Henri; she looked as if she'd made a major discovery. 'You risked your lives to save ours.'

He closed his eyes briefly and I suspected he was trying to hide his irritation with her for getting us all into this mess in the first place. 'Put your shoes back on, the ground is hot. Hurry.'

He took Ashley in his arms and gripped my hand. I took hold of Dee's. We were barely able to keep up as he led us out of the smoking wood, past burning branches to the blackened field and in the direction of the town.

-

The walk home seemed to take forever. I breathed a sigh of relief when we reached the garden gate. We stopped and turned in unison to stare silently over the fields to where fire fighters dampened the small fires that sprung up closer to the village, each of us lost in the trauma of what we had experienced.

He lowered the little girl to the ground.

'Thank you,' Dee said, bending down to hug her tightly. Ashley stared up at him.

Henri cleared his throat looking a little embarrassed. He moved his weight from one foot to the other. 'I must return to my farm.' He ruffled Ashley's hair, gently removing a stray leaf and bent down, his face level with hers. 'You were very brave, *ma petite*. Now, I must check my animals.' He moved back to give Dee and Ashley space to pass.

I watched them go inside the house, looking for Leo. The enormity of what we'd just survived began to dawn on me and I started to tremble. 'Thank you for coming to find me,' I said, certain I'd never been as grateful to anyone else.

He stared at me, his expression solemn before taking hold of me and pulling me against him in a hug. I could feel his warm breath on my neck. 'I had no choice,' he whispered, leaning slightly back to be able to give me a slow, exhausted smile. 'I must go.'

I leant against the roughness of the warped wooden gate staring at the devastation in the distance. I shivered, despite the heat, at the thought of what could have been had Henri not managed to find the three of us. Where had he learnt those survival techniques? I ran into the garden to the house.

Where was Leo?

'That girl,' my mother said, glancing up at the ceiling. 'If it hadn't been for her foolishness, you and that dear little girl of hers would have nearly perished in that fire.'

I went to argue. I still needed her to explain her shocking revelation that she had killed a man. Then I noticed my mother's face was ashen. I walked over to her and put an arm around her shoulder.

'Sera, you're filthy, go and shower.'

I smiled. After everything that had happened, her main concern was me being dirty.

I spotted Dee coming back downstairs. 'She's right, though, you could have got us all killed out there today. Why did you run off like that?'

Dee glared at me. 'You wouldn't understand.' She flounced out of the room and I chased after her. I'd had enough of her moods and this was going to stop.

I took hold of her arm, stopping her in her tracks. 'I'm taking a shower and then you and I are going to sit down and sort a few things out.'

She snatched her arm away from my hand. 'Really? You're calling the shots again?'

What the hell was wrong with her? 'Hey,' I said, too emotionally drained to have a full-scale quarrel. 'Mum and

I have been good to you, putting up with your moods. I think the least you can do is try to clear the air between us. I want to help you, if only for Ashley's sake. That poor child must be wondering what the hell is going on right now.'

'Ashley is my business, not yours.'

'That's where you're wrong, Dee,' I shook my head. 'We're all fond of her and I'm not letting you fob me off any longer.' I started walking up the stairs leaving her behind. 'I'll catch up with you shortly.'

I stripped and showered. I had endured enough of Dee's self-indulgence. I didn't know if it was a reaction against what we'd faced earlier, but I'd had enough and wanted answers. Whether she liked it, or not.

Someone had to stand up for Ashley. Leo was obviously more concerned with Dee's feelings than hers. I didn't understand how he hadn't noticed the little girl's frailty.

Dressed in an old cotton sundress, I sat down at my dressing table and began brushing my hair. Catching my reflection in the mirror, it dawned on me how frightened I still looked. The reality that Henri had only just found us in time chilled me. I tried to push away the image of Katie standing alone by the window with Mum, wondering when I'd return. My little girl could have been an orphan before she was five years old, and it would have been my fault for making the decision to run after Dee. Damn Dee for her selfishness.

I cursed the day I'd bumped into Leo. Ever since that morning, my family's lives had been dictated to by his sister's moods. I pulled my hair back, twisting it up into a French pleat and attached a hairclip to hold it in place. I braced myself for the onslaught.

'Dee?' I called, barely able to contain my rage. 'You've got ten minutes to get yourself down to the kitchen.'

—

I checked my watch. It was early evening and I wasn't going to spend one more night under the same roof as these people without giving them a few home truths. I checked on Katie and Ashley who were playing quietly in Katie's room before going downstairs to pour myself a glass of rosé. I carried it out to the garden. The hot breeze cooled the dry air a little, so at least it wasn't as humid as it had been for the past few weeks.

I walked over to the garden gate and pulled it open, glancing in the direction of Henri's farm and then over to the wood. The fire engines were still dowsing the area and the air smelt of burnt foliage and smoke. Thankfully the wind direction had changed. We could rest easy, for now at least.

I leant against the wooden frame, staring over towards the farm and took a sip of the cool drink. I'd been furious with Henri for investigating Mum, but after him risking his life for me I didn't think I had the right to criticise him about anything. In fact, I owed him. I was just contemplating inviting him over for Mum to answer a few of his – and to be honest, my own – questions, when I spotted Leo out of the corner of my eye. He was coming towards me.

'Hi, how's it going?' He seemed a little awkward, which I'm sure I would be too, if I'd disappeared like he had.

'Where the hell did you get to?' I asked, bewildered by his disappearance. 'I thought you'd gone to find your

258

sister and Ashley. Instead you came back here while Henri and I risked our lives for them.'

He frowned. 'I did look for her, but I don't know my way around like you do.' It was a feeble excuse and we both knew it. 'I assumed Dee had seen the smoke, come to her senses and returned here.'

I was still furious with him, but what he said made some sense. 'I'm fed up of keeping my mouth shut. I'm about to speak to Dee about the way she's behaving.'

'I think she's suffered enough today.'

I moved away from the gate and glared at him. 'I think I probably know better than you what she's gone through today. I was happy for you both to stay here, but I'm tired of her constant disruption to Mum and Katie.' I shrugged. 'Ashley can stay here until Dee is settled somewhere, but I'm not going to put up with her unsettling this household any longer.'

I noticed Dee moving past the coloured glass in the upstairs hall window. Good, she was on her way down. Perhaps now I could resolve this mess.

'Please, Sera,' Leo lowered his voice. 'You don't know what wounds you'll open if you push for her to tell you things.'

'It's too late for that.' But I wavered for a second.

He shook his head. 'Don't say I didn't warn you.'

I was sick of these underhand threats. They'd held me back from speaking out for too long. After this afternoon I was determined to drag this house back to some semblance of normality.

–

Dee looked at us from the open back door before descending the steps and joining us. I noticed her hair

259

was still wet. Maybe she was also ready to finally resolve things, too?

'Shall we go and sit over there,' I suggested, gesturing towards the garden furniture.

Dee nodded. She accompanied me, but not before I spotted her ignoring a pointed look from Leo.

'Right,' I said, when we were all seated. Leo folded his arms across his chest, tapping one of his feet on the grass.

'Go on then,' Dee said. 'Let's get this over with.'

'Leo explained about the dreadful time you suffered at the hands of your ex,' I admitted.

'That's considerate of him,' she said, giving him a side-ways glance. 'Go on.'

I raised an eyebrow, not certain why she was suddenly in a hurry to speak to me. 'I sympathise with you, Dee. We were good friends once and I care about you.'

I thought about how ballsy she had always been. The one to encourage me to do things we both knew our mothers would frown upon. Pinching sweets from the nearby newsagent's, creeping out of our rooms to meet at the back of the chippie and generally making our lives more fun. I hoped we could find a way to get back to some sort of comfortable friendship.

She smirked and shook her head. 'Do you care for me like you would a sister?'

Her question threw me. I didn't know what she was going on about. I went to answer, but before I could, Mum interrupted.

'Stop this now,' she shouted as she rushed to join us. She looked flustered and glared at Dee. 'You should be ashamed of yourself.'

'Why? Because I know your secret and your precious daughter doesn't?'

I glanced at Mum, confused, but she was too busy staring at Dee to notice.

'Haven't you caused enough chaos today?' Mum bent down, her face almost nose to nose with Dee's. 'If anyone is going to tell Sera, I will, not you.'

I gazed at the two of them, like two lionesses fighting for seniority. A sense of dread crept up from my gut.

'What are you both talking about?' I asked, aware the tables were about to be turned on me. 'What secret?'

Dee smiled. 'The secret your mother's been determined to keep from you all these years.' She sneered. 'Do you want to know what it is?'

Chapter Twenty-Eight

1990 — Scotland

Mimi

Where was Hazel? Knowing it was unlikely that she would have gone off somewhere in the early hours of the morning by herself, I went to step into my jeans. Then, remembering where I was, I put on the green cocktail dress. I ran a brush through my hair and checked my face. I hadn't bothered to remove my make-up and spat on a tissue, rubbing it under my eyes to make my face passable. I pushed my feet into the satin shoes that matched my dress and left the room to look for her. I told myself there was probably a perfectly rational reason for her to go for a wander around the enormous house at nearly three in the morning. There didn't seem to be anyone about, which was a relief.

Walking along the corridor, trying to shift the heavy feeling pressing down on me, it dawned on me that I had little choice but to go to Vinnie's room to look for her. I was nervous, but couldn't turn my back on her now I knew how dangerous he could be. I walked quietly towards his bedroom, stopped outside, and leaned my head closer to the door and listened. Voices came from inside. If I'd have stood here listening to him in his bedroom with someone else a few hours earlier, I would have been hysterical with jealousy. Now I was just frightened. I heard a muffled cry and recognised it as Hazel's voice. She was pleading with him and sounded terrified.

My heart raced, and I took a deep breath to try and control my rising panic. I placed my hand on the door handle and slowly turned it, relieved, yet horrified, when it twisted and the door opened. Pushing it ajar, I could hear her cries more clearly now.

'Please, Vinnie, I couldn't do it,' she cried, her swollen lips distorting her voice. 'He's disgusting.'

Her pleading was lost on him. I bent my head to look around the door and peered inside. He was crouched over her. Her nightie had been torn from her shoulders and now barely concealed her bruised body. She was too busy shielding her face to notice me. Her right eye was swollen shut and her thighs grazed and bruised. Vinnie knelt between her legs.

How could I have thought myself in love with this monster?

Holding her down with one hand around her neck, he bent his arm back. 'You're a fucking bitch,' he hissed, saliva spraying through his gritted teeth. 'Your childish behaviour has embarrassed him and he's called off our deal.'

'I didn't mean to upset him,' she sobbed, trying to protect her face.

'So, why overreact and claw at his sodding face then? He wants us out by the morning and it's all your fault.' He clenched his fist, getting ready to strike her again.

Desperate to stop him, I glanced around the room and spotted a heavy glass ashtray. I grabbed it, lifting it high.

He turned to face me, shock at what I was about to do registering on his features. I knew how much stronger than us he was and that I had one chance to make this count. Squealing in revulsion, I slammed the heavy object as hard as I could against his temple, watching in dazed horror as it split his skin, shattering into pieces onto the carpet.

He stared at me, momentarily stunned. Then, closing his eyes, he dropped like a slaughtered bull onto the carpet next to Hazel. She pressed her hands over her mouth to stifle her screams. Shocked by what I'd just done, I bent down to lift his leg off her and helped her to stand.

'You killed him,' Hazel whispered.

My heart pounded painfully. I let go of the remains of the ashtray still in my hand, and shivered. 'What do we do now?' I asked, swallowing a wave of nausea. 'We can't leave him here. They'll come for us.'

'You saved my life, Mimi,' she panted. 'But did you have to hit him so hard?' Hazel continued, trembling.

'What? You'd rather I make him angry by tapping his head?' I tried not to panic. 'He'd have killed us.' I pointed at Hazel. 'He's already battered you.'

Vinnie's warm blood oozed across the rug reaching my feet and making them sticky. I stepped back.

Hazel grabbed Vinnie's dressing gown from the chair and pulled it over her ripped nightdress. Tying the cord belt, she took hold of my shoulders. 'We have to get rid of him.'

What did she just say? I stared at Vinnie, humiliated to realise how easily his movie star looks had distracted me from his dark personality. 'How? Where?'

Hazel's hands shook, and I wished we could go back twenty-four hours.

'Get a towel,' Hazel said. 'Put it around his head before he really starts to bleed.'

I glanced at a large glass shard embedded in Vinnie's skull, relieved to note it was stemming the blood flow.

'Quickly,' Hazel said. 'We'll need to get rid of this rug. We don't want blood seeping through to the carpet. We don't have time to clean this place.'

My legs trembled, as I walked to the bathroom to find a towel. A terrifying thought occurred to me as I carried it to Hazel to wrap around Vinnie's head. 'If he's bleeding, doesn't that mean he's still alive?'

'Only just, by the look of him.' Hazel retched as she lifted his head. 'Help me.'

We struggled to wrap the towel around Vinnie's head. Once done, Hazel sat back on her haunches. 'That will have to do for now.' She raked her hands through her messy hair. 'I'm going to get dressed, wait here.'

'You can't leave me alone,' I said, horrified at the prospect of being left with him.

'If someone comes, answer the door, just don't open it.' Hazel grimaced as she pulled a handkerchief out of his dressing gown pocket. 'If they think he's in here with you, they'll be too scared to insist on coming in. Make some excuse,' she hesitated. 'Say he's in the bathroom.' Hazel winced as she walked to the door. 'You'd better wash his blood off your shoes.'

I did as she said. I couldn't stop crying as the red water ran from my feet and down the sides of the sink. Spotting one of Vinnie's ties, it dawned on me that if we were going to make him disappear, then we needed to make it look as if he'd left of his own volition.

We needed to hide his things. Vinnie was too proud of his personal effects to leave them behind. I ran across the room, tiptoeing around his body. I pulled his suitcase from where he'd left it next to the wardrobe. Wrenching his bespoke suits from hangers, I threw them and his underwear from the drawers untidily into the case.

Hurrying into the bathroom, I opened his leather wash bag. I held it above the sink and brushed my shaking arm across the glass shelf, sweeping his toothpaste, aftershave and razor into the bag. Then, taking his toothbrush from the glass, I dropped that in. I pushed away a mental replay of what I had done to him, and hurriedly zipped up the bag, before throwing it into the case.

I scanned the room for anything I might have missed. 'Wallet,' I whispered, remembering the brown leather wallet he always had crammed with notes and ready to hand to tip someone lavishly. Though I was now sure it was more to show others how successful he was, than generosity. I pulled open the bedside drawer, retrieving his wallet and a pair of gold cufflinks.

The light reflected off his heavy gold watch. Taking a deep breath, I unclasped it, cringing at the touch of his flesh as I removed it from his wrist. 'Damn,' I groaned, aware that I also needed to pull off his pinkie ring. It was a bit of a struggle and I gritted my teeth, forcing myself to complete the grim task. The heavy gold chain around his neck was all that remained for me to take from his body.

Finally, exhausted and sweating, I pushed the last vestiges of Vinnie's possessions into a side pocket in the case.

The door opened. I froze until I spotted Hazel's hair.

'What are you doing?' Hazel frowned, spotting the open case. I explained hurriedly. 'Good thinking. Make sure we've got everything. Is his wallet in there?' I nodded.

'Because we're going to need money. It's our only way of getting out of Scotland.'

My trembling hands made it difficult to close the catches on Vinnie's case. 'I'll take this to our room,' I whispered to Hazel, desperate to get away.

–

After checking that there was no one else in the hallway, I crept to our bedroom. I couldn't bear the thought of returning to Vinnie's room, but knew I had no choice. I took a few deep breaths to calm myself and got going.

'Do you think it'd be safe for us to return to London?' I wondered, not ready to leave the city I had fallen in love with. 'Everyone at the club knows we came here with Vinnie and his mates. Won't they ask us questions if we go back without him?'

Hazel considered. 'I suppose they will. We need to get rid of him before we think about running away. Help me roll him onto his back,' she said. 'That's it. Now lift his arm over your shoulder and I'll do the same.' We groaned with the strain. 'It's going to be an effort, but I've done this a few times with my brothers when they're drunk. I'm sure we can manage to get him out of here if we're determined.'

He was heavier than I expected. The effort of carrying him in the warm night air was exhausting.

'Where are we going?' I asked, as it dawned on me that we hadn't discussed the next step of our plan.

'This way.'

We dragged him along, his head flopping between our bodies. Too late, I wished I had thought to change out of my heels.

'There's a back staircase,' Hazel said, nodding in the direction. I noticed that despite our struggle to move him, Hazel's voice appeared stronger. 'I checked it when I went to change,' she said. 'It's late so hopefully we won't be disturbed out here.'

We hoisted him up a little further onto our shoulders.

'Shit, he's heavy,' Hazel whispered, her voice strained with the effort.

'Where exactly are we going?' I asked as we rounded a corner at the end of the corridor.

Hazel gestured to a service lift. 'There are some woods out the back.'

Once down on the ground floor, we manoeuvred Vinnie outside.

Hazel stopped abruptly. 'Shh.'

'What?'

'I heard someone.'

We waited. When there was no further sound, we moved away from the doorway.

'I'm scared,' I admitted, pushing aside the thought of someone discovering us with the body. I wasn't sure I could go through with this.

'Shut up,' Hazel whispered. 'You were the one who smashed him over the head, remember?'

The idea that this was my fault frightened me. I choked back tears. I didn't want to end up spending the rest of my life in prison. 'I was trying to stop him killing you.'

'I know.' Hazel's voice softened. 'But you were the one who killed him, not me. I'm trying to help you hide his body. Now let's get a move on. The sooner we do this the sooner we can get far away from this place.'

After almost dropping him, we eventually reached the wooded area. I was grateful for the denseness of the thick leaves overhead. They diminished the pearl whiteness of the moonlight and gave us much needed cover.

A revolting thought occurred to me. 'We need to strip him and dump his clothes.'

'Good idea,' Hazel agreed. 'I'm going to find something for us to dig with. They must have a gardener's shed where we'll find spades.'

Hazel had run off into the darkness before I had time to stop her. Pushing away my squeamishness, I stripped Vinnie. I kicked his once beautiful bespoke grey suit out of the way, and stood up. This was a living nightmare. I noticed Hazel coming back. She was holding up a huge shovel that looked as if it was used for coal rather than soil.

'I also found this smaller spade.' She handed the larger one to me. 'Quick, we don't have much time.'

We dug for what seemed like hours. We needed to hide all traces of him. Even though he was dead, he still had the power to hurt us. The thought was terrifying.

Then his head moved.

I dropped the spade and covered my mouth to stop from screaming. 'He's still alive,' I grimaced, swallowing bile rising in my throat.

'Shush.' Hazel's controlled tone was chilling. 'We have no choice. We must get rid of him. Now, dig.'

I slammed the blade of the shovel down into the hard earth with as much force as my exhausted arms could muster. 'Surely this is deep enough now?' I whispered a few minutes later, my body trembling with the effort of trying to remain calm.

Vinnie groaned. The sound seemed to echo through the night air.

I was too scared to look at him, even though I could hear him battling to breathe inches from my feet. 'He's still alive.' I shuddered.

'I can see that,' Hazel spat. 'Keep going. We'll soon be finished and then we can forget about everything that's happened tonight.'

You might be able to, I thought. My shoulders were agony and my blistered hands stung. My heart almost stopped in my chest when Vinnie opened his swollen eyes and slowly drew his gaze up from my feet to stare at my face. I could barely breathe.

'Mimi, for fuck's sake stop staring at him. Dig. We're nearly done.'

Yearning for the nightmare to end, I frantically continued digging.

'That should do it,' Hazel said, eventually. 'Right, I'll grab him under his armpits. You take his ankles.'

I reached down, recoiling when my palms connected with his hairy flesh. 'Do we have to?'

'After what's happened; what do you think? Right, one, two, three…'

His warm blood made his ankles slippery and difficult to hold. We hoisted him barely an inch from the ground, dragging him the few feet towards his makeshift grave. Straining with his weight, we then released our grip on him, dropping him into the muddy hole. He landed with a sickening thud.

'It's not big enough,' I panicked, barely able to breathe, my heart was pounding so hard. By the look of the stunned expression on Vinnie's battered face, I wasn't the only one who couldn't believe this was happening.

'Shut up,' Hazel snapped, jumping into the hole next to him.

I grimaced as her feet landed heavily next to his tanned stomach, and watched as Hazel's muddied hands grabbed behind his knees. She pulled them up with difficulty until his feet fitted into the shallow grave. 'There, now help me out.'

Terrified that he might grab Hazel's ankles, I didn't hesitate. I took Hazel's outstretched hand and pulled. Standing upright next to me, she withdrew her hand from mine and wiped my hands vigorously against the skirt of my ruined cocktail dress.

He whimpered quietly. I saw him staring at me, as if he was imprinting the image of our murderous faces to savour for eternity. We stared in petrified silence as bloody bubbles dribbled from his bruised mouth. I turned away and vomited.

'Don't think about it,' Hazel said, elbowing me. I winced from the force of the nudge to my ribs. 'We need to cover him up.'

I noticed the sky had lightened to a salmon pink. Soon dog walkers could come through the woods for their early morning stroll. It wouldn't do for one of them to sniff our handiwork. I shovelled the heavy soil over his body as quickly as I could manage. Closing my eyes, I willed the image of his final silent plea to disappear from the back of my sore eyelids. The muscles in my neck and back ached. I straightened up with a little difficulty and took a deep breath of the fresh morning air, relieved that we had almost completed our gruesome task.

I opened my mouth to speak, when the earth shifted near my left foot, revealing Vinnie's hands and face. I squealed and dropped the spade.

'Keep going; hurry,' Hazel cried.

Picking up my spade, I frantically shovelled soil until he was hidden once more. We needed to disguise the freshly dug soil, so Hazel and I dragged a heavy, rotting branch, resting it over Vinnie's grave.

'We need leaves, lots of them,' Hazel said knowingly, as if she did this sort of thing often.

Sobbing from the trauma of what we were doing, I wiped my eyes with the back of my dirty hands. Then I searched for more camouflage to conceal our handiwork.

Finally, we were done. Hazel and I studied the area, to see if anyone could tell what was there under the branch and leaves. We had done a good job. No one passing by would ever suspect that there was a body buried here.

'We must make a pact never to speak about this to anyone,' Hazel said.

I willingly agreed. Who would I tell and why would I tell them?

'Do you promise?'

'Of course I bloody do.'

We stared at each other. I wondered if my face had hardened as much as Hazel's appeared to have done since the beginning of our trip to Scotland.

'Where to now?' I asked, glancing across the lawn at the rear of the imposing building.

'I've no idea, but we need to go inside and get our things,' Hazel said. 'And remember, if you hear anyone coming, run for the shadows.'

We took a deep breath and ran out of the darkness of the wood, across the dimly lit backyard, and into the servants' entrance at the back of the building.

Chapter Twenty-Nine

2018 – Oakwold, New Forest

Sera

'You and Hazel killed a man?' I still couldn't take in what she was telling me. I stared at her, trying to focus on the fact that this was my mother talking. All these years I'd suspected she wasn't telling me everything about her past, after all, as far as she was concerned she didn't really have one to share with me. It never dawned on me she could be capable of something like this. How could I have missed this other side to her character that had remained hidden from me until now?

'What?' Dee looked at my mother then me, open-mouthed. 'Are you insane?'

My mother looked anything but insane to me. I thought of the many times she'd become absorbed by a character she was playing in a film. 'You are serious, I suppose?'

She nodded. 'Who would lie about something like this?'

I realised I didn't know her at all. I took a deep breath to try and calm down, pressing the heel of my palms against my eyes to relieve the throbbing headache I could feel stirring. This couldn't be happening.

She moved over to sit next to me and rested her hand on my back. I looked sideways at her. She looked the same and sounded the same. I opened my mouth to ask the identity of the man she and Hazel had murdered, gasping when an answer occurred to me that was so horrendous I had to close my eyes to speak.

'Please,' I whispered, my voice barely audible even to me. 'Tell me you didn't kill Jack.'

She frowned. 'Who?'

'Mum's boyfriend,' Leo said, his face pale and tense.

She gazed at me, her mouth open in confusion. 'Hazel's—? No, of course I didn't kill Hazel's boyfriend. What do you take me for?'

After what she had just dropped on us, the irony of her question wasn't lost on me. I shrugged her hand off me and stood, glaring at her. How could she retain that cool veneer of control at a time like this? The nerve of her being angry with my reply made me want to shake her.

'Mum, you've just announced you killed a man. If he wasn't Henri's father, then who the hell was he?'

She stared at me as if the name of her mysterious victim refused to part from her lips.

'Vincent Black?' Leo murmured eventually, nervously looking from me to Dee. 'Was that the man?'

Where had I heard that name before? I realised Mum was crying. 'Was it him?'

She closed her eyes. Incredible that with these revelations being thrown about her only reaction was to allow a few tears to fall. She nodded.

'I once stupidly thought I was in love with him,' she said, her voice quiet as if it was the first time she was allowing herself to hear this nugget of information.

274

I walked away from the three of them, desperate for enough space to be able to think clearly. My world was falling apart and I wasn't sure how much more I could take. I bent to pick a head of lavender, lifting it up to my nose to breathe in the familiar, calming scent. She was my mother and the only other person I'd trusted since Marcus' death. She might be able to convincingly play the part of a killer in a television movie, but for her to be able to end another person's life in real life—

'What did he do to you?' I asked, walking back to join them. 'You must have been terrified of him to kill him.' I looked at her tall, fine frame. She didn't have the strength to fight a man, so this can't have been something she had chosen to do lightly.

'I need a moment to think.' She leant her head back and stared up at the blue sky. 'I never meant tell you.' She gave Dee a pointed glare. 'I'd give anything to have kept this from you.'

She recounted her story, her usually loud voice quiet and the look in her eyes haunted. I watched her pick away the skin from around her perfectly manicured nails and wished I could put my arm around her to comfort her a little, but any interruption could cause her to stop speaking. I daren't move until she finished explaining what had happened.

'This is ridiculous,' Dee shouted, standing up and knocking over my glass.

I bent to pick it up before she stood on it. The idea of broken glass in the grass under the children's bare feet wasn't something I needed to deal with on top of everything else. 'You knew?' I asked, irritated she was overreacting yet again.

Dee shook her head frantically. 'No. I didn't know anything about this man, or his murder.' She almost spat the last word as she jerked her head around to glare at my mother. 'You're trying to tell me that my crazy, pisshead of a mother helped you bury a man you were both in love with?' She sat down heavily, burying her face in her hands. 'You're completely mad.'

'Dee, that's enough.' My mother's booming voice shocked us all. Dee looked across at her, hate filling her eyes.

I willed someone to tell me it was a sick joke. I recalled what Dee had said to start off this whole sorry confession and realised there was more to come. 'If you weren't going to tell me about the murder, what was the big secret you were so determined to share?'

Mum grabbed hold of my hand and squeezed, patting it with the other hand. I could feel her trembling. 'Dee was going to tell you that Vinnie was your father.'

My mouth dropped open. 'Sorry, what?'

'And mine,' Dee said, her mouth slowly drawing back into a sardonic smile.

'What?' I repeated, unable to force my brain into a cohesive thought.

'I asked you a question earlier,' Dee smirked. 'Would you care for me like a sister?'

My mind raced. Nothing made sense.

Mum nodded. 'She's right,' she said quietly. When I didn't move, she turned her attention to Dee. 'When did Hazel tell you?'

My new-found sister and I stared at each other. All these years, I'd had a sibling, and no one had thought to tell me. No wonder I had felt a part of Hazel's family, I almost was. 'Why didn't you tell us we were sisters when we were little?' I asked, my words sounding as if they were muffled behind a cushion. 'We'd have been delighted back then.'

'It might have changed many things, don't you think?' Dee asked.

I agreed. 'Mum? Why didn't you, or Hazel, tell us this before now?'

Sadness seemed etched in my mother's face. 'Because we knew you'd probably ask awkward questions.' When we didn't say anything to this, she continued. 'You were both such inquisitive children, you would have wanted to go and look for him.'

She was right, we would have done. Both of us loved any excuse for an adventure and those were sorely lacking when we were younger. This news would have come as an exciting change in our mostly uneventful lives.

'We were trying to hide the fact that we'd killed a man,' she continued. 'Don't forget we had to be as inconspicuous as possible.'

I needed to glean as much information from her as I could while she was opening up to us. 'But you lived so near to each other, yet let us believe you weren't friends, why?'

'We didn't want anyone to see us together. We were scared Vinnie's cronies were looking for the two of us, and—' She hesitated. 'It was complicated between Hazel and me. That night scarred us both. Every time I saw her I was reminded about what we'd done. It was easier to keep away from her.'

It sounded plausible. 'But why end up in Oakwold?' I asked.

'We didn't plan it this way,' she admitted. 'We just wanted to get away from that place and took several trains until we ran out of money.' She closed her eyes wearily, looking her age for once. 'It's hard knowing that at any moment your secret could be discovered. Neither of us had any other family we trusted enough to care for our children if one of us ever did have to go away.'

Leo cleared his throat. He'd been very quiet. I'd almost forgotten he was there. 'Obviously he couldn't have been my father?'

Mum shook her head. 'No, he died four years before you were born, Leo. Sorry. I've no idea who your father is. You'll have to ask your mother that.'

'This is madness,' Dee interrupted. 'How can you expect us to believe that you, an actress who's spent decades on television, has been hiding from anyone who might have known you back then? Didn't you think someone would recognise you?'

Mum nodded. 'There was a possibility, but I was very young when this happened, my make-up was different. It was easy enough to change how I looked.' She seemed almost proud of her achievement. 'Even subtle changes to your appearance with colours, contouring and hairstyles can make a difference.'

'Do you think the police looked for him?'

'Would you waste resources on a villain you were delighted to see the back of? I wouldn't.' She crossed her arms. 'I suppose they might have made perfunctory enquiries, but the people we were worried about were his cronies. Except no one came to find us. Hazel and I assumed that someone was ready to step into Vinnie's shoes and take over where he'd left off. We probably inadvertently did them a favour.'

'But your acting parts?' I asked, wondering why she'd continue in a job that could put her in front of those looking for her.

'As far as my publicity people and the papers were concerned, I was a mid-list actress, no one made too much fuss of. I reverted to being called Maureen. It was relatively simple, but it worked. Hazel and I took false surnames and came to live here.' She paused, as if reliving it all. 'It's easier to hide in plain sight sometimes, you know. People tend to look hardest at a distant point and fail to see what's right under their noses.'

'Well, none of us had a clue this had happened, so you must be right,' Dee said sarcastically. She hesitated for a moment. 'I'd like to know, which one of you killed our father?'

'Yes,' interrupted Leo. 'Are you, or is Mum, Vincent Black's murderer?'

Her face contorted with what I assumed must be revulsion at the memory of what they had done. I recalled her wearing a similar expression in a television movie a couple of years before when she had played a murderer then. Was she acting this part too?

'As I said, I was the one to hit Vinnie over the head,' Mum said quietly. 'But Hazel insisted we bury him and that's ultimately what must have killed him.'

The three of us sat in stunned silence taking in what she had just told us.

'Hang on a sec,' Dee snapped. 'Are you saying he was still alive when you buried him?'

Mum shifted in her seat and cleared her throat.

'Mum?' An icy shiver ran down my back. I willed her to reassure us that was not the case. Every part of me was trying to push this experience away.

Eventually she nodded. 'Yes.'

'Why?' I shrieked in disbelief. 'How could you do such a thing?'

Discovering my father was some low-life creep who beat up women was one thing, but finding out that my mother had buried him alive was another entirely. I went to speak again, but could see she was flagging. Something else troubled her. What now? My head ached. She seemed to have aged ten years in as many minutes.

Each of us stared at her, lost in our own troubled thoughts. Something niggled in my mind. I recalled the burnt piece of her letter she had made me deliver to Hazel all those years ago.

'Let me get this straight,' I said. 'The message I took to Hazel the day before she disappeared, what did it say?'

She turned the dress ring on her right index finger round and round. 'I'd discovered they were digging up the woods near the country house where we'd buried Vinnie. We were both always frightened they might find his body, but as the years went by and nothing happened, I began to relax. Then, when I read in the newspapers that the house was empty and the area was being turned a housing estate, I knew I had to tip her off. I wanted her to be careful and keep her mouth shut.'

Leo stood up and walked around to the back of Mum's chair. 'Instead, Mum panicked and ran away with us.'

I could understand Hazel wanting to take her children away from the threat of her crime being discovered. 'But what's that got to do with Jack?' I still couldn't believe the fun-loving, occasionally possessive Frenchman had been Henri's dad.

The three of them stared at me.

'What's he got to do with this?' Leo asked.

It occurred to me that neither of them knew his real identity yet. 'Jack's name was actually Jacques. J-A-C-Q-U-E-S,' I spelt it to make myself clear. 'He was Henri's dad.'

They looked more stunned by this news than that of our mother's joint murder of Vinnie. There was a stilled silence as Leo and Dee took in this nugget of information and glanced at each other.

'Henri's father?' Leo raised his eyebrows.

'Yes,' Mum said. 'And the reason Henri's leasing the farm is because his father disappeared in the summer of 2003 and he wants to find out what happened to him.' She studied each of them in turn. Was she paying them back for forcing her to confess to everything today? 'You wouldn't know anything about that, I don't suppose?'

'Mum, of course they wouldn't.' Why was she trying to shift the focus on to them? I could see by the granite-hard glint in her blue eyes that she was relishing telling them this news. She didn't take her eyes off them, and for once I could imagine her being capable of doing something far worse than I'd ever considered before.

'Well?' she asked. 'I've been honest with you two, it's your turn to return the compliment, don't you think?'

Leo looked over at me. His face paled even more as I watched him, and his normally straight shoulders slumped. 'She's right, Sera. We do know more about Jack than we're letting on.'

'He's dead,' Dee said, matter-of-factly. 'Killed that night before we left.'

'No. I'm not listening to this anymore.' I had had enough.

This was too much for me to take in. I didn't want to hear any more about Jack, not yet. I had enough of my own past to process first. Jack was dead, though. I would have to tell Henri.

'I'm going to check on the girls. I hope they haven't heard any of this. Then later, when they're asleep—' I didn't add, 'and when my brain has caught up with this insanity', 'I want you to tell me everything you know about Jack. I'm going to have to tell Henri what happened to his father.'

Leo shook his head. 'You're not telling him anything,' he said severely.

I went to argue with him but something about his manner stopped me. 'Fine, I won't,' I lied. Henri had a right to know, but with all the talk of violence I didn't like the way Leo was looking at me and wasn't going to tempt fate by challenging him. Not yet, anyway.

-

I heard Katie's voice calling from the upstairs window for me and made an excuse to leave them and go to her. I didn't feel safe and could sense the evening ahead would reveal more secrets yet. I had no intention of keeping Katie here in case things did turn nasty and decided to take her to a guest house for a few days. Somewhere away from here until everything was sorted out. I ran up the stairs to find her, guilt flooding my veins. I would give anything not to have to leave Ashley in this house tonight, but she wasn't my child to take.

'What is it, darling?' My faith in human nature healed slightly when I looked down at my little girl's cherubic face, her arms outstretched for me to pick her up. I bent down to lift her, hugging her tightly. 'I think it's time you went to bed, don't you?'

'But I haven't had my bath, Mummy.' She gave me a hopeful grin.

'You can go to bed without one tonight, just this once.' She giggled. 'Come on, let's give your face a quick wash and clean your teeth, you do have to do that. Where's Ashley?'

'Sleeping,' she whispered.

That was a relief. I gave her a quick wash and changed her, settling her in her bed. I needed time to pack some of her things. As soon as she began to drift off, I took a change of clothes, her swimming costume and a cardigan, packed her toothbrush and favourite teddy that had dropped from her arms, and snuck down the stairs and out of the front door to put them in the car.

I stepped back inside the house and turned to close the door as silently as possible.

'Where do you think you're going?' Leo barked from behind me.

My heart jolted. 'Bloody hell, Leo, you almost gave me a heart attack. What's wrong with you?'

'You didn't answer my question.' He stood close to me, not fooled by my bravado.

I refused to let him see how much he frightened me. 'Firstly,' I said, pointing my finger at him and stepping back slightly to make space between us. 'This is my house and you're a guest. You don't have to stay here if you don't like how I behave. Secondly, and most importantly,' I lowered my voice to give it as much gravitas as possible, 'I don't need to ask permission from you, or anyone else. Got it?'

He lowered his head and moved in closer to me. 'Sera, I have a feeling you think you're addressing someone else. Probably that bloody Frenchman.'

I swallowed to moisten my throat, which for some reason had gone incredibly dry. If Leo thought he was going to intimidate me when my child was sleeping upstairs, he was sorely mistaken.

'Leo,' I said, very slowly. 'Don't you dare think you can boss me around, I'm not Dee and I don't need you for anything. Now, move out of my way.' I put my arm out to push past him and hid my relief when he moved. I didn't want to give him any ideas about my plan to take Katie out of the house, so marched out to the garden to find Mum.

'Mimi's gone to bed,' Dee said. 'Told us she couldn't talk about this anymore, and left. I can't say I'm sorry.'

I looked at my half-sister and tried to imagine how different things could have been between us if her family hadn't left when they did, or if we'd been brought up knowing our connection. Or if Jack hadn't been killed that night in 2003.

'What did happen to Jack?' I asked Dee, unable to hide the tremor in my voice after my confrontation with Leo.

'That night changed all our lives,' she said, her voice distant as her thoughts drifted off elsewhere.

It was then I realised that the trauma of what she'd been forced to live with all these years had altered her beyond any point of recovery. She wasn't the girl I'd known and loved when we were teenagers. Her spirit died that night, along with Jack.

'Can you tell me how he died?' I asked, wanting to find out as much as possible for Henri's sake. I suspected Leo was going to stop her telling me anything more than I already knew.

She stared into space at some unseen horror. 'Jack didn't want us to leave the farm. Mum refused to tell him why she was so insistent on going, so he thought she was just being ridiculous. They argued.' She took a deep breath. 'When he refused to help her put things in the car she panicked that we were taking too long to pack and became hysterical. He slapped her.' She looked at me. 'I saw it all, but Leo was out by the car trying to fit everything into it. He only came back into the room when Mum fell over with the force of Jack's slap. She hit her side on a table and yelped.'

I clasped my hands together in an effort not to show how much I was shaking. I wanted her to tell me everything, aware I didn't have long before Leo came back outside and shut her up.

'Leo charged at Jack. Jack grabbed Leo, who was only skinny then, if you remember, and slapped him. I think Mum falling had shocked Jack and he was almost demented with her out-of-character behaviour and then Leo having a go at him.' She looked at me. 'Thinking back, I don't think Jack meant to hurt Mum, but it was incredibly hot and her reaction to Maureen's letter and their fight pushed the atmosphere to breaking point. Mum was desperate to leave, you see. I was frightened and not sure what was going on. I panicked because she refused to give me enough time to visit your house to let you know we were going. And Leo was desperate to protect us.' She stopped talking and took a shuddering breath.

I walked over to her and crouched in front of her, resting my hands on her knees. 'Go on, what happened?' I asked, keeping my voice as level as I could. I could see the back door out of the corner of my eye, aware that Leo could appear at any moment.

She stared at her hands. 'I'm not completely certain, but one minute I was in the living room crying, the next

I was in the kitchen grabbing a steak knife from a dinner plate one of us had used earlier. I ran back to Mum. I don't know what I thought I'd do with it, threaten Jack to keep him from stopping us leave maybe. But Jack turned to leave the living room, just as I was running back in.' She flinched and closed her eyes.

'Oh, Dee,' I whispered, picturing the horrific scene. I hugged her, wishing I could comfort that teenage girl who had altered her life forever in a single second of mistimed madness.

'I'll never forget the look on his face,' she cried, large tears dripping down her face. 'He was stunned. We stared at each other; time seemed frozen until Jack dropped to the floor, clutching his stomach, blood seeping through the gaps in his fingers.'

'Dee, shut the hell up.' Leo bellowed from the doorway. Then turning his anger at me, shouted, 'Are you happy now? You had to know, didn't you?'

'So she's told me,' I said as cockily as I could manage. 'So, what? It was years ago. No one should have to keep something that devastating secret,' I said, recalling that my mother had done just that. 'Come and comfort your sister. I need to I check on Mum.'

Not waiting for him to argue and knowing Leo well enough that he would want to grill Dee about exactly how much she had admitted to me, he and I crossed paths and I ran to the house. I turned to watch Leo and Dee briefly from the back door. They were whispering animatedly to each other. I left them to it and stepped inside.

–

'Why did he mind Dee admitting she'd killed Jack?' I asked Mum when I joined her in her bedroom and sat on the end of her bed. I couldn't seem to stop trembling.

Despite everything that had happened, she was sitting at her dressing table, as she did every night before retiring, removing her make-up and applying her night cream to her face and neck.

'I'm not sure,' she murmured, studying her reflection in the mirror to ensure she'd rubbed every bit in to her youthful-looking skin. Satisfied, she came over to the bed, pulled back her summer duvet, stepped in and settled down against the large, downy pillows. 'Maybe he's being clever.'

'How so?' I asked, watching her and wondering if I'd ever really known her.

'If neither of them confessed to killing Jack they could blame it on their mother.' She stared out of the window. 'As much as Hazel annoyed me, I don't like the way they described her earlier. We must try and find out how she is.'

It was odd hearing her talking about Hazel in a caring way.

'She could be steely tough when you least expected it, but as you know, she had a timid side to her, too,' Mum considered. 'If, as they say, Jack's murder was an unfortunate accident, they shouldn't have run away. Henri must have gone through hell all these years wondering what happened to his father.'

'True.' A thought occurred to me, and as much as I tried to suppress it, I couldn't help asking, 'Don't you ever think about Vincent Black's family and what they must have gone through?' When she didn't react, I added,

'Wouldn't they have wondered why he didn't return from Scotland?'

She took a jar of hand cream from her bedside table and silently unscrewed the large silver lid. She dipped two finger tips into the white cream, handed the jar to me to reseal and began working the cream into her fingers, around her manicured nails and then over her tops of her hands to her wrists.

'I think about them every day,' she admitted. 'I did a terrible thing. I can't blame Hazel for it – even though we were both involved in his death.' Her voice faltered at the last word in the sentence and she stopped what she was doing and looked directly at me. 'Do you see me any differently now you know this?'

I wanted to lie, but she knew me far too well for me to get away with doing so. 'Yes.' She flinched, so I added, 'But only because you've always been a nurturer to me and Katie.' I laughed. 'And to some of your younger boyfriends.'

She didn't smile at my stupid attempt at lightening the mood. 'I don't want Katie to ever learn about this.' She swallowed and cleared her throat. 'I want her to always think of me as kindly Nana Mimi who buys her pretty dresses and ice creams.'

I placed the jar of hand cream on her bedside cabinet. 'I can't promise not to tell her, Mum. I've resented your secrets my entire life. I will do my best to make sure she doesn't judge you. I'm sure she'll always love you. I do.'

'Good.' She took both my hands in hers. 'None of us ever knows what we're capable of until we're faced with a situation. I can't tell you how terrified I was that night.' She studied my expression. 'And the hundreds of nights afterwards when I waited for someone to discover his body and come looking for me and Hazel.'

'And now Henri has done just that.'

She nodded. 'Yes, the man who saved your life today, the one to whom I'll always be grateful, is probably going to be the one who sees me answer for my crime. Fate is having a laugh at my expense.'

I gave her hands a squeeze. 'I don't think he's going to do that, Mum.' I had to speak to him.

'He's a detective, Sera. His life has been about tracking people down and making them pay for crimes they've committed. Why shouldn't he want the same result for Vinnie?'

I wasn't certain, but thinking back to what he'd assured me, I said, 'No, I truly believe he's here to discover what happened to his father, and now he has. He can tell his family what became of Jack, and put it all to rest.'

She looked sad and suddenly fragile; almost not like my mother at all. 'He'll want Hazel's children to pay for what they did.'

'Yes, we can't expect him not to want them to answer for killing his father.' I rubbed my tired eyes. 'I want to go and see him,' I admitted, glancing at the door and lowering my voice, just in case Leo was standing outside listening. 'Hang on a sec.' I stood up and crept over to the window, peering down at the garden. They were still there, heads close together in conversation. I returned to Mum's bed and bent down to whisper to her. 'I put a few things in the car earlier, in case I needed to get Katie away from here.'

'From me?' She looked horrified.

I shook my head. 'No, of course not from you.'

I explained about Leo waiting for me in the hallway when I came in and his determination not to let me go anywhere. 'I think he suspects Henri would be my first stopping point if I left here.'

She sat up a little straighter. 'Why would you take Katie there, you barely know the man?'

She was right. 'I'm sure I can trust him to look after her for me. But I'm not so sure I'm happy having her here around Leo and Dee. They seem to be unravelling with every discovery, and I don't think it's going to be easy getting them to leave.'

Mum threw back the duvet and slipped her feet into her slippers, pulling on her fine dressing gown. 'Come on,' she said, opening the bedroom door. 'There's more I need to share with you, and I may as well tell Dee and Leo at the same time.'

Chapter Thirty

1990 – Bournemouth

Mimi

'Where are we going and what are we going to do when we get there?' It took me a couple of seconds to realise we were on a train as Hazel's terrified whisper woke me from a disturbed sleep. 'We've got barely any money and they'll probably come looking for us.'

I yawned and stretched my aching legs as far as the space in front of the train seats would allow. This was our second train journey. My entire body ached from the effort of taking Vinnie outside and then burying him. We had dumped some of his belongings in several bins around the main station and we'd loaded stones into the case before dropping it into a river nearby with the rest of his stuff. Then we'd caught an antiquated bus for a brief trip to a different village to get on another train. We were hot and sticky, and I just hoped we were getting far enough away from the country house.

'Because the first train we could catch was going in this direction,' I whispered when she asked me for a second time. 'We'll have to do whatever we can with any opportunities that come our way.' I didn't hold out much hope but was simply happy to be distancing myself away from

Vinnie's body more each second. I stared out at the fields as our train passed them by.

'I was thinking, you need to dye your hair and I'll cut mine.' She pulled miserably at her long curly tresses she'd always been so proud of.

'No,' I said. 'I'll cut mine. I've always wanted to see what it looked like shorter. You can dye yours red and cut it into a different style.' I gave her a soothing smile. 'We'll be fine.'

'You're sure?'

I wasn't, but I couldn't let her carry on getting into more of a state than she was already. I nodded. 'How are you?' I asked, unable to forget the sight of her bruised thighs and other areas Vinnie had abused so cruelly.

She groaned. 'Sore.' She picked at the skin next to one of her thumbnails. 'Ashamed.'

I put my arm around her trembling shoulders. 'You've got nothing to be ashamed of and don't you bloody forget it. Neither of us could have known what he'd do.' I reflected on my times alone with him and shivered. 'We both thought he was perfect.'

She began to cry. 'I can't believe what we did to him.'

Neither could I. 'Shush, you don't want to alert the other passengers, we have to stay as incognito as possible.' I was concerned one of them might read the papers the next day, assuming Vinnie's disappearance would make the press, and connect us to him.

'Were we right to—' she murmured, leaned slightly forward and glanced around at nearby passengers, '—you know, do what we did?'

'I don't know,' I said honestly. 'It's too late to do anything about it now, isn't it?'

She huddled up, bringing her slim legs up and hugging them. 'I need to sleep.'

I was relieved. I didn't know how to soothe her. I was grateful for the time I'd spent practising make-up techniques. They had come in handy when I needed to camouflage her bruises earlier, so we could go to the station.

It was slightly alarming that Hazel, after her bravado at Vinnie's grave, had now dissolved into a frightened girl again. I wasn't sure I had the strength for both of us. I stared out of the train window seeing Hazel's sleeping reflection and my own pale expression looking back at me. I would have given anything to turn back the clock and find a way to change things. I felt so alone and for the first time in my life, truly frightened. The one thing I did know was that Hazel and I could never return to our parents' homes again. If the police were looking for Vinnie they would probably try and find us there first. I might have been desperate to leave home, but it never occurred to me when I left that I was seeing my family for the last time.

The soothing monotony of the train wheels against the rails must have sent me to sleep because when I woke, it was morning and this time when I looked out of the window, it was at miles and miles of golden cornfields. The sunrise shone on the thin mist shrouding the town. It would soon burn off and as I looked up to the perfect, cloudless sky, it was hard to fit this picturesque scene with the horror of the previous night. I tried to clear my mind and wake up slowly, gazing at the perfection outside the window.

We needed to concentrate on making new lives for ourselves and somehow disappear. I wasn't sure how we were going to manage it. At least, I mused, the very worst we had to deal with was over now.

I was wrong.

—

'Psst, come here.' Hazel waved me over at the café where we both worked. We'd been in Bournemouth for almost eight weeks, since earning enough money working in a café in Tenby on the Welsh coast to travel even further from Scotland.

We hadn't spent much time getting to know the town, mainly because we wanted to save what money we still had. We knew nothing much about the area and had only chosen to come here in the first place because Hazel said she had read somewhere about there being lots of tourists – she'd thought we'd find work easily.

We liked it here, but both knew it wasn't far enough from Vinnie's body for us to build a new life. It was the first place someone had offered us a live-in job and not knowing how difficult it was going to be elsewhere, we took our chances.

'What?' I said when she called me again. 'I've got an audition with one of the summer shows this afternoon.' I carried on wiping the outside metal tables and emptying the filled plastic ashtrays into the disgusting bucket I had to carry around with me for this task.

She came closer and began straightening chairs when the owner walked past from his daily visit to the nearby guesthouse where we assumed he had a girlfriend. He was carrying a packet of his favourite cigarettes. I glanced down at the stinking bucket, waving away a waft of dank, wet ash with my hand and wondering what pleasure people got out of smoking.

'I think I'm pregnant,' she whispered.

I stopped what I was doing, nearly dropping the bucket. 'Are you sure?'

She nodded, her eyes brimming with tears.

I thought back to the sickness I'd been experiencing in the mornings for the past few weeks. 'Me, too,' I admitted, not only to her but to myself for the first time.

'Vinnie lives on, after all.'

Chapter Thirty-One

2018 – Oakwold, New Forest

Sera

'I wish you'd confided in me before now,' I said when Mum had finished speaking. 'So, you both struggled alone. Mum, that's awful.' I hated to think of two girls younger than me looking for a way to cope with such a frightening situation.

Dee was ashen; she stared at me for so long it was unnerving. I wished she would say something.

'So, Sera,' she said finally. 'Yet again you come out on top of things.'

I frowned. 'How do you work that out? I've had problems, too...'

'I meant about our father.'

Not this again. 'We're both his children, Dee.'

'Yes, but you're the result of a romantic, if not a little sleazy, fling. I'm the product of rape. Brilliant, not something to boast about to the grandchildren, isn't it?'

'Stop it!' Mum shouted. 'How dare you? Your mother loved you regardless of how she became pregnant. In fact,' she said, looking like she wanted to slap Dee, 'she probably over-compensated you for what happened.'

'Rubbish.' Dee slammed her palm down on the table making the plates we'd used earlier rattle. 'Every time she looked at my face she must have seen the man who raped her.'

'That's not Mum's fault,' Leo said. 'She always favoured you over me, and you know it.'

I pictured Dee's room with the pretty decorations and little touches making it so much better than any of her friends'. 'They're right, Dee,' I said. 'Whatever you choose to believe, Hazel did adore you and was always trying to show you in small ways.' I wasn't sure why I was trying to be so nice to her. I decided to try a different approach. 'Surely the point we should both remember is that our mums could have chosen to get rid of us.'

I gave Mum a sideways glance. I was saying this for her benefit as much as Dee's. 'I'm sure it would have been much easier for them to make new lives for themselves if they hadn't had babies to consider.' She didn't argue, so I added, 'Hazel managed to give you a magical childhood, at least up to that summer when it all changed. Maybe you should focus on that aspect of your life rather than the negatives that happened since.'

We stared at each other. Sisters; enemies.

'Maybe,' she said, her tone almost threatening. 'But you have no idea what happened after that night, do you?'

No, I didn't. 'I know about your ex, but no, not about anything else.' I didn't bother to remind her that my life hadn't been so perfect either, but this wasn't a competition to see who had dealt with the most misery. 'Look, do what you want, but don't bring your nastiness to this house.'

'Or you'll what?' Leo said, standing slowly until he reached his full six feet plus. He loomed over the table. I went to retaliate, but was too drained to care what he might do to me if I did stand up to him. Before I uttered a word, the doorbell rang.

Leo looked at his watch. 'Who the hell is that, it's nearly nine o'clock?'

Making the most of his distraction, I leapt up and ran past him up the steps, into the back door and through the hallway, with him thundering after me. 'Leave that fucking door closed,' he bellowed.

My heart raced. I reached out, grabbing the doorknob with one hand and the key with the other, turning both simultaneously, pulling the door back. 'Henri,' I almost wept with relief.

His eyes widened to see me as I almost catapulted myself into him. He wrapped his arms protectively around me. I looked over my shoulder at the furious man bearing down on him. 'It's okay, Sera. I'm here,' he whispered, like a soothing kiss. He turned with me, so that he was between me and Leo. 'So, you bully women?'

Leo stood inches in front of Henri, glaring at him, his breathing heavy, as if more in temper than an exerted effort to catch me. 'Get out of this house, this has nothing to do with you.'

'No. This I will not do, unless Sera or her mother instructs it of me.'

Leo laughed, hands on his hips, head thrown back. 'Seriously? You think you can tell me what to do? You're a pathetic excuse for a man.' He pushed Henri's damaged right shoulder, hard. 'You're only half a man, look at you.'

My instincts told me that to defend Henri would be the worst thing I could do, so I said nothing.

Henri tensed. 'This half-man, as you say, will knock you down if you push me one more time.' Henri reached back with one hand and found mine, giving it a brief squeeze to assure me everything was fine. I didn't know how much of this was bravado; I'd seen Henri struggle to run some days, but he was fit, and working on that farm must have gone some way to building his strength back up since his accident.

Mum came out to the hallway, closely followed by Dee. 'Henri,' she said, relief filling her voice. 'I want you to take Sera and Katie to your farm for the night, while I sort things out with Dee and Leo. I'm afraid there's been a few misunderstandings.'

'She's not going anywhere,' Leo said. 'Sera, get back into this house.'

My blood coursed rapidly through my veins, not with fright, but with fury. 'Shut up, Leo. I don't know who you think you are, but in my house, you're nobody. Take your sister and that poor unfortunate little girl. Better still, leave Ashley behind. I don't mind keeping her here, but you two need to leave tonight. Go and sort through your issues somewhere else.'

'Or you'll do what, exactly?' He sneered at me and I couldn't help likening myself to Mum and how she must have been fooled into believing she was in love with Vinnie all those years ago. I'd been stupid enough to think that something of the shy little boy Leo had once been remained in this tall, handsome man. But thankfully I didn't even like Leo, despite what I'd fooled myself into believing when he'd first arrived at my home.

'The chances of them finding any body at the estate now are almost nil, I should imagine. The entire area has been built on for years. I'll call the police without hesitation,' I said. He went to say something, but I held my hand up to stop him. 'No, don't think you can threaten Mum with anything, she'll deny it.'

'She's right, you know,' Mum said, looking relieved.

Bolstered by him wavering, I added, 'You, on the other hand, have a confession to make to Henri.'

'Me?' Henri looked at me, surprise registering on his face that I might be referring to his father's disappearance.

I nodded, placing a hand on his shoulder. 'Yes, we know what happened to your father.'

I addressed Leo again. 'Jack's body can be identified through forensics, if it hasn't been already. He was killed at your family home and missing from the date you two and Hazel vanished. I think there's too much evidence against you to even think you can get away with this.'

'You mean you won't inform the police of our involvement if we leave now?' Dee asked, coming to stand next to her brother.

I patted Henri's shoulder. 'That's up to you,' I said. 'You have every right to call them, if you choose.'

He slid his arm around my waist and pulled me forward to stand by his side. 'I will decide when I have listened to what they tell me about my father's death.'

'Fair enough,' Dee said, defeat in her voice. 'You deserve to know the truth. I only wish we'd been honest years ago.'

I realised I'd been right. She had been haunted by what she'd done that night.

'Me, too,' Henri said. I could only imagine how much of his life had been taken up looking for and wondering where his father could be. All that frustration and confusion would never have happened if these two had told the truth about Jack's death earlier.

I looked at Dee. 'I'd have loved for us to become close again, but I can't see that happening any time now. Go with Leo. Leave Ashley here with me, at least until you've sorted out a new life somewhere.' She opened her mouth to argue. 'I promise I'll take care of her for you,' I said. 'I'm her auntie, after all.'

'You want me to leave her here?'

'Why not?' I said. 'She'll be perfectly safe. You can come and get her any time. You and Leo need to sort things out quietly, you can't do that with a child accompanying you.'

She didn't look convinced. I caught movement out of the corner of my eye and spotted Katie and Ashley holding hands at the top of the stairs, both with muzzled bed hair and eyes puffy from sleep.

'Mummy, why is everyone cross?' Katie asked.

'It's nothing. Go back to bed, sweetie, I'll come and tuck you in soon.'

'Ashley's scared,' she said.

I opened my mouth to speak, but Dee stepped forward to the bottom of the stairs and looked up at the two sleepy little girls, so like her and me when we were small.

'Ashley, would you like to stay with Auntie Sera while Mummy finds us a new home?'

I felt a pang in my heart at her use of the words 'Auntie Sera' and waited for the little girl to reply. She looked terrified, then nodded slowly.

'Okay, then. You go off to bed with Katie and I'll come up and see you in a bit.'

I took hold of Henri's hand and led him forward, past Leo, now quiet and deflated, and through to the kitchen. It was soothing to feel his calloused hand in mine and I gave it an appreciative squeeze. I heard them follow us into the room and motioned for Henri to sit. Mum sat down next to him. I noticed they were on the side closest to the door, so Leo and Dee had no choice but to walk around the table to get past us if they wanted to leave.

'Right, you two have the chance to put your case to Henri.' I let go of his hand as he sat down and stood behind him, both my hands resting on his broad shoulders. I studied my childhood friends for a while, a part of me feeling pity for what they'd gone through. 'I'll go and check on the children and leave you four to chat.'

I hurried up to the girls' bedrooms, checking on Ashley first. 'You okay?' I asked, stroking her cheek. She nodded. 'Katie is going to love having you to stay with her.'

She smiled. It was the first time I recalled seeing her so relaxed and childlike. 'It'll be fine,' I soothed. 'You mustn't worry about anything.'

She didn't take her eyes off my face while I straightened her pillows. 'Then will my mummy come for me?' For the first time she said enough for me to pick up on her French accent.

I nodded. 'She will, as soon as she and Uncle Leo have found you a new home.'

Her smile faltered. 'No, my real mummy.'

Chapter Thirty-Two

2018 – Oakwold, New Forest

Sera

'Sorry?' I asked, thrown by her odd question. 'What do you mean?'

She sat up and beckoned me close, curving her hand around her mouth and whispering through it. 'My maman, at home.'

My brain froze. She lay back down again, an expectant expression on her face, waiting for me to answer her. Her chin began to wobble. I assumed she was being open with me because she'd seen me stand up to Leo. Her face crumbled. I could see she was frightened and didn't know what to do.

'Hey,' I whispered, stunned that Dee had stooped lower than I could have imagined and kidnapped a child. 'It's okay. I promise I won't tell anyone what you've asked me.' My mind whirled trying to make sense of this latest shock. I hoped Ashley was playing a silly game and that Dee was her mum. The alternative was too horrible to contemplate. 'I'll do my best to find your mummy for you, okay?'

Her panic receded a little. 'Yes.'

I put my finger up to my mouth when I heard footsteps on the stairs. 'Don't say anything. Leave it to me.'

She closed her eyes. By the time Dee reached the bedroom door, I was leaving. 'She's fast asleep,' I said quietly, willing her to leave the child alone.

She glanced in the room and I had to hold back a sigh of relief when she retraced her steps to join the others.

I went into Katie's room and sat on the edge of her bed trying to make sense of my jumbled thoughts. What the hell was going on here? Who was this kid? All I knew was this little girl, whoever she might be, trusted me and I needed to ensure she was returned to her real mother.

The first thing I needed to do now that Dee and Leo had agreed to let Ashley stay with me was to get them to leave. After that I could find a way to track down the little girl's mum. I went to the hallway outside her room. I opened the bedroom door and with my heart pounding, strained to hear any sound coming up from the kitchen. There didn't seem to be any raised voices. I calmed down a little, willing my vague seed of a plan to work.

I needed to rejoin them before they became suspicious of my absence. I listened at the kitchen door to get the gist of what was being said. That's when I heard Leo's voice saying, 'I don't see any reason for us not to leave first thing in the morning.'

I checked my watch; it was almost nine-thirty.

'No, you will leave tonight. If, as you say, my father's death was an accident,' I heard Henri say. 'And you didn't intend to kill him, then I will allow you to leave, but only tonight. If you go now, I will take you to the station. There are trains leaving Southampton through the night. If you insist on staying, then I will call the police and have you arrested. It is your only choice.'

I could have kissed Henri for giving them very little option but to leave straight away.

'You want us to go now?' Dee asked.

I stepped forward and entered the room. 'Why wait?' I said, determined to see the back of them before Henri changed his mind, or they changed theirs. I sat down next to Henri.

Leo watched me. Did he realise that I'd discovered the truth about Ashley? Or that I'd worked out that he had only brought Dee here to hide her and Ashley away from whoever might be looking for them? He seemed to be mulling over his next move. I didn't catch his eye, but forced a smile in Dee's direction.

'You don't have to, of course.' I hoped the reverse psychology Mum always used on me would work for her. 'But I'd have thought you'd want to get as far away from here and the farm as soon as you could.'

The reminder of the farm seemed to do the trick. Dee grabbed hold of Leo's sleeve. 'She's right, I hate it here. I have to go tonight, and if you care anything about me at all you'll come with me.'

'But what about Ashley?' he asked, glancing at me. I kept my expression neutral and patted Mum's hand for something to do.

'The child will be perfectly fine here,' Mum said. 'She has Katie to play with and you can come and get her when you're settled elsewhere.' She caught my eye. I could see she'd picked up that I was trying to hide something. 'Why don't I come and help you pack, Dee? Who knows, the change of scenery might be exactly what you need.'

Dee nodded. 'You're right. Leo, we're going.'

He didn't argue, but got up and followed Dee and Mum out of the kitchen, stopping at the door to give Henri and me a brief look. The heat of Henri's leg against mine was comforting and I was deeply grateful for his return to the house. Neither of us spoke. He placed his hand over mine and kept it there until we heard Leo's voice from the first-floor landing.

'He is a dangerous man, Sera.'

I nodded. 'I realise that now. I'm so relieved you came here tonight. Do you mind not informing the police about what happened to your father?'

He shook his head. 'It is in the past and they were children. I have been able to solve the mystery of my father's disappearance, and for me, right now, this is enough.'

I heard footsteps coming down the stairs. 'Thank you,' I whispered.

'Thank me when they've gone.' He hesitated, staring at me intently. 'Sera, what is wrong?'

I pointed towards the open doorway. 'I'll tell you later.'

I went to the kitchen and waited while Henri joined Mum and the others. She said her brief goodbyes to Dee and Leo mainly to witness their exit before they left with Henri for the station, hurriedly closing the front door and locking it behind them.

'I thought they'd never leave,' she said, coming back into the kitchen and resting against the worktop. She looked drained, her shoulders drooping. 'Henri is a good man, Sera, I misjudged him terribly.'

'All I care about right now is that they've gone, Mum. I hope he makes sure they get on to a train – any damn train – and leave Southampton for good.'

She stifled a yawn with the back of her hand. 'Would you mind if I went to bed now?'

'No, of course not. I'll stay down here for a bit.'

She closed her eyes for a moment. 'You should try and rest if you can,' she said. 'Henri told me he'd come back in the morning. He said you should get some sleep.'

She sighed. 'Who knows what we'll have to deal with tomorrow.'

I dreaded to think. 'I'm shattered too.' I walked up to her and gave her a hug. 'I'm sorry for inviting them into our home.'

'You didn't know what would happen, darling.' She linked arms with me and, leading me out of the kitchen, stopped to wait while I switched off the light. 'I can't believe they've actually left.'

'Nor can I,' I said, hoping I didn't wake up and discover this was all a misleading dream. I decided to wait until the morning to tell her what I'd discovered about Ashley; she had coped with enough shocks for one day. It wasn't as if I could do anything much tonight anyway, I reasoned. I checked the house doors were locked and we went upstairs.

I was about to get into bed when I remembered the small photo I'd taken from Hazel's room of her and Jack in 2003. I walked over to the corner of the room and knelt. Dragging back the edge of the carpet I lifted the small end of the floorboard to reveal my childhood hiding place where I stored all my secret bits. I rummaged around with my hand until I came across the silver frame and pulled it out. Wiping the dust from the glass against my pyjama shorts, I lifted the picture and studied it. Would it be the right thing to do to offer this to Henri? Or should I take the picture out of the frame and cut Hazel's body from the photo? Unsure what to do, I decided to let him choose.

Chapter Thirty-Three

2018 – Oakwold, New Forest

Sera

I barely slept and was washed and dressed by the time Henri rang the doorbell at 8.30 the following morning. Mum took the girls out to the shops so that we could chat about him dropping Leo and Dee off at the station.

'Where could they be now?' I asked, willing him to say Outer Mongolia, or better still, Mars.

'East, although they might have got off at the next stop, or any after that,' he said, looking as exhausted as I felt.

I would have loved proof of their destination, but that wasn't going to happen. Eventually Mum came back with the girls and we left them to go upstairs to play in Katie's room. She joined us and I finally told them what Ashley had said to me the night before.

Neither of them spoke. I waited until they'd digested this latest shock.

'She's an odd child, Sera,' Mum said. 'Are you certain she wasn't just messing with you?'

'Mum, she's five, supposedly,' I argued, realising how little I knew about the child upstairs with my daughter. 'How would she think up something so weird? She has a French accent.'

'She's grown up there, so that's not surprising,' Mum said. 'Henri, what do you think? Should we take this seriously?'

He looked surprised at her question. 'Of course. If it is not true then we have lost nothing, but if it is, this child must be returned to her parents immediately.' He rubbed his stubbly chin. 'I will contact my ex-colleagues. Maybe they can find information about a missing child. Do you recognise her accent?'

'No,' I said, aware I had no idea about different accents in France. 'I suppose it could help narrow down the search for her family,' I said. 'I wish I could help.'

'She has never spoken in front of me, so I cannot tell,' he said, giving me a reassuring smile. 'I'll find out everything I can. We must act immediately, before they return and try to claim her.'

Mum looked horrified. 'Thank you, Henri,' she said. 'I'm incredibly grateful to you for this and for being so generous about not pressing charges against those fiends. I don't think I could have stood having them here for a moment longer than they were.'

He tilted his head in a half nod and left. I spent several hours catching up with my work. I had forgotten it was my day to have a stall at the market and decided that even though I was hours late starting, it would still be better to spend some time there than none. Mum was happy to have the children, saying it was too hot for her to go out anywhere.

—

Despite the humidity of the ongoing heatwave, I needed something else to take my mind off everything that had transpired over the past twenty-four hours. I took the photo of Hazel and Jack with me, pushing it carefully into my back pocket, so I could drop it off to Henri on my way home from the market.

I usually preferred to be somewhere in the middle, but had missed the opportunity by being so late to arrive at the town square, so ended up being at the far end of the pitches.

'Ahh, Sera, we thought you weren't coming to join us today,' the elderly lady with the fruit stall said, as I gave the change to my first customer of the day.

I laughed. 'I forgot what day it was,' I admitted, which was partially true.

The heat was unbearable and because I'd only got the last stall in the market, the canopy didn't shade me as much as I would have liked. I drank some water from a bottle and fanned my face with one of the booklets I gave away with each of my sales to advertise the rest of the stock.

I lifted the signs down at the end of the day, wrapping each one carefully and placing them in a box ready to take home. When I stood up I spotted Henri moving slowly through the thinning crowds.

'Henri,' I shouted, standing on my tiptoes to wave at him. 'Over here.'

He stopped and held his hand up, moving as quickly as he could towards my stall.

'Any news?'

He nodded. 'It is not good.' His tanned face was strained. 'I am sorry.'

'So, Ashley was telling the truth?' His distress was obvious. 'What do we do now?'

He came around to my side of the stall. 'I've spoken with your mother. She has packed up Ashley's belongings and is taking the girls to a soft play centre for the morning and then to pre-school for the afternoon. She is getting them away from the house in case Dee and Leo return. The pre-school leader has been informed and will keep the children there with your mother until the police arrive.'

'I can't believe it,' I said, stunned at how low Dee had sunk in my estimation. 'Let's go.'

He helped me pack my signs into the back of my car. 'We must not go to your house, not until this has been sorted. We have no way of knowing if Leo and Dee will be there and I cannot take the chance they might follow us to Ashley.' He was so in control and I realised what a loss he must have been to the police service.

'I'll drop these off at the studio. You follow me there and then I'll come to the school with you.'

On the way to the school he filled me in on the rest of what had happened since I last saw him. It was hard to imagine that only four hours had passed since then.

'Her real name is Sophie.' He barely contained his emotions as he explained more of what he'd discovered. 'Her parents moved to France a couple of years ago, so didn't know many people there. Dee was a volunteer at the school; she helped the little ones with their reading.'

'That's how she got to know Ashley, I mean, Sophie,' I said almost to myself.

'Sophie's mother recently started a new job, I am told. She worked long hours, sometimes arriving late to collect her daughter. Dee always offered to stay behind with the child. One day, the mother arrived late to collect her and they had both vanished.'

I pictured the horror on that poor mother's face discovering her child missing. 'Poor woman.'

'Yes.'

An icy tingle ran down my spine making me shiver. 'How didn't we know about her being missing? Wasn't the story reported in the international papers?'

'No. The papers probably printed something about it, but they're mostly publishing stories about this heatwave and fires, deaths caused by the situation. No one was looking for a kidnapped child around here. It's not your fault you didn't know.'

'What happens when we get to the school?'

'Her mother is on a flight. A benefactor is flying her on his private jet to the nearest airport. She arrives in an hour.' He put his foot down harder on the accelerator. 'We must hurry.'

Chapter Thirty-Four

2018 – Oakwold, New Forest

Sera

I held Katie in my arms as we watched Sophie clinging to her mother's neck being carried to a waiting car. This little girl looked completely different to the one who had stayed at my home for the past few weeks. Her mother turned and mouthed a thank you to me. I could see how like her Sophie was. Sophie waved with one hand, holding tightly onto the teddy Katie had given her with the other. I didn't care that tears were running down my face as we waited for them to get into the car and drive away.

Henri went to speak to two of his ex-colleagues who had accompanied the mother on the plane. I hugged Katie, unsure how I would ever be brave enough to leave her at pre-school again.

'She's fine, darling,' Mum said, reading my thoughts and stroking my arm. 'And so is Sophie, now she's back with her own mother.'

'I can't believe Dee could do such a thing.' I swallowed the lump restricting my throat.

'Or Leo, he covered for her all this time.'

'We've been harbouring two fugitives and a kidnapped child.' I choked on the last words. Thinking I was going to be sick, I handed Katie to Mum and I ran inside to the bathroom. I leant over the sink resting my forehead on the cool tiles behind, trying to come to terms with the fact that I'd inadvertently helped keep Sophie from her mother.

'Sera, Sera,' Henri called from the hallway. He must have heard me because the next thing I knew he was in the Ladies with me, hugging me tightly. 'It's okay now. Sophie is back with her mother and will be home soon.'

'But I should have realised something was wrong. I knew she was withdrawn and unhappy, it just never occurred to me it could be because of something this horrendous.'

He held me close to him. '*Chérie*, you looked after her. Katie was her friend and you discovered the truth in the end. The child trusted you enough to confide in you, that is a good thing.'

I sniffed. 'Her poor mother.' He handed me a tissue and I blew my nose. 'What about Dee and Leo?'

'They are looking for them now. The police believe Dee became obsessed with the little girl after her own baby died.'

'I can't believe she did such a thing.' As soon as I'd spoken, I couldn't help hoping that Dee would manage to find some other way to cope with the loss of her own baby.

'Maybe their past helped make them act this way.' He placed a finger under my chin and lifted it slightly. 'I will be prosecuting them now for what they did to my father, Sera.'

'I know.' I didn't blame him at all.

'Before, I assumed Papa's death had been a tragic accident. These two people have proved how cruel they can be by taking the little girl, so now I am happy to press charges against them. The authorities are also checking out my theory that Leo started the fire at the barn.'

I couldn't believe it. 'But why would he do something like that?'

Henri shook his head. 'I believe he started the fire to cover up any tracks left behind from the killing, when he realised he needed to hide Dee and Sophie at your home. He hoped to dispose of any evidence before bringing them.'

'And in the process ended up causing Jack's body to be discovered,' I concluded, aware of the irony of his actions.

'Yes.'

Did I ever know Leo at all? I wondered. 'So you think he meant for me to see him that day in Southampton?'

Henri nodded. 'Do you take the same route each time?'

'Yes, several times a week, and usually at the same time, too.' I thought about the plans Leo must have made to cover up what his sister had done, all the lies. 'I'm pleased you're prosecuting them for your father's death,' I said honestly. 'Which reminds me.' He watched silently as I pushed my hand into my back pocket to retrieve the picture. 'I didn't know whether to cut Hazel from this, or not, but your dad looks very happy and I didn't want to ruin the picture. I'll leave it up to you to decide.'

He took it from me as if I was handing him the most delicate trinket and stared silently at his father's image. 'Thank you, Sera,' he whispered, looking down at the photo cupped in his hands.

'I took it from Hazel's house after they disappeared,' I admitted. 'It's been hidden in my room since then.'

He smiled at me. 'We have many of the answers now.'

'Yes,' I said. 'Answers to questions we didn't know we should be asking.' It was all too surreal. 'It's going to take a long time for me to trust my instincts again. I thought I knew those people.' I didn't add I'd also thought I'd known my mother, but she'd turned out to be capable of far worse than anything I ever imagined. 'How can we ever be certain we truly know the people closest to us?'

Henri hugged me tightly. Placing his right hand behind my head, he kissed me. My upset and fear caused by everything that had happened instantly dispersed. I kissed him back, confident that with him in my life everything was going to be all right.

He moved back slightly. 'To answer your question, we can't ever be sure who to trust,' he said. 'But we need to be brave and I promise you can trust me.' He kissed me again as if to further reassure me. 'Don't let what happened change you, Sera. You have me. I will not let anything bad happen to you ever again. Be brave. Enjoy your life and the people in it.'

'You know what, Henri?' I said, finally free from my past. 'I think I will.'

A Letter From Ella

I would like to thank you for reading *The Darkest Summer*.

This story was initially inspired by my own experience of losing a teenage friend who disappeared from my life one summer's night with her family many years ago. Her story is nothing like this one, thankfully, and we did meet up again years later. One day I was thinking about how I felt when she had gone and used this as the basis for Sera's story.

I hope you enjoyed reading *The Darkest Summer*. If you did, I'd love to hear what you think. Please consider writing a review as they can also help other readers discover new authors and their books. Or maybe you can recommend *The Darkest Summer* to your friends and family...

I'm fascinated by people's pasts and how what they experience changes them as they grow older. I love losing myself in my characters' emotions and imagining why they react in the ways that they do.

This is the story of two friends, Sera and Dee and how their experiences and the choices they make taint their futures. Sera has had to cope with the loss of her best friend at a vulnerable time in her life and the unexpected death of her husband when she is only in her twenties. She has returned to live in her childhood home with her mother and her little girl and everything in her life is settled until the night of the fire at a neighbour's farm and her reunion with her two closest childhood friends.

Thank you for joining me for Sera's story.

I love hearing from readers – so please get in touch on my Facebook or Goodreads page, twitter or through my website.

And if you'd like to keep up-to-date with all my latest releases, just sign up at the website link below.

Thank you very much for your support, I really appreciate it.

Ella Drummond

https://www.herabooks.com/authors/ella-drummond/
https://deborahcarr.org/contact/
https://www.facebook.com/DeborahCarrAuthor/
https://twitter.com/DebsCarr

Acknowledgements

Many thanks to everyone at Hera Books, especially Keshini Naidoo, Lindsey Mooney and editors Jon Appleton and Jennie Ayres, it's been a wonderful experience working with you all on this second book, *The Darkest Summer*.

Thanks also to my extended family, but especially to my husband, Rob and children, James and Saskia.

My fellow Blonde Plotters, Kelly Clayton and Gwyn GB deserve a big thank you for their continued encouragement and support especially when I was working on edits for this book and they were left to do so much of the preparation for our first MYVLF.com event.

To my agent, Kate Nash and everyone at the Kate Nash Literary Agency for their constant support.

To you, the reader, a massive thank you for choosing to read *The Darkest Summer*, I hope you enjoy this book.